I0740817

Julia C. R. Dorr

In Kings Houses

A romance of the days of Queen Anne

Julia C. R. Dorr

In Kings Houses
A romance of the days of Queen Anne

ISBN/EAN: 9783743397507

Manufactured in Europe, USA, Canada, Australia, Japa

Cover: Foto ©Andreas Hilbeck / pixelio.de

Manufactured and distributed by brebook publishing software (www.brebook.com)

Julia C. R. Dorr

In Kings Houses

LIST OF ILLUSTRATIONS.

IN KINGS' HOUSES.

CHAPTER I.

"Nay, but tell me, granny! Think you the King will ride to-day?"

Dame Dorothy laughed as she drew out the shining flax, and then let it coil, a fine silver thread, around the spindle. Robin watched the process as he sat on the floor at her feet, and in the interest of the moment he almost forgot the unanswered question.

Yet the sight was by no means unfamiliar. It seemed to the child that Dame Dorothy was always spinning, spinning. But presently he bethought him.

"You do not tell me," he cried, impatiently. "Will the King ride to-day?"

The dame dropped the thread, and drew the child closer to her side.

"The King? Truly, I know not. How should I? He may ride, if it pleases him, and then again he may not. If it be damp, or the east wind blows, he may choose to stay by the fire, and smoke his Dutch pipe. Rheumatism is no respecter of persons, my lad."

"But you should know all about it, granny, — you who have lived in king's houses. Who should know better than you if the King be likely to ride or no?"

Dame Dorothy laughed again, rumpling the child's dark curls, and then smoothing them down with a tender touch. She gave him a swift kiss, and resumed her spinning before answering this last remark.

"'In kings' houses?' Faith, I see it behooves one to be careful of speech with such sharp ears about. But, laddie, I know naught of the King. He is not at the castle now. 'Tis said he likes not Windsor since Queen Mary died; and God knows he liked it none too well before."

The child sighed. "Who is at the castle then, if it be not the King? For when we carried the eggs to market this morning, Betty Macthorne marvelled much at the many flags a-flying, and I saw great clouds of smoke coming from the big chimneys of the kitchen and scullery."

"No doubt, no doubt, my Robin. But there are mouths enow to be filled at the castle, — mouths of great folk and small folk, — whether the King be there or no. It is not he does all the eating."

Then a sudden thought striking her, she turned to the child so sharply that her thread broke.

"But why do you ask about the King?" she said. "What matters it to you whether he ride or no? The King knows naught of you, nor you of him."

"He knows naught of me," answered the boy, slowly twirling a shred of flax between his fingers. "But last even-song I heard the priest—"

The child's voice died away, and he sat gazing thoughtfully into the fire.

"Well," said the grandmother, after a pause, "what about the priest?"

"Granny," was the irrelevant answer, "tell me about the King's daughter."

"The King's daughter? The King has no daughter to my knowledge. But what about the priest?"

"Why, at even-song, last night, he said the King had a crown of pure gold on his head. And one other day he spake of the King's daughter. He said she was all glorious, and that her kirtle was of wrought gold. I never saw a king, nor a princess," he went on, plaintively. "But you, granny, you have lived in kings' houses!"

Dame Dorothy dropped her hands despairingly. "Now grant me patience!" she cried. "Why, child, the priest spake not of William III. He spake of God, the King of all the earth,—and of his daughter, the Church. It is she who has 'put on glorious apparel.'"

"Oh! I thought he meant King William," sighed the child. "But that's no matter, granny. Tell me a story of the days long ago, when you dwelt in kings' houses. Was it King William's house? Was he your master?"

The woman's cheek flushed crimson, taking on the color of an autumn pippin, and for a few moments the room was silent save for the monotonous whirring of the wheel. Then she said, softly:

"Nay, he was not my master; and he is not now, save as the King is master of us all. It was long ago, laddie, in the days of Charles Stuart—"

"Who had his head cut off?" interrupted Robin, excitedly.

"Hush thee, hush thee, child," whispered the dame, dropping into the thee and thou, as she was apt to do whenever greatly moved. "Thou must not speak of such things. Have I not told thee more than once? No. It was when Charles II. reigned. But I was not of his household."

The wheel turned slower and slower, till it at last stood still. The dame's eyes were fixed upon the bed of coals glowing on the hearth, and her foot, that had slipped from the treadle, kept its steady upward and downward movement unawares. The child waited a moment, and then pulled at her apron.

"Go on, granny," he said. "Tell me more."

She started, picked up her thread, and resumed her spinning with her story.

"'When I dwelt in kings' houses?' What a child thou art! The story is naught, Robin; and if it were much, you have heard it a thousand times. It was in the year of the Great Plague. Ah, what a time was that! 'Twas the terror by night, and the pestilence that walketh in darkness, and the destruction that wasteth at noonday."

Again she paused, lost in the maze of memory.

"Oh, do go on!" cried the child. "Granny, why do you always stop and look in the fire when you get to the plague and the dead folk?"

"Why? Laddie, you will understand some day. They all died, — my father, and my mother, and my young brother, and weeks afterward, though not of the plague, my own babe that slept in my bosom. Well, it was two or three weeks after this, when I was out in the paddock one morning, feeding the fowls, I heard the trampling of horses and the sound of wheels, and looking up, I saw a great lady in a carriage, and beside her a fine gentleman whose face I knew well. It was the young Sir Henry Valdegrave, my father's landlord, and my husband's also.

"He beckoned to me, and bade me approach. I took off my apron of heavy linen, — which was none too clean, in sooth, for I had gathered up a brood of chickens in it, — and threw it behind the hen-coop. Then with my two hands I smoothed down my hair, which the wind had roughened, and went forward somewhat abashed, and wondering if the lady required a bowl of milk, or mayhap a flagon of ale, for the day was hot. But I said not a word, — as was fitting, — only made my obeisance and stood with my eyes cast down, waiting their commands. I can hear, even now, how the bees hummed in the laburnums that morning, and in the great lime-tree that overhung the wicket.

"Very like it was not two minutes; but it seemed to me I stood there two hours, while the lady and gentleman talked in low tones that I could not understand. Then the lady nodded, and shrugged her shoulders, settling her mantle with a word of displeasure about the dust, while the gentleman motioned me near with a little wave of his hand, — I having remained all the while half hidden by the paling.

"'Methinks she will do, if she pleases your ladyship,' he said, after a little; 'I know her to be of good stock, and she is not uncomely.'

"'She seems a sturdy wench, which is more to the point, and modest withal,' answered the lady. 'I care not much if she be comely. Better otherwise, Sir Henry," and she laughed a little. Whereupon they went on talking about me as if I had been a stick or a stone, while I got red in the face, and stood like a gawk twirling the corner of my kerchief, and wondering what all this pother was about.

"But presently the lady cried out with a great sigh, 'Faith, but 'tis hot! I cannot bide here longer. Bid the wench come to the palace to-morrow, Sir Henry.'

"Never was my head in such a whirl, and my heart was like a hammer thumping and pounding in my breast. But Sir Henry spoke never a word then, save to tell me to go in out of the sun. As he bade the coachman drive on, and the wheels began to move, I heard him say, 'I will give her instructions before night, Lady Frances.'

"Then I went into the house, picking up my apron as I went, and sat down in the empty foreroom, wondering what this strange thing might be that had come into my life. For I had not heard enough of the conversation to understand what was wanted of me, — only that I was to be summoned to the palace by order of this grand dame, whose smile was cold and haughty.

"As I sat there all in a maze, trembling, and hot and cold by turns, Allan came in."

"My grandsir Allan?"

Dame Dorothy laughed softly as she dipped her fingers in the cup, moistening the flax.

"Who else should he be? But he was not your grandsir then. He was my young husband, scarce twenty-five years old, six feet in his stockings, straight as an arrow, and with eyes as blue as the speedwell you picked yesterday. Well, he was sore troubled at the plight he found me in, and began to comfort me about the baby that had died, and to talk to me of our eldest born, who was named Robin. He could talk, and was a sturdy chap, and when our troubles came we had sent him to his granny — his father's mother — to be taken care of."

"Just as I was sent over sea to my granny," remarked the child, gravely.

The dame nodded.

"Yes. And I remember how my Allan bade me dry my eyes and be cheery again, saying death was God's will, and all that. But I answered it seemed to me that mayhap men and the devil had as much to do with the plague and other ills as God had. However, we did not dispute about that. I did not tell him of the morning's strange happening, for I did not understand it myself, and thought it no use to trouble him till I knew what was wanted of me.

"So presently I bestirred myself and made ready a bowl of pottage, — black beans, with some savory herbs added thereto. And lo! as he was eating it, with a loaf of black bread on a trencher beside him, I heard the tramping of hoofs again, and Sir Henry leaped from his horse, throwing the bridle-rein to the groom who rode a gray nag behind him.

"He strode into the low room without so much as a knock, but doffed his hat and smiled on me ere he spake a word. And I bethought me that there was one bottle left of the cherry cordial mother had made last year, and brought him a small draught, which he drained every drop. Mother was skilled in all the secrets of the still-room, and was esteemed a fine cook in her day."

"She was no better skilled than you, I warrant," observed Robin, politely. "But what happened next, granny?"

"Why, then he told me I was to go to Richmond the next day, to be nurse to the Lady Anne of York. It was the Lady Frances Villiers whom I had seen in the carriage that morning; she who had been appointed governess to the Lady Mary and the Lady Anne, the two little daughters of James, the Duke of York. And because of the great plague, the children had been removed from Twickenham to the palace at Richmond, whither I was to go at once.

"All this Sir Henry told me as I sat shivering with cold and fright (though it was so hot outside) and holding on to Allan's hand for dear life, while he said never a word, whether he would that I should go, or stay.

"At last I said, 'But, your honor, I cannot go to

nurse the Lady Anne.   I have to keep the house for Allan ;' and then Allan smiled at me, and squeezed my hand the tighter.

"Then Sir Henry talked to us both very kindly and wisely.   You are too young to understand it all, dear heart.   But he made us see it would be to our great advantage if I were to go to Richmond for awhile.   And of course I knew it was a great honor for one like me to be sought for as nurse to the Lady Anne.   Her mother, the duchess — she that was Anne Hyde — was thought to be near her death just then, and the whole country talked of it.   As I thought of this, and of my own baby lying cold in its small grave, my heart yearned over the little one in the palace.   We are all alike, my laddie, when pain and sorrow come.

"Moreover, I knew I could not help myself anyway.   Who was I, to set up my will against that of my betters ?   There was no use kicking against the pricks.   So when Allan said quietly that he could go and stay with his own mother for awhile, I consented to what I saw must be.

"Sir Henry said I would have fair wage, and my clothes furnished, — and more than all, that Allan would have leave to see me now and then ; and that if I would be reasonable and content, Lady Frances had promised him I would be allowed to go home one Sunday in each month.   Then he chucked me under the chin, bidding me dry my eyes and be a good wench, leaped on his horse, and rode away to London."

"And that is how you happened to dwell in kings' houses ? "

"Yes, that is how it happened. I thought it was to be only for a few weeks, or, mayhap, a twelve-month at the most. But the days went on and on ; and for more than six years I was head nurse to my little Lady Anne Stuart. Most of the time we were at Richmond. But wherever she went, I went also."

"And you saw many fine doings at the palace ?— great lords, and great ladies ?"

"Oh, yes ! They were plenty as blackberries ! Lady Frances Villiers had six gay daughters of her own; and there was constant coming and going, with boating on the river, and fine games, — tennis and the like, — and dances, and much splendid array of man and beast. I saw many a fine sight as I sat in the nursery window — a carved oriel looking down upon the great court — or strolled in the pleasaunce with Lady Anne."

"I wish I had been alive to be there," sighed Robin, plaintively. "The fine doings all came too soon for me. But go on ! You haven't got to the Black Day yet."

"What a memory thou hast, child ! Dost thou

forget nothing I tell thee?   Well, one day out of all
the year, the great palace was hushed and quiet.
There was no merry-making then, I tell thee, and no
flaunting in gay apparel.   On that day the command
went forth, and all in the household of the Duke of
York put on mourning garments, — aye, all, — from
the least unto the greatest.   They fasted and prayed.
Truly they wept when they remembered Zion."

"Ho, now, granny, you do not tell it right!"
cried the boy, tugging at her gown ; for her hands
lay idly in her lap, and her thoughts were far afield.
"You never saia that word before!   What was
Zion?   They wept when they remembered Charles
I., and how — "

Dame Dorothy caught the child in a swift embrace, smothering his words with kisses.

"You are growing too wise, laddie!   I shall have
to stop telling you these old stories.   Run away
now and play with your kitten, while I make ready
the porridge for your supper."

"Nay, let Betty Macthorne make it.   There's all
that about the young stepmother to come yet."

"Humph!   The duchess did not die for two or
three years after I went to the palace, in spite of
the doctors.   And then — in due time, of course —
the duke married Mary Beatrice of Modena.   That
was a gay time, you may well believe!   The new
duchess was very young, only four years older than

the Lady Mary.　When the duke brought her home, he said to his daughters, 'See! I bring you a new playfellow.'　She was almost as much a child as they.　They liked her well enow at first. But Lady Anne's chief friend and playmate was a girl older than herself, — one Sarah Jennings.　A proud minx she was in those days, with nothing to be proud of but her pertness.　But she is my Lady Marlborough now, I hear, and rules her mistress's household."

"I don't care to hear about Sarah Jennings," said the child.　"Tell me about the little Lady Anne. Was she pretty, granny?　Are great ladies always pretty?"

"Well, no, — not always, if one may make bold to say so.　But my little lady was pretty, with lovely brown hair that curled like the dandelion ringlets you bedecked the cat with yesterday; and red lips, and cheeks like roses.　She had beautiful hands and arms, and the sweetest voice ever heard.　Her uncle, King Charles, used to bring the great folks to hearken to it, and she used to recite versicles to amuse them when she was but a little child.　Very proud was I of that, though verily I had little to do with it."

"And did you tell her stories, as you do me?"

"No doubt, no doubt.　But if she begged for stories, they must be about the fairy folk, or else tales of my own childhood. She teased not for tales of 'kings' houses' as you do."

"Why should she? She knew all about them without the telling! But was this long, oh, very long ago, granny?"

"Sometimes it seems very long, and sometimes but a day. I cannot count the years. I only know I first went to Richmond in the year of the Great Plague, when Charles II. was King of England. Then reigned King James, till William and Mary came overseas and drove him from his throne. Now William rules alone. Yes, child, it was long ago, as you count years."

Dame Dorothy put the wheel away, and Robin ran out into the low slanting sunshine to play until called to supper.

CHAPTER II.

DAME DOROTHY'S cottage stood on the outskirts, the very edge, of Windsor Forest, not far from a great oak that was known for many years as "Queen Anne's Oak." Beneath its branches, tradition saith, she was accustomed to mount for the chase. But it did not bear this name when Robin played in its shadow, nor till long afterward.

The cottage was of gray stone, low and broad, with small-paned, latticed windows, and a door divided horizontally in the middle, after the manner of those in old Dutch pictures. It was a veritable nest of green. Scarcely a bit of the gray stone was to be seen, for the ivy, the beautiful luxuriant ivy of England, had clambered all over it, framing the windows, curtaining the cornices, and climbing to the very top of the red chimney. On each side of the door grew two great rose-trees, one pink, and one white, whose long, slender branches were held in the friendly clasp of the ivy, and went wandering with it whithersoever it would, throwing out red and white banners from roof and crosspole.

In front of the cottage was a small garden, sweet

with thyme, lavender, and rosemary.   Behind it was
the croft where a dun cow was grazing; and at the
left was a low bench on which were three beehives,
their brown inmates coming and going in the sun
with a low, continuous monotone.

Within, the cottage was comfortable, though by no
means fine.   There was a little entry, with small,
low-ceiled rooms on either side, and a tiny kitchen
farther back.   This was all, save for the loft, which
was reached by a ladder-like stairway leading from
the kitchen.   But there were two great fireplaces,
with black iron fire-dogs and wide hospitable hearths,
each with its wooden settle; and, whatever the
weather might be, the rooms were warm and bright,
and sweet with the odors of wildwood and garden.
There for some months had dwelt Dame Dorothy
and Robin, and a well-grown lass of fourteen or
thereabouts, called Betty Macthorne.

The good dame, even though she had lived "in
kings' houses" at one period of her changeful life,
hardly felt called upon to keep a servant.   But she
was by no means poor; and the time had come when
she found it pleasanter to sit by the fire and spin, or
to potter about among her bees, her birds, her fowls,
and her garden, than to do all the rough work of even
so humble an establishment.   And as for Betty Macthorne, — a waif from the city streets, who had been
blown about by fierce winds, and tossed hither and

thither by adverse fortune, — she thought she had found paradise when Dame Dorothy's kindly voice bade her braid up her elfin locks, wash her hands, and learn how to bake the bread and fry the bacon.

"You can save my old bones many an ache, and my joints many a twinge, if you prove but willing and faithful, lassie," the dame had said. "The bit you eat I shall hardly miss. And as for clothing, — there is wool and flax for the spinning ; and for these many days yet, my gowns and petticoats can be cut down to your size when they are too much worn for my using. So come in God's name, child, if you like, and we will do our best to travel on together, in peace and quietness."

Betty needed no second bidding, — and very happy she was, for life had gone hardly with her till that day.

If one were to stand to-day where the cottage then stood, and were to look to the right and left, his eye would follow a long, straight drive, or walk, bordered on either side by stately elms, — a three-mile stretch, from St. George's Gateway on the north, with the massive towers of the castle rising in long array above it, to Snow Hill on the south, crowned by the equestrian statue of George III., standing in bold relief against the sky. Hundreds of fallow deer toss their antlered heads to-day in the great park that was once Windsor Forest.

Wild deer roamed that forest then; and as Robin played about the door he sometimes caught sight of one, a mere shadow in the far distance. But they were shy things in those days, very unlike the tame creatures that now browse there undisturbed. In place of the long, straight drive, wildwood paths ran hither and thither; ferns and wild flowers nodded in the breeze; and over every rock, and wherever a hunter's cabin or a woodman's hut had encroached upon the solitude, the mantling ivy had crept, hiding man's poor handiwork in the folds of its own soft verdure.

One morning, about a week after Dame Dorothy had, for the hundredth time, told Robin how it happened that she had once dwelt in kings' houses, she sent Betty on an errand to the small town lying at the foot of the castle. An hour had not passed when the girl came flying back in a state of great excitement. Dame Dorothy was tying up her wall-flowers, that had been beaten down by a sharp shower the night before, while Robin was making a fleet of pea-pod boats. The child looked up wonderingly.

"Why, granny, whatever is the matter with Betty Macthorne?" he cried. "Look! look! She is running as if the Coverly witch were after her!"

"Reach me my scissors, there's a good child," answered the dame, without lifting her eyes. "A thoughtful wench is Betty. Haply she is afeard the porridge will burn. She hung on the pot before she went out."

But, as it proved, Betty's thoughts were not on the porridge-pot.

"Oh, good mistress," she cried, panting, as she dropped down on a garden stool, "such a marvellous thing as has happened to me! I never could ha' believed it, — and as I live, I know not now whether I be dreaming or no!"

"Well, if you can gather your wits together, and get your breath long enow to tell me about this wonderful happening," said her mistress, slowly, as she went on carefully brushing and blowing the soil from a red stock-gilly that had been bent to the ground, "mayhap I can help you out. Have you seen the Black Wizard, or haply Beelzebub himself, with his horns and hoofs, running loose in Windsor streets this fair morning?"

"Nay, mistress, do not jest," answered Betty. "I have seen neither Beelzebub, nor the Wizard. But just as I was turning into the forest, walking quietly along with my basket on my arm, and thinking about a red ribbon in the haberdasher's window, I heard some boys shouting, and making a great pother, and lo! there I saw, before my eyes, just turning the corner from Eton way, a fine carriage, with postilions, and footmen, and outriders, and gentlemen in scarlet coats and gold lace; and there were ladies in the carriage all silks and feathers, and shining jewels, and — and — "

" Yes, yes, child," said Dame Dorothy, " no doubt, no doubt! But if you live near Windsor long, you will get used to such sights, and make little of them. There be always great folk at the castle, — lords and ladies, and the like, — whether the King be there or no. And they do always be riding in state, and taking their pleasure. It is the way of the quality."

Robin had dropped his pea-pods, and was listening with eyes and ears, as it were, too absorbed for even a word.

" But there is more to come, mistress! I drew to one side to make my obeisance, as was fitting, and was standing still, with my eyes cast down, and my basket on my arm — "

" Don't tell any more about the basket!" cried Robin, who had found his tongue at last. " Tell about the lords and ladies!"

" But, Master Robin," exclaimed poor Betty, desperately, " the basket is the nib of the whole story! As I stood there, waiting for the carriage to pass by, I took from under the cover a handful of double jonquils I plucked this morning, — well, knowing you would be willing, mistress, as I was meaning to give them to the sick girl who lies by the window of the last cottage under the hill. It was near the place, and I thought to have them ready. But just then the carriage halted, for one of the ladies caught sight of the flowers, and cried out, softly, ‘Oh, stop! stop! See those beautiful jonquils!’ The gentlemen leaped from their horses, and the grandest of them all doffed his hat to the lady, while he asked if I would sell the flowers. And I said nay, they were not for sale; but I laid them in his hand. The lady smiled and thanked me kindly, and bade a younger lady, who sat beside her, to keep them well in the shade, that they might not wilt from the heat. For, said she, ‘Never saw I such lovely jonquils, and they just match in color the gown I mean to wear this evening.’”

“Well, well!” cried Dame Dorothy, “I little thought my jonquils would come to such honor as that. Yet I knew they were wondrous fine, the bulbs having been sent to me by my cousin, who is head gardener to my lord the Duke of Devonshire. Neither did I think they would bloom for me this year, so late was it before I planted them. It was a miracle that they bore a single blossom, for it is long past their season.”

“But there is more to come yet!” said Betty. “One of the ladies took note of the bit of lace you bade me show to the mercer. It hung over the edge of the basket, having clung to the jonquils as I drew them forth, and she at once remarked the pattern, saying it was a rare one, and finely wrought, — like the work of one she knew long ago. Whereupon I made a curtsey, and said the lace was made by my mistress, Dame Dorothy, who was skilled in all fine spinning and lace-weaving. 'Dame Dorothy,' quoth the lady, 'verily the one I knew was called Dorothy, also.' Now is not that strange, mistress?"

"But what happened next?" cried Robin, greatly excited. "Was it the Queen, mayhap? Did the lady wear a golden crown? I wish I had been there!"

"The Queen? England has no queen, child," interposed Dame Dorothy. "But had the lady been a queen she would not have worn her crown this morning, when she was but out a-pleasuring. Crowns are only for great days and great pageantries. How looked the chief lady, Betty?"

Betty pondered.

"She was large and stately, mistress, but methinks my eyes were dazzled. I could not look on her face."

"Methinks you were just frightened, Betty," remarked Robin. "Sometimes my eyes feel that way."

"Did you hear aught of great doings at the castle, — or of strangers quartered in the state apartments?"

"Indeed, no," answered Betty. "I asked no questions. There were gawks in plenty gaping and staring at the street corners. But," deprecatingly, "you

know you have told me how a modest lass should de-
mean herself, and so I just passed through the crowd
and said nothing. And then came this great happening !"

" Nothing ever happens to me," wailed Robin.
" To think that granny gave me leave to go to town
with you this morning, and I chose to stay behind
and make little boats out of pea-pods ! But tell the
rest, Betty. What came next ?"

" That was all. Only the gentleman who took the
flowers tossed me this crown piece, the lady smiled
and nodded, the carriages swept on up the hill, — and
here I am, alive and breathing after it all ! I couldn't
ha' believed it. But, verily, mistress, it is borne in
upon my mind that this will not be the end of it."

" Young lassies are apt to imagine vain things.
But we have wasted time enough over this. Go
you to your work, Betty, and I must in to my
spinning. Robin, put your boats in safe harbor
under the beehives, and come you in and read me
your lesson out of the horn-book."

" I will come if I must, but I am sore tired of
that horn-book," said the lad, as he stowed away
his boats. " I know every word from a to izzard
already. Are there no other books in the world,
that I must aye be reading that one over and
over ?"

The good dame looked bewildered. " Tired of

the horn-book?   Now who ever heard the like?
'Tis not every lad who gets a chance at it, I can
tell you that.   But, come in, child, come in, and
do your best at it to-day.   Mayhap I can get you
a better book of Father Hunt."

Pausing on the threshold, she called to Betty, who
was flying round to the croft door.   "But what said
he about the lace, — the mercer?"

"That you were to make a piece like it, forthwith," she called back.   "But, body o' me, the porridge is burning!   'Twill be only fit to throw to the
farrow."

CHAPTER III.

BETTY was right. This was not the end of it.

The next afternoon Dame Dorothy sat with her cushion on her knee, tossing the bobbins "in and out, and round about," while the narrow web of lace grew beneath her fingers. The sun had gone behind a cloud, and Betty had made a small fire on the hearth. There were few days when dwellers in the forest did not find a bed of smoldering coals, or a bright blaze, both cheery and comfortable.

She had been, as Sir Henry Valdegrave had said, not uncomely in her youth. She was far more comely now in the serene and tranquil dignity that had come to her as the years went by, —a dignity that had nothing to do with place or station. It was something innate; and many a high-born dame, many a lady of high degree, might have envied it. Quietly, and without resentment, she bore the burden of her years, with a form unbent, a step still light, a face unfurrowed by petty cares, or unholy passions.

It was a pretty picture the small interior presented that afternoon: the clear hearth, the unobtrusive, friendly fire, the shining pewter-ware on the dresser, the brass candlesticks on the narrow mantel-shelf, the gay cushion on the high-backed settle, where a great black cat was taking its ease, the lozenge-shaped window-panes, and the broad ledge underneath, where grew a pot of basil, Robin sailing his boats in a pan of water, and, finally, Dame Dorothy herself, in a gown of puce-colored flannel, white linen kerchief and apron, and a close cap, or hood, of muslin, with broad lappets that reached nearly to her waist.

Betty came flying in. "Ah, mistress, mistress! There be carriages coming down the road," she panted, "and fine ladies, and — I know not what! Run you to the window, Master Robin, quick, quick, that you may see the grand sight!"

But Robin had waited for no bidding. His nose was already flattened against the window-pane. Before Dame Dorothy could lay aside her cushion, it became evident that something more than seeing was demanded of her. Robin was too much over-awed for speech when the foremost of the two carriages came to a halt, and one of the footmen in scarlet livery leaped to the ground, strode up the garden path, and gave a thundering knock upon the door.

The dame herself opened it, and to the man's own amazement, possibly, his hand was raised to the level of his brow, instinctively.

"Doth one who is called Dame Dorothy dwell here?" he asked.

"I am she," was the answer, with a low curtsey.

Whereupon a tall, stately lady, with beautiful chestnut curls, beckoned to one of the gentlemen-in-waiting.

"I will alight," she said. "Drive ye all on for an hour, while I sit in the cottage. But let Gloster be brought hither. He will remain with me."

"I will alight also," said a handsome, imperious dame, from the carriage. "It is not fitting that your Grace visit the cottage unattended."

The Princess Anne hesitated for an instant, tapping the ground with the toe of her shoe.

"I require no attendance, my Lady Marlborough," she said, looking up quickly. "Drive on, and leave me for an hour."

She waited silently while a fair, blue-eyed boy was lifted from the second carriage, and ran towards her, delighted. Then taking his hand in hers, she stood quietly till the equipages were out of hearing ere she turned to Dame Dorothy, who had remained in the doorway, awaiting her commands.

Now the latter stepped forward ; and meeting the

300577

princess half-way down the path, she would have knelt to kiss her hand, had she not been forcibly prevented.

"Nay, nay, thou art too old for that. We'll have no bending of the knees. Kiss my hand if thou wilt; but thou hast kissed my cheek ere this. Dost thou not know me, Dorothy?"

"Surely I know thee, I know thee," said the dame, lifting the hand extended to her lips. "Thou art mine own Lady Anne Stuart. Or rather, thou art now the Princess Anne of Denmark."

"And thou art mine old nurse Dorothy, who has rocked me on her breast many a time," the lady answered. "It is as I thought when I saw that rare, quaint pattern of lace yesterday. I knew it for thy handiwork. Did not the lass tell thee?"

"Yes, my lady, and I wondered much. In truth, I slept little, last night, thinking of the years gone by. But I knew not thou wert at Windsor; and if I had, I could not have ventured to bring myself to thy notice after so many years."

For answer, the lady laid her hand on Dorothy's shoulder, smiling kindly.

"Come, come, Dame Dorothy, have you forgotten your manners?" she said, lightly, after a moment's pause. "Am I not to walk into your house, and have a seat by your fire? My shoes are none too thick, and I shall have twinges in my legs if I stand

longer on this ground, which seemeth to me somewhat damp."

"I crave your pardon, my Lady Anne. Come in,
come in! Glad indeed am I if my house may again
give shelter, if but for a moment, to one of the house
of Stuart."

The princess looked sharply at her hostess for an
instant. Then passing by her, she entered the cottage."

"Dorothy, Dorothy," she said, in a voice that was
marvellously sweet and musical, "I bid you be careful of your speech. Do you not know that light
words are dangerous? None can be too careful in
these days."

"Yea, I know it; but I fear not thee. Thou art
a Stuart, — and a daughter," she added in a whisper,
as she brought forward the best chair.

Meanwhile the small Duke of Gloster had followed
his mother into the house, and stood erect and silent
by the door, holding his plumed hat upon his hip.
The two women had forgotten his presence. Robin,
perched on the window-seat, with one small, brown
hand clinging to the casement, was as motionless as
the marble cherubs in St. George's Chapel. His
eyes were fastened on the small figure at the door in
an earnest gaze strangely compounded of curiosity,
awe, and boyish adoration. Surely something had
happened at last, even to him!

But presently Dorothy caught sight of the little duke, who was looking quietly about him with thoughtful, observant eyes.

"I crave pardon of his Grace," she said, springing forward, and leading the child to a seat. "It is not fitting that he should be thus left in the background when he visits Dame Dorothy's poor house. It is your son, Lady Anne?—the little Duke of Gloster?"

"It is Gloster," she answered, gravely. "Come hither, Willie. Look at Dame Dorothy, that you may know her well. When I was but a little creature, and, indeed, until I was more than six years old, she nursed me, and took tender care of me. Will you remember?"

"Indeed I will," the boy answered, stoutly. "But did she ever scold you? Tell me that, mamma."

"Nay, I have no such recollection," said the mother, laughing. "If she did, no doubt I deserved it. How was it, nurse? Pray you inform the young man. Did you ever scold me?"

"Nay, if my memory serves, I never ventured on that, my Lady Anne," retorted the dame. "In good sooth, I left the scolding to my Lady Frances."

"Which was well done and wisely. She had a sharper tongue than you, Dorothy. It stung like a lash when things went not to her liking."

"And did Dame Dorothy tell you fairy stories, and comfort you when you were ill, madam?"

"Yes, that she did."

"Then I will give her a kiss," said the child, suddenly leaning forward and kissing Dorothy's cheek as she knelt beside him.

Tears sprang to her eyes, though they did not overflow. She threw her arms about the princely boy for an instant; then kissed his hand. "God bless the lad!" she said, fervently. "God keep him, that he may sit upon the throne of his fathers."

This was too much for Robin. "Indeed I have kissed my granny more than a thousand times every day since I was born, and she did not cry about it!" he exclaimed, scrambling down from the window and rushing to the group by the fireside, with dark eyes kindling and cheeks aglow.

Dame Dorothy put her arm round him and drew him close to her side.

"Indeed and indeed thou hast. Thou art a good child to me, my Robin."

"But methinks thou didst begin the kissing right early," laughed the princess. "Thou wert a precocious youth, surely. Come hither, lad, and let me look at thee. The child is wondrously fair, nurse. Your grandson, did you say?"

"Lift your head, and speak to the princess, Robin. She would know who you are. Tell her your name."

"My name is Robin Sandys; and I am grandson

to Dame Dorothy Sandys," the child answered, quickly, as if repeating a lesson.

"And a right good name it is. Now tell me. Do you know who I am?"

The child answered gravely, lifting his dark eyes to the fair, kindly face of the princess:

"My granny has often told me how, in the days when she dwelt in king's houses, she nursed the Lady Anne Stuart, and all about the fine palace, and the shining river, and the gay barges going up and down, with all their flags a-flying. Truly I think you are her Lady Anne," he said, shyly.

"And who is this?" she asked, with her arm about her little duke.

"Oh, I know him! I have heard about *him!*" Robin cried, turning a glowing face towards Gloster. "He is to be the king one day, when he is a man grown. My grandmother has told me; and how I am to be his faithful servant till I die. I will love him now, if he will let me."

"Truly, truly I will," was Gloster's eager answer, as he seized Robin's hand. "Do they call you Robin? Do you want to be a soldier? Have you a sword and a cap, or guns and cannon?"

"No! I have no such toys. I would rather sail the high seas with a great fleet of ships."

"I am a soldier already," said his Grace, the duke. "I have command of a regiment."

"Kings have to be soldiers," said Robin, sententiously. "They have to learn things. I never learned."

Just then Gloster's eye fell upon the pea-pod fleet in the corner of the room, and the great round sea of the milk-pan.

"Oh!" he cried, in delight. "Are those your ships? Did you make them? See the masts and the little sails! May I touch them?"

There was a moment's whispering, then, "Mamma! Mamma! may I go with Robin to sail them?"

"Yes, yes. Run away," said the princess; and, at a sign from Dorothy, Robin lifted the pan with great care, lest the ocean should overflow, and the two boys went out to play in the garden.

"A pretty pair," said the princess. "Your little lad is well spoken for one of his age and breeding."

A "slow, wise smile," significant of much observation, passed over Dame Dorothy's face.

"Think you so, my lady?—I crave pardon of your Grace. But even against my will, my tongue forms the name by which I called you when you were a child in my arms, the Lady Anne Stuart, whom I loved."

"Call me what you will, Dorothy. I like to hear the Lady Anne from your lips. But we were speaking of the lad."

"I have tried to do my best for the child," Dame

Dorothy went on. "If he seems to you well-spoken, mayhap it is because he has seldom played with children, and has had naught to do with rough folk. I have kept him close under my own wing."

"But has he neither father nor mother?"

"'Tis a long story, madam. My son Robin went, as your Grace may remember, to the colonies in Virginia, for the bettering of his fortunes. But he found death there, not gold; and his young wife died soon after. Their one little son, who bore his father's name, was sent overseas to me by the hand of one who had grown homesick for old England, and was fain to return to the land of his birth."

"He brought the small craft he piloted into a safe and goodly harbor," said the princess, looking round her. "You seem well-to-do, nurse Dorothy, and in no need."

"In no need, thanks be to God," she answered. "I have been rarely prospered. When I was nurse to the Lady Anne I had no occasion to use my wages. All was saved that my husband might buy the rental of a bit of land in Deptford, on which his heart had long been set, — some fields adjoining those his father tilled. And when my term of service was over, my lord, the duke, — your honored father, madam, — added thereto a goodly sum. Then I have deft fingers, as your ladyship knows, and my wants are few. And, thanks be to God, I have had wit enough to take care of what I had. The battle is half won when one has learned that."

"When did I see you last, — and where?" asked the princess. "It must have been long ago."

"I know not the number of the years, my lady. I am not good at such figures. But it was when his Majesty, James II., was on the throne. I remember it well. It was at the Cock-pit."

The Cock-pit, so-called, was a part of the great palace of Whitehall, and was for some years the home of the Princess Anne and her husband, Prince George of Denmark.

The princess had risen from her chair, and was moving nervously about the room, now looking out of the window at the children, now giving a twirl to the small wheel that stood against the wall, now breaking a leaf from the pot of basil, and crushing it between her fingers. At length she seated herself in the corner of the settle, and leaned her head against the high back.

"Go on," she said, softly. "Tell me about it. It was at the Cock-pit?"

"Yes, madam. I had come up from Deptford with some exceeding fine yarn I had spun at the order of my Lady Somerset; and having bought me some stuff for a new petticoat, and a bit of taffeta ribbon withal, I turned from the Strand into White-hall Street, on my way homeward. Now I had in

my pocket a gay ball, knitted of many-colored wors-
teds, and bright with tinkling bells, such as might
please a child's fancy; and I thought mayhap the
little Lady Mary, — your daughter, — whom I heard
was ailing, might be diverted thereby. So I stopped
at the Cock-pit, and made bold to ask the housekeeper to devise means to bring it to her notice.
'Surely, surely,' quoth she, and while I was drinking a bowl of posset, she carried off the ball and
presently brought me word that I was to go to your
chamber."

"It had passed from my mind, but I remember it
all, now," said the princess, "and that I knew the
ball was of your knitting as soon as ever I saw it.
But go on."

"Your Grace was in the small tapestried chamber
over the eastern gate, — the one with the oriel window. The two little ladies were with you."

"And they are both gone, Dorothy! Only Gloster
is left to me, — only he of all my children."

"Dear, my lady!" said the elder woman, tenderly,
and then was silent. Leaving the painful theme, she
resumed her story.

"After awhile your ladyship bade the nurse-maids
take the children into another room; and then, just
as you were speaking with me kindly of my own
small matters, and asking about the crops, and
how we were getting on, lo! there was the sound of

footsteps in the corridor, and the gentleman usher announced in a loud voice his Majesty, the King. I was that frightened that my heart was in my mouth; and seeing there was no way to escape, save by the corridor, I would fain have hid behind the arras. But you bade me withdraw into the oriel window, and wait, — just out of hearing. I peeped out from behind the curtain, — as who would not? — for it is not every day that a woman like me gets a chance to look on a king, — and she in the same room with him! Dost thou remember how he looked that day, madam? Tall and stately, with a fine color, and the Stuart dimple in his chin, and the fine, straight nose of him? He wore a crimson doublet, slashed, and a jewelled collar, and a tall hat with feathers. Methought he was not like a king at all, but just like any common father when he sat down beside you, and kissed your cheek, and passed his hand over your bright curls. Ah, how he loved you, my Lady Anne!"

The princess frowned, and seemed about to speak as she moved her small hands nervously. But some strange fascination held her silent, and the old woman went on.

"That was what I kept thinking all the time, — 'how he loves her!' 'Twas sometimes said the King was a stern man, and a hard. But he seemed not so that day, — only grand and tender, as befitted his high office."

"Peace, Dorothy!" cried the princess. "I will not have you talk thus. Why call you James II. king? He is king no longer."

"Nay, I know that right well. But, lady, thou art a Stuart, and I dare to tell thee that I love the Stuarts with every drop of the red blood in my veins! I like not Dutch interlopers and changes and revolutions, and the banishing of good, true men for the crime of being loyal to their anointed king. Who is this William of Orange? He, to lord it over Englishmen! While Queen Mary was alive, the old line was upon the throne, and that was something, even to those of us who were fain to believe in the keeping of the fifth commandment. But now!"

The Princess Anne, whether she were a loyal daughter or no, — as, alas! she was not if history tells the truth, — was at least not overfond of her Dutch brother-in-law, who had for years taken every means to humiliate and annoy her, even while he acknowledged her son as his heir, and herself as next in succession. Certain it is that there was no love lost between them. Doubtless this had much to do with the fact that she quite ignored the sharp sting in this plain-spoken old woman's reference to the fifth commandment. Looking at her steadily for a moment, she said:

"Grant me patience, Dorothy! These be too

great points for women to meddle with. I am only sorry my father brought things to such a pass as they were at. If he had not, no doubt he would be on the throne now."

"Would God he were!" cried Dorothy.

"And again I say to you, Dorothy Sandys, that you must bridle your tongue! Such talk is not safe. Do you not know it?"

"Yea, madam, I know it well. But think not I am such a fool as to cry aloud in the market-place. I know where, and to whom, I speak. Dost not thou, too, love the Stuarts, my princess?"

"Thou wouldst fain make me believe I do, in spite of all," cried Anne. "But enough of this. Let us have no more such talk! Dorothy, do you mind the foaming glass you used to mix for me? I know not what you called the draught; but it was hot and smooth and sweet, and of a golden yellow, with a great drift of white sea-foam on the top. I liked it well."

"It was Queen's Broth, my lady," cried Dame Dorothy, delighted. "And to think your ladyship remembers it after all these years! It was made with a fresh-laid egg well beaten, a spoonful — "

"No matter for the recipe, nurse, as I am not likely to compound it myself. But I would fain know if the sweet draught still has the olden savor."

As the dame hurried away to prepare it, in a
pleasant flurry of excitement, the Princess Anne
leaned her head against the back of the settle, and
watched the little flickering fire with eyes that saw
only the past.

CHAPTER IV.

MEANWHILE the sun had come out from behind the clouds, the wind had gone down, and the small garden lay basking in the light and warmth of the afternoon, bright with color, and sweet with flower scents, and the pungent odor of aromatic herbs. Pansies, sweet peas, and scarlet runners bloomed in humble content side by side with those belated jonquils.

The two children had grown tired at length of their pea-pod boats, and had been chasing each other up and down the garden paths, with an occasional excursion around the croft, where the dun cow was grazing, until the little duke, who was not strong, had dropped upon a bench opposite the beehives, and was fanning himself with his plumed hat. Robin sat on the ground at his feet, looking up at him with adoring eyes. He was very happy. The great world of kings and princes and fine ladies, of palaces and castles, of gay pageants and magnificent spectacles, which had so stirred his childish imagination, as he listened to his grandmother's stories, did not seem as far off as usual. For this little lad at whose feet he sat, a lad no older, — nay, perhaps even younger, — no stronger, and in some respects no wiser than he; this lad who had been running races with him, and had been just as anxious to touch the goal first as was ever Betty Macthorne herself, — was he not to be King of England some day?

But Robin was very curious; and in the sweet freemasonry of childhood, he did not in the least hesitate to ask questions.

"How do you like it?" he said, throwing himself back on the warm grass, and, with hands clasped under his head, taking in every detail of the small figure above him, from the sunny hair, and the lace collar falling over the blue velvet coat, to the silken hose and pointed shoes.

"'Like it?' What do you mean?"

"Why, how do you think you will like it, — to be king?"

"I don't think about it more than I can help," said the heir to the throne, shying an acorn at a squirrel. "All that is a great way off. I may like it well enough when I am a man, and I may not. Kings have a great deal of trouble."

"But how does your Grace like getting ready to be a king? You have to do that, don't you? You have to learn how?"

The little duke laughed outright.

ROBIN AND GLOSTER IN THE GARDEN.

"You are an odd boy, surely. No one ever asked me that question before. What made you think of it? But, look you, Robin. You are not to call me 'your Grace.' I will not have it, for you know we are to be friends, — and we are only lads now," he added, bearing in mind, no doubt, some slight knowledge of the etiquette of courts.

"All right," said Robin. "I don't quite like it myself, now that you have said — what you did just now. But what shall I call you? You will have to tell me, because I don't know about such things."

"Call me Gloster. How do I like getting ready to be a king?" he added, going back to Robin's quaint question. "I never thought that was what I was doing till this minute. But I suppose it is. I have to do it whether I like it or not, you see."

"But is it hard work to learn how? Don't you like it?"

Gloster pondered. "I like the soldiering part well enough," he said, gravely. "But, you see, that's a small part of it, and sometimes I wish I had no tutors and governors. There are so many things to learn, and I tire of it when my head aches. But I should like to be Prince of Wales," he added, confidentially, lowering his voice, and looking round as if for eavesdroppers. "A prince does not have to be so wise as a king; and then I like the Welsh people, on account of Lewis Jenkins. He's

a Welshman, and a good friend of mine. He says
I may be Prince of Wales some day," the lad went
on, dreamily.   "But why am I not now, as the
others were? Tell me that, if you can?"

This was a conundrum quite beyond Robin's solv-
ing. "What others?" he asked, with a puzzled air.

"Why, the other lads who were getting ready to
be kings, as you say I am. They have all been
Princes of Wales, and I am not. But who is Prince,
then? I asked Bishop Burnet, one day, and he only
shook his head, and told me not to ask questions."

To Robin's mind it was much as if Gloster had
asked why he was not the angel Gabriel. But
had he been older, he would have seen that his new
acquaintance had been kept in ignorance of the existence of his grandfather James II., and of the little
exiled Prince of Wales, who was scarcely older than
himself.

He still lay on the grass, looking thoughtfully up
at the blue sky above him, over which a few light,
fleecy clouds were slowly sailing. Then he brought
his eyes down to the level of the pretty boy beside
him.

"I never knew that kings had trouble," he said,
laying his hand tenderly upon the small foot that
was swinging to and fro. "I thought any lad would
be glad and proud to be — what is it they call you?"

"Heir to the Crown of England," said Gloster,

sententiously. "But what of that? I took my aunt Mary's crown in my hand once. It sparkled grandly, yet —"

This was an absorbing talk for Robin. "Why do you stop?" he said, impatiently.

"Oh, I was thinking of one day at Kensington, when I heard my mother ask her if it was not heavy."

"And what did she say?"

"That crowns were not always so heavy as they seemed. Well," with a long-drawn sigh, "I don't understand it all, but I know I would rather be Knight of the Garter, and have the blue ribbon. I hoped to have had it for a birthday present. But what do you think? They gave me a parrot instead!"

Robin's eyes opened wider and wider. Here was a boy who talked of jewelled crowns as lightly as if they were cricket balls or marbles. And what was it to be Knight of the Garter, and have a blue ribbon?

"I — I think I would have liked the parrot better, myself," he said, hesitatingly.

"That's only because you don't know," answered Gloster. "But no matter. I'll explain it to you sometime."

Then, with a long-drawn breath and a flourish of his hat, he changed the whole subject.

"What are we sitting here for, talking of these dull things?" he said, seizing Robin's hand and giving it a strong pull. "You know I said you must belong to my regiment. Let us go in and consult madam, — my mother."

But it was too late for any further negotiations that day. Just as they reached the threshold, the returning carriages drew up before the cottage. The ladies therein would fain have alighted, for this unattended visit of the princess to her old nurse had excited no little curiosity in their innocent breasts. Anne, however, radiant and smiling after her sup of Queen's Broth, waited for no summons, and appeared upon the scene at once.

"Methinks it will rain again, shortly," she said, glancing at the sky, over which one or two innocent white clouds were idly floating. "We will make no further delay. Hasten, Gloster! the Lady Fitzhardinge waits."

The boy was accustomed to obedience. Making hurried adieux to Dame Dorothy, who stood curtseying in the doorway, he hesitated for a moment, and then threw one arm across Robin's shoulder.

"I will come again," he whispered, "and I will not forget. You are to be one of my men."

Some one lifted him into the high-hung carriage, or chariot, and he was whisked away out of sight, while Robin stood gazing after him with a new expression on his speaking face. After awhile he went slowly into the house, as one in a dream.

"Granny, one never knows what may happen," said he, standing gravely by the fire with his hands clasped behind him, and his eyes fixed upon the smoldering coals. "Little did I think, when I made those pea-pod boats, that Gloster and I would play with them together, and then have such a long talk about kings and crowns afterwards."

"And little did I think, when I stuffed the new cushions for the settle, who would be first to use them. But, *Gloster* did you say?" asked Dame Dorothy, suddenly. "The young duke's name seems to slip from your tongue quite glibly, my laddie. Did you hold much discourse with his Grace out there by the beehives? Betty, the cow is lowing. 'Tis high time she were milked and quartered for the night. Child, 'tis not well to be too familiar with the quality. Sometimes they take offence when one would not think it."

Child as he was, Robin felt the implied rebuke, and his face crimsoned. He did not answer; but his breast heaved, and Dorothy saw he was striving valiantly to keep the tears back.

"Nay, nay, 'tis nothing to grieve about," she said, pushing her wheel away, and drawing her chair nearer to the hearth. "Come hither, laddie, and tell me all about it. Dost thou like the young duke?"

"*Like* him! I love him, and we are to be friends. He said so, and that he liked me well. He told me I was to call him Gloster, and that I was not to say 'your Grace.'"

Overwrought and excited, the boy broke at last into a flood of passionate tears, clasping his arms around her neck, and burying his face in her bosom.

"There, there, dear heart!" she whispered, "hush thee now! Thou art tired and must rest. We will talk no more of it to-night, but to-morrow thou shalt tell me all about it. Wipe thine eyes, my laddie, that are too young for such salt tears, and I will sing thee one of the little songs thou lovest," and she crooned to him in the twilight till he fell asleep.

Perhaps the dame was not sorry when, two hours after, Robin awoke, bright and happy, hungry for his supper, and eager to talk of the events of the afternoon. It must be confessed she was anxious to know what had passed between the two children.

"Well, well," she said, "here be news indeed! And so my young master, the duke, wants my laddie for one of his soldiers, does he? Truly, we are in for fine doings. Mayhap we will have to join the army in Flanders. Who knows? And what else said he?"

"I told him," answered the child, in a low voice, "that you had lived in kings' houses, and he said that it might be I would live in kings' houses myself, some day. What think you of that, granny? Would you like it?"

"Indeed and indeed, that is a question not to be answered lightly," she said, after a long pause. "When you are older, if there should be chance to get you place in the household of some noble gentleman who would have you trained in all things fitting — But no more of that now," she went on, clasping him closer. "You are not ready to fly from the nest yet, thank God! We are quiet and comfortable here now, with bread enow and to spare. There's no hurry."

"But — granny!"

"Well, what now?"

"Can you teach me Latin?"

"Gramercy, no! — Latin? I can read my prayer-book well enow, and now and then make out a chapter, or a few versicles, thanks to my wits and a good pair of eyes. But as for Latin! — no, child, I can't teach you that. One tongue is all I can manage."

"And who will?"

"And you must learn the Latin?" she said, at length. "God bless me, but what put that notion into your head? You have never seemed any too eager to learn your horn-book, let alone harder stuff."

"Because — I did not know," the child answered, in a low voice. "But now — I must be getting ready."

" Ready for what ? "

" To be a man — and to be Gloster's friend.   Do you hear, granny?   I am to be Gloster's friend, — and you told me yourself he was to be King of England one of these days.   He is getting ready now."

"Stars and garters!" the dame exclaimed, in utter amazement.   "The young eaglets are pluming their wings, sure enough!   So!   The little duke is getting ready to be king, is he?   And how, if I may make bold to ask?   Methinks the lad is in something of a hurry."

"Don't laugh, granny.   You do not understand. 'Tis not that he is in a hurry, — but he has to do it. He has tutors and governors, and he learns the Latin, and he studies the maps, and how to build forts and direct armies; and he is trained — oh, listen, listen, granny! — he is trained in all ' knightly exercises.' That is what he said.   I remember the words well."

" Poor little lambkin!" said Dame Dorothy, shaking her head.   "'Tis no wonder he is slight and delicate, and has not thy fresh color, laddie.   But, tell me!   How wouldst thou like that sort of life, boy?   Thou art young to be thinking of matters like this, Robin."

" I am older than Gloster, and he thinks of them. Why should not I?   But, granny, may I learn the Latin, and begin to make myself ready?   'Tis high time!"

She laughed.

"You must make yourself ready for bed," she answered. "Dear me, laddie! 'tis ten o' the clock. But about the Latin? Have patience, for I must talk to Father Hunt. Mayhap he can put you in the way of it, if it pleases him."

Dame Dorothy sat long by the fire that night, pondering deeply over things past, present, and to come. Few women of her day, and certainly very few of her station, had led lives as full and varied as hers. If her outlook was wider, and more comprehensive than theirs, it is not to be wondered at. There was much to think of, much to consider; for she felt instinctively that a new and vital force had entered her life and Robin's. What would come of it?

At length she arose, and put the brands together, covering the embers carefully; and then stood leaning against the settle, while one hand grasped the high mantel-shelf, and the other drew back her skirts from the hot hearth.

"God in heaven knows all," she sighed, at last, glancing at the bed in the opposite room, where the beautiful child lay sleeping soundly, his cheeks flushed with the warmth of slumber, his brown hair a mass of tousled curls, and his long, dark eyelashes curving softly. "I cannot look far ahead. But the lad must have every chance in life that I can compass for him. I must see Father Hunt."

CHAPTER V

Royal children learn worldly wisdom early.

"And to whom, pray, have you had the honor of making so long a visit?" asked the Lady Fitzhardinge of her charge, as he seated himself in the carriage.

Perhaps the child noticed a slight touch of sarcasm in the voice of his governess.

"To an old friend of my mother's," he answered, gravely, after a moment's pause.

"And the lad whom you caressed, — who may he be?"

"He is her grandson, Robin Sandys by name, and a friend of mine own," said Gloster, settling himself back in his seat, and removing his hat while he toyed with the feather, and allowed the soft summer wind to rumple his fair hair. "I like him much."

"Humph! Put on your hat, sir. We shall have you ill again, and there will be another pother with diet-drinks, and doctors. I thought surely he must be some young prince when I saw you embrace him so warmly under her Royal Highness's very eyes."

"He is a — kind of prince," retorted the child,

laughing good-naturedly, and quietly obeying the mandate as to his head-gear. "I like him much," he repeated. "He is — interesting. He makes me think."

"As how, for instance? Did you discuss affairs of state with this fine young gentleman?"

"I don't know just what your ladyship means by that," said Gloster; "but we talked of many things. He asked me how I liked getting ready to be a king. Now, no one ever asked me that before, — not even Lewis Jenkins, or Bishop Burnet. No one ever cared!"

"Methinks when you name the two it would be well to give precedence to my lord Bishop rather than that Welshman," remarked Lady Fitzhardinge. "Sit up, Gloster. It is not seemly to loll on the cushions in that manner. Hold yourself erect, and do not fail to acknowledge the salutation of the guards."

This was said as the carriage swept up Castle Hill and through the gateway of Henry VIII. into the lower court.

An hour later, a little figure in blue velvet flashed along the east terrace, scrambled up a flight of narrow, winding stairs, and then dashed through sundry intricate passages, till he reached a chamber in one of the towers, called the Queen's Closet. It was the favorite apartment of the Princess Anne. Here the child paused, panting for breath, after his rapid flight, and wiped his forehead with his small handkerchief before he knocked.

A voice bade him enter; and with some difficulty he lifted the wrought-iron latch, and the heavy oaken door swung inward. In an instant, his eye swept every corner of the room, and Gloster flew into his mother's arms with a cry of joy.

"What! is it you, my Willie?" the princess said, caressing him tenderly. "And alone? You know I do not like to have you run about the castle unattended."

"Yes, I know, I know, mamma! But 'tis just this once, and I wanted *you*. I have business. So I stole away when nobody knew it. This is how it was. I had just had supper, with Lady Fitzhardinge and Lewis Jenkins in attendance; and then my lady was fain to go to her chamber, and Lewis went to carry her train. Then I flew, — and here I am!"

The princess tried to frown, but laughed instead.

"So I see, so I see, and I greatly fear it was a naughty trick, my Will. But tell me now — where was my Lady Fitzhardinge's page, that Lewis Jenkins found it needful to play the part of train-bearer to her ladyship?"

"Harry Hamilton? Why, my lady allowed him to see the cricket match this afternoon over at Eton. But won't there be a pother when they find I am gone!" and the boy's blue eyes danced with glee at the thought.

Truth to tell, those of his mother danced also. Anne was punctilious, and knew well the etiquette of courts; but as far as it touched her family life and loves, she found it burdensome. It was always a delight to both when she could have her little son to herself, out of reach of tutors, governesses, and gentlemen-in-waiting.

One great fear had long harassed her, — the fear that he would be taken from her by King William, and placed in charge of some nobleman, or ecclesiastic, during the period of his education. This was quite according to precedent, and had been for many ages. But the small duke was a frail child, and had been reared, even thus far, with difficulty. To tear him from his mother's watchful, brooding care might mean disaster, if not death. It is not strange if Anne felt that the stern, hard brother-in-law to whom she had yielded the throne held in his hands a weapon by means of which he might easily reach her heart.

But presently the lad withdrew from the arms that held him close, and, drawing forward a small tabouret, seated himself at his mother's knee.

"Now for business," she said, smiling.

"Yes," Gloster answered, very gravely. "I said I had business. Mamma, I want to talk to you about Robin."

"Dame Dorothy's little lad? Well,—what of him?"

"I want him for one of my men—my soldiers. I spoke to him about it. Do you think Dame Dorothy would object?" he asked, anxiously.

The princess laughed, undeterred by the grave, earnest face, with thoughtful blue eyes that sought her own inquiringly. "Verily," she said, "one would imagine the objecting might be on the other side. But what do you want of this Robin, pretty lad though he be? Haven't you men enough already?"

"Not so many as I had in Kensington. I had two whole companies there. But that is not all, mamma. A soldier is one thing, and a friend is another. I must have Robin for my friend."

"But have you not friends enough already? Did I not send to Eton for four lads to bear you company? See now, while I tell them over. There are Peter Bathurst and his brother, and Arthur Churchill, and Peter Boscawen, to say nothing of Harry Hamilton, and the other boys. What need have you of more? Do you not like them?"

"Yes, mamma, I like them well enough. But not as I like Robin. I love him greatly."

"Well, well! but this seems to be a case of love at first sight. And does Robin love you?"

"Indeed he does. We said a rhyme together,

and shook hands on it. May I repeat it to you, mamma?"

"Certainly. I shall hearken with great pleasure. I am rather fond of love songs," said the princess. "Go on."

The child rose and stood before her, clasping his small hands, while he repeated, in a low voice:

> " We will be friends
> Until life ends;
> Until death parts
> Our loving hearts."

"Heaven save us!" cried the princess, "but this seems to be serious business. Which made the rhyme, you or Robin?"

"We made it together, mamma. I made the first two lines, and Robin the last two. But tell me, mamma! May I have Robin here at the castle? Do not stop to think," he cried, dancing about impatiently. "Jenkins will find me in two minutes. May I have Robin?"

But just then an obsequious knock was heard, followed by the voice of the faithful Welsh usher, asking if the duke was within.

"Gloster is here. You shall have him presently," answered the princess. "Now go you quietly with Jenkins," she added, "and tell him you were naughty to run away from him. Nay, you must have pa-

tience, child. I will think of this matter, and talk
with you again. But now good night."

Two days after this, a groom in the scarlet and
gold livery of the Princess Anne drew rein before
Dame Dorothy's porch. He bore to her the command of his royal mistress, that she should present
herself at the castle next morning by ten of the
clock, bringing with her her little grandson, Robin
by name.

Dame Dorothy curtseyed.

"Make my reverence to her Royal Highness,"
she said ; "I will do her bidding."

"Good lack !" cried Mat Hansel. "Of course
you will ! It is not every day that a woman of your
order is summoned to the castle by command of the
princess herself. 'Tis a great honor. If it were
Mistress Randee, the housekeeper, now, it would be
quite another matter. But 'tis the princess, herself,
I say."

However, he accepted graciously a stirrup-cup of
foaming beer presented at that moment by Betty
Macthorne, and drained it to the dregs at one
draught.

"Truely a fair and comely damsel," he said, with
a low bow, after the manner of his betters, as he
returned the flagon. "I give you thanks, Dame Dorothy, for the day is hot and my throat was parched.
But to business. You are to be at the foot of St.

John's Tower by ten o' the clock ; and there you will be met by one who will convey you to the presence of her Royal Highness. Do you understand the matter ?"

"Surely I have wit enow for that," was the answer. "It is not so wondrous hard. Hear now! God willing, I will be at the foot of St. John's Tower to-morrow morning at ten o' the clock. Is that right?"

"Good day, then," said the groom, replacing the cap he had removed while drinking. "Might this young damsel be your daughter?"

"She might be, but she is not," Dame Dorothy replied, somewhat curtly. "Good day to you, and thanks for your kind offices. Run into the house, Betty," she added, in a low tone, as the girl lingered in the doorway. "No need to stand staring there like a gawk."

She did not intend that Betty's head should be turned by compliments at so early a stage in its career.

"It is time to spread the cloth for dinner, child," she said, kindly, as they went indoors. "Put out the veal pasty I made last night, with a manchet of brown bread, and a bit of cheese."

But Betty lingered, with her hand on the door-latch, and her eyes on Mat Hansel's flying figure.

"Is it true, mistress ?" she asked, in a low, tremulous voice. " Am I 'fair and comely,' as he said? Why, the very boys in London streets used to jeer and hoot at me, and call me a blackamoor, and other hard names, till I cried for very shame, and thought I was but a blot on the face of the earth. Is it true what he said ? "

" Nay, but that is all nonsense, child. Fair, or foul, you are as God made you. Not but that you're well enow ; yes, you're well enow. Many a lass looks worse. But as for these young, foolish gallants, like him of the scarlet coat yonder, never do you heed what they may say, my Betty. They have plenty of fine phrases that they scatter about, never heeding whether they be fitting or no. But you're well enow, child, if you do but keep yourself clean and tidy."

Betty ran off to her work, half forgetting, in this new interest, that her mistress and Robin had been summoned to the castle. But when she went to dip water from a clear, running spring behind the cottage, she looked long and earnestly at the face that peered up at her from its depths — a mirror framed in green mosses.

She frowned as she looked. " I am not 'fair and comely,' " she said. " He was but jesting — that man. My hair does not curl, and my nose is awry, and my mouth — "

But here she broke into a laugh, and spoiled the

picture as she sent the bucket splashing down into
the cool, green depths below.   Not a doll's face, certainly ; but the clear, steady eyes told their own tale of
truth and loyalty ; and the mouth she had so laughed
to scorn would one day settle into curves of mingled
strength and sweetness.   Mat Hansel was not so far
out of the way, after all.

The gray cottage was astir betimes the next morning. Betty was jubilant, fully believing that this great
honor had come to her mistress and Robin through
her.   Never was the breakfast-table more daintily
set forth ; and, as an offering acceptable to the pro-
pitious gods, a brown stone jug overflowing with jonquils had the place of honor in the middle.   A rasher
of bacon and some eggs gave out delicious odors, but
Dame Dorothy ate little and Robin even less.

"Master Robin, you do not eat your breakfast.
You will need plenty of strength to-day, with all the
fine doings," Betty remarked, anxiously, as she flitted
in and out.   "Come now, mistress, will it not be well
for me to make him a posset of new milk with a sup
of raspberry cordial in it ?   It might hearten him up
a bit."

Dame Dorothy laughed, but shook her head, while
Robin made brave but futile attempts at doing trencher duty.   He said nothing, but glanced now and
then at the sun that was rising high in the heavens.

"There's no need of haste, sweetheart," said the

grandmother. "Even my old legs can carry me to the town in half an hour, and there's no use standing about, staring, before we are wanted. Come hither, and let me make thy collar straight, and fasten thy hose that they do not be dangling about thine heels. I would have bought thee a new pair of garters, if I had but foreseen what was coming."

As the child stood before her, patiently submitting to the touch of her deft fingers, she was struck anew with a sense of his remarkable beauty. Surely there would be none fairer than he in the old castle on the hill. He wore a little suit of brown frieze, the very color of his eyes and hair, faced back with scarlet, and a scarlet cap with a silken tassel. His broad collar and deep cuffs were of fine linen, thanks to Dame Dorothy's own skill. She bought no linen of the mercer, not she !

As for herself, she wore the petticoat of puce-colored flannel that she had worn on the day of the princess's visit, with an overgown of gray wool, and the same muslin hood and deep lappets. But in honor of the occasion she had brought forth from the depths of an oak chest a fine white apron, edged with drawn-work. Robin, boy-like, had taken but little note of his own array, but he looked with approving eyes on his grandmother. "You look very nice," he said, smoothing down the white folds of her apron. "Almost like a lady. I suppose you looked like this always, when you lived in kings' houses."

"Ah, no! I was young then, laddie, and my cheeks were like the damask roses. But—like a lady! If I were a real lady, now, and were called to her Grace's presence, I should wear a coif set with seed pearls, and a veil of Flanders lace. But God forgive me! The muslin hood is fine enow for me, and I am well content with it. Come now,— we'll be going."

Hand in hand, in the sweet morning stillness, they went on their way to the castle,—down what is now the Long Walk, but which was then but a wildwood road through a mass of tangled verdure, with glimpses of the blue sky shining through the overhanging boughs. But ever and anon the gray towers and turrets rose before them, with the massive, stately keep dominating all.

The little town seemed asleep as they turned into High Street, for it was not market-day, and the business of the place had scarce begun. Robin's eyes grew large and dark, and his hand clasped that of his grandmother tightly as they passed under King Henry's Gateway and, entering the lower court, walked slowly up the hill.

"And whither do we go now?" the lad asked, looking up at the great Round Tower. "Granny, granny, do you know the way to go?"

"Never fear, laddie, I can find my way to St. John's Tower.   Hark!"

For just then they were passing St. George's Chapel.   A bell was tolling softly, and through the open door came the deep, rolling thunder of the organ.   "Would you like to look in?" she said. "There will be services later, but it is not time yet. Shall we go in for a minute?"

But the child drew back.   "Oh! may we?" he whispered.   "Is it not the King's church?"

"It is the house of the King of kings, and the lowliest may enter in," said the old woman, drawing him through the portal.   The beautiful chapel, with its vaulted roof, its richly stained windows, its lofty choir, with the emblazoned coats-of-arms and the banners of the Knights of the Garter drooping idly above the carved stalls, seemed to the sensitive child like a passing glimpse of the house not made with hands.   He trembled and his eyes filled.

"Not now, granny, not now," he cried, shrinking into the shadow of a stately column.   "Sometime I will go in mayhap, but not now."

"Come on, then," she said.   "In truth we must not loiter, for the great clock yonder hath given its warning, and it will soon strike ten."

CHAPTER VI.

Skirting the great keep, from whose hoary battlements the banner of England floated, with the
colors of the Princess Anne fluttering from a lower
flagstaff under it, they passed through a gateway at
the right into the upper quadrangle, and crossed the
court to St. John's Tower. Here, in a small Gothic
porch, they awaited further orders; and here, presently, Mat Hansel joined them.

"So you are here in good time," he said. "That
is well. Her Royal Highness doth not like to be
kept waiting, as I have learned to my cost," and he
shrugged his broad shoulders. "Faith! She hath
a little temper of her own, mild as she seems, for
women are women. Hast ever had speech with her
Grace?"

"Nay, I care not to discuss the business nor the
tempers of my betters," she answered. "Will it
please you to tell me how I may be brought to the
presence of her Grace?"

"Why, that is just what I am here for," he said,
flicking the dust from the sleeve of his red jerkin.
"I am to conduct you to her bedchamber woman,

Mistress Abigail Hill, who will bring you where you may have speech of her. Come on, for the clock strikes."

They had passed the guard-house, when a quick roll of drums came from the windows of St. George's Hall, just above their heads, — with loud shouts, shrill, childish voices, outcries, and merry laughter. And in a moment, down a great stairway, Gloster came flying, dressed in full regimentals and wearing a sheathed sword that clattered on the stones as he ran. At his heels followed his adjutant, a lad much older than himself, while at the head of the stairs swarmed the whole army, in showy red caps and coats, armed cap-a-pie.

"Halt! go back!" shouted the small commandant. "Back to the Hall this instant! It is not soldierly to leave your posts. Go you, too, Boscawen, and proceed with the drill. I will myself return presently."

Meanwhile Robin would fain have lingered, but Mat Hansel was stalking on ahead, looking neither to the right nor the left. Dame Dorothy kept fast hold of her grandson's hand, half dragging him onward.

"Stop! Stop! Do you not hear me, Robin? This is the place!" a clear voice called after them. "Robin, Robin, come back!"

Dame Dorothy paused irresolutely, but did not

retrace her steps. Robin, however, with a bound and a spring, drew his hand from her grasp, and was at Gloster's side in an instant.

"This is well, this is well!" cried the latter. "You are just in time. Come you up to the Hall, Robin, and Boscawen will have you armed and equipped in a trice. Come on!"

"Now here's a fine pother!" cried Dame Dorothy, approaching the pair, who stood with clasped hands, smiling radiantly at each other. "Nay, nay, my young master, this may not be. I am loath to displease you, but Robin cannot go with you. He must come with me to the chamber of her Grace, your mother, with no delay, for yon young gallant who was sent to guide us is well-nigh out of sight this minute. Neither is it good manners to loiter, for we were to be with my lady at ten o' the clock. Come, Robin, make no more delay."

"Yes, you must go," said Gloster, ruefully. "By my sword, but this is a disappointment. I thought it was all settled. But hold up your head, and don't be afeard, Robin," he whispered. "I told her Grace about the rhymes, and she did but laugh."

Away he sped up the stairs again, while Dame Dorothy and her charge followed swiftly the receding figure of Mat Hansel.

He led them out on Queen Elizabeth's Terrace, and thence by a roundabout way to a flight of winding stairs, at the foot of which the new bedchamber woman, Mistress Abigail Hill, who had lately obtained this place by the intervention of her cousin, — my Lady Marlborough, — was waiting to take them in charge.

"This way," quoth Mistress Hill, leading the way up the stairs, that wound round and round, corkscrew fashion. The tower was high, and the ascent was lighted only by narrow slits in the deep masonry, while the steps were worn into great, uneven hollows, where the feet of the generations had trodden from age to age.

Robin was overpowered by the strangeness of it all, the sense of mystery, the vastness, the silence, and a new, unexpected dread of what might be coming. He clung to Dame Dorothy's hand, and his breath came quickly.

"My heart thumps in my breast, granny," he half sobbed. "I cannot breathe! These stairs are so long."

"Yes, laddie, and they are steep. It's aye hard climbing. Many a man has learned that. But you must not be afeard, my lamb. You came not hither of your own wild will, but because the princess commanded."

Mistress Hill left them in a small anteroom. Presently she returned; and lifting the heavy hangings of faded tapestry, motioned them to enter the presence of the princess.

It was a large oblong chamber, with a heavy ceiling of carved and panelled oak, black with age. · In an alcove was a richly canopied bed, the curtains and coverlet being of green velvet, embroidered with silver thread. The great mirror that hung above the low toilet-table was framed in silver, and on the table itself was a glittering array of bottles, pounce-boxes, brushes, and other toilet articles, all mounted in the same precious metal. A green cockatoo swung in a silver cage, and on a silver salver was a green chocolate service, inlaid with silver arabesques. All was green and silver, reminding Robin of a certain green recess in the forest, where the young ferns and mosses crept to the margin of a silver stream.

The princess, in a silken morning gown, sat in a high-backed oaken chair, with one small, slippered foot resting on a velvet cushion. She had been extremely pretty in her early youth, with her round, pliant figure, her fair, fresh English complexion, her luxuriant, dark brown hair, and her dainty hands and feet ; and although she had of late years grown too stout for perfect comeliness, she was still fair, with a royal dignity in the poise of her well-shaped head, and much of the charm that belongs to beautiful womanhood. At least, this was the impression received by Dame Dorothy, as with one keen glance about the room she passed swiftly down its long length, dropped on one knee, and kissed the hand extended to her.

"God bless my Lady Anne Stuart," she said. "It does my old heart good to see her thus in the palace of her fathers, — abiding her time."

The princess smiled, but did not reply directly. Resuming the work she had dropped, — for she had been deftly mending a rent in a bit of lace, — she dismissed Mistress Hill, and motioned the old woman to a seat on a divan near her.

"Now is not that well done?" she said, displaying her handiwork. "If I cannot spin and weave, or even darn and set fine stitches, like you, Nurse Dorothy, I am not one whit afraid to match my needle against that of other folk. But I wanted to speak with you about the lad. Come hither, child."

Robin had scarcely ventured to set his foot within what seemed to his reverent little soul the sacred precincts of that chamber. He stood in the doorway, one hand grasping the tapestry that screened it, while his eyes took in at one glance the unaccustomed splendor, the princess, the green cockatoo, and a little girl who sat at an embroidery-frame in a deep oriel window at the further end of the room. So intent was he, and so absorbed in his observations, that he did not hear the summons of the princess.

"Robin!" cried Dame Dorothy, "dost thou not hear, or hast thou lost thy wits a-looking at that cockatoo? Come hither, and make thine obeisance to her Grace."

The lad's color deepened perceptibly, till his olive cheek glowed like the innermost heart of a rose, but there was no awkwardness, or self-consciousness, in his manner, as he knelt at the princess's feet.

"I crave pardon," he said, "but if I have lost my wits it is not because of the cockatoo."

The princess clapped her hands, with a low, musical laugh. "Verily, Dorothy," she cried, "the boy is a born gallant! In what school didst thou learn to make fine speeches, sirrah?" she continued, drawing him to her side, and looking curiously at his small brown hands.

But the incipient courtier was evidently puzzled. Like "the hand that rounded Peter's dome," he had builded wiser than he knew. He looked inquiringly from Anne's face to his grandmother's.

"Nay, madam," he said, after a little space, "I know naught of fine speeches. But I never saw so fair a room before, nor so many fine things; and I meant to say that if I had lost my wits, and did not give proper heed when your Grace called me, that was the reason of it."

"And so my poor room meets your approval?" asked the princess, smiling on the boy and casting an amused glance at Dorothy.

For a moment he looked about him with wondering eyes. He did not by any means fully understand this light badinage, yet he caught a glimpse of its meaning, half unconsciously. "My grandmother has told me much about kings' houses," he said, at last, in a low tone, "for I would always be asking her. But — she did not tell me the half, after all."

"And would you like — but never you mind! Run away now, and look at the cockatoo. Where got the lad that queer expression about 'kings' houses,' Dorothy?" she said, when he was out of hearing. "It sounds wondrous quaint."

"I am no scholar, my lady," was the old woman's answer, "but I can make shift to read the lessons, with some spelling of the long words, and I have read them to him daily. Dost thou not remember how it saith in Matthew, the eleventh chapter and the eighth verse, 'Behold, they that wear soft clothing are in king's houses'?"

"Nay, verily, Nurse Dorothy, if you quote Scripture to me, chapter and verse, I shall soon get beyond my depth," laughed Anne. "The texts will never stick in my memory, whether I read them in my closet, or hearken to them of a Sunday. But now about Robin."

There was a knock at the door, and Peter Boscawen, dropping on one knee, informed the princess that her son craved audience.

"Bid him come in," was the answer. "But, Boscawen, stay you without. How now, Gloster? You seem in haste. Is the army routed?"

"Not so, madam. But there is about to be an engagement between the French and English. Both armies are even now in battle array. I came with my aide-de-camp, to ask permission to take Robin to the Hall — or to — to — the field, I should say —"

The little duke had given the military salute as he entered, and stood now, an erect figure with sword and belt, his hand lifted to his high, plumed cap.

"Certainly," his mother said, with utmost gravity. "Only I hope there will be no bloodshed — or at least, as little as comports with the circumstances. When the battle is over, you will report here, with Robin."

The young commander bowed profoundly, and was about to withdraw when, unfortunately for the maintenance of his dignity, he caught sight of a wistful little face bowed over the embroidery-frame in the oriel window.

"Oh, mamma!" he exclaimed, forgetful of his rôle, "may Anne go with us? Say yes, mamma!"

"But she has her task to do."

"She can do it when she comes back. Girls!" he went on, half pitifully, half scornfully, "what good is their tapestry work? All day long pulling the silks in and out. Pray let me take her to see the battle, mamma."

"But what if she were to get hurt? Really, it is no place for a little maid, Gloster."

"Ah, but I should have told you, madam. Mistress Randee came to the Hall, on one of her own errands, and I besought her to stay, telling her she would be quite safe in the minstrel's gallery. I will put Anne in her charge; or she can sit in one of the window niches, where no harm can come to her."

A pair of wistful, pleading eyes looked up from the embroidery-frame, and a flush burned on the cheeks of the small maiden beside it, who was bending forward and listening eagerly.

"Well, well. I suppose she can go for once. Come hither, Anne. But first get your hooded cloak. It may be cold in the Hall."

"'Tis in the antechamber, madam," said the little girl, coming forward with a low obeisance, and a word of thanks. "I will put it on as I pass out."

Now, for the first time since he entered the room, Gloster turned to Robin, extending his hand.

"Come!" he cried, "let us hasten;" and the three children disappeared behind the tapestry.

The eyes of the princess followed them, and she was silent for some minutes, while the cockatoo fluttered in its cage, and a fly buzzed loudly in the oriel window.

"Dorothy," she said, at last, "Gloster has fallen fathoms deep in love with your laddie, and, in good truth, I do not much wonder. Thou hast had great good luck in rearing him, my old nurse, or else God hath given him such a nature as he gives not to all."

"Nay, my lady, doth he not give to each according to its need? One gift to the birds that fly in the air, and another to the fishes that swim in the sea. He knoweth the wants of his creatures. But Robin is a fair child, and a good. I am not gainsaying that."

"Why, it is as good as a play, or a story-book," and the princess laughed outright. "The lads have been making rhymes and love-ditties, a kind of compact. Did you hear of it? Something about 'hearts' and 'parts,' and being friends until life ends, and all that. Gloster stood up and repeated the jingle to me with quite an air."

"Ah! dost thou remember, dear my lady, how thou wert wont to repeat little versicles thyself? and how thine uncle, his Majesty King Charles, used to bring the great folk to hear thee?"

"Yes, indeed, but I did not make the versicles. I left that to the verse-makers, like one who read his poem to me in my dressing-room but yesterday, likening me unto Diana, and I know not what. Methought 'twas stupid stuff, but I bade Lady Marlborough give him a gold piece and send him packing. A beggarly set, these poets! Then Robin did not tell you of the verses, which seemed to be a sort of covenant between them?"

"Nay, he did not tell me of the verses. But he

told me of much else that passed between them,— talk of his Grace's studies, and of the coming days, and of much at which I marvelled greatly, thinking it beyond their years. Be not offended with me for repeating it, my lady, but my young Master Robin declared he was henceforth sworn friend of the duke's, and must be learning the Latin, forsooth! He made such a pother about it that I was fain to go and see the priest yesterday, thinking his Reverence might put me in the way of having him taught. Learning is a great thing, no doubt, whether for gentles or commons."

"The 'priest,' say you, Dorothy? Talk you still of priests and popery? Their day is over, thank God!"

The old woman shrugged her shoulders. "My Lady Anne Stuart knows I am no papist," she said. "But when the land changes its religion with its king, being papist to-day and Protestant to-morrow, it is not always easy for an old tongue to order its speech aright. I did but speak as I spake in my youth. I went to Father Hunt, who was once parish priest of St. Mary's."

"And now?"

"Now he visits the sick, comforts the dying, and succors all who are in need, whether they be papists, Church folk, or non-conformists. He teaches many lads, also, and is now tutor to the sons of Lord Herbert of Somerset."

"Very like, very like! Chaplain too, no doubt. But what said the godly man about the Latin?" .

"That if Robin was so fast for learning it, it were a sin to gainsay him, and that he would himself put him in the way of being taught. That is all, your Grace."

There was silence in the room for some minutes. Then said the princess, "Will you give the boy to me, Dorothy? to be one of Gloster's suite, and to dwell under this roof?"

Dame Dorothy sprang up trembling, with a low exclamation that was like a prayer. Her cheek flushed and paled, and her eyes filled.

"Oh, my lady, my lady!" she cried. "How can I answer you? How can I know what is right? Give the boy to you, — is that what thou sayest?"

"Yes, — to be one of Gloster's suite," repeated the princess. "Is that so dreadful?"

"Thou canst not think that, dear Lady Anne, for thou knowest how I love thee. But it is so sudden, and he is so young. None can know so well as I how fair he is and how full of promise. Often I have lain awake till the dawn broke, thinking of his high thoughts and ways, and dreaming I know not what! Yet now, — nay, nay, my lady. I cannot put him from me yet. He is too young. He is but a child."

"I know, I understand," said the princess, her

own voice trembling. "Have I not feared Gloster would be torn from me? I will not take the lad from you, my old nurse, yet I would fain let Gloster have his way in this matter. Besides, — sit you down again, Dorothy, and listen to me. But first see if there be any in the antechamber, for I cannot abide eavesdroppers, and these walls be full of them. All's well? Now hearken! Gloster must be trained in all warlike sports. Such is his father's will, and the King's command, and no doubt it is needful. The King's heir must not be a milk-sop —"

"The King's heir?" interrupted the old woman. "Surely he is *your* heir, my lady. What right has William to the throne that you — a Stuart — do not grant him?"

"Well, well! I do but speak as I am bidden. Gloster has, as you know, this troupe of village boys whom he calls his 'men,' and whom he drills daily. They are well enough, as lads go; but, nathless, many of them are rude and ill-taught, and interlard their speech with oaths, and such coarse words as I am loath to have him hear. Neither can I order the speech of the grooms; and the lad greatly affects the stables, and all that pertains to horse-flesh. They tell me curses and foul words are becoming to a youth, giving promise of manliness and brave deeds. I know not, — it may be so," she went on, with a long-drawn sigh. "Prince George doth but laugh when I fret, and say women are overnice. Surely he ought to know better than I. And yet — I like it not."

"Yet my young master has companions of gentle breeding. Did I not hear some talk as to the four young gentlemen your Grace brought from Eton?"

"Yes. But they are all older than Gloster, and more like caretakers than companions. I would he had a friend and playmate of his own age, — and he will have none but Robin."

Suffice it to say that, after a long and confidential talk, in which great plainness of speech was used on both sides, it was settled that Robin should continue to live at the gray cottage with his grandmother, but should come daily to the castle, sharing in the little duke's sports, and in some slight degree, at least, in his studies.

"He shall be taught the Latin, if he is so set on it, and no thanks to Father Hunt," said Anne, laughing. "Dorothy, I will see that no harm comes to the lad."

CHAPTER VII.

"Go you on ahead, Boscawen," said the small duke to his adjutant, as the children waited in the anteroom while the little girl put on her hooded cloak. "Go you on ahead, quickly, lest the men should be getting uneasy. Let them stand at ease till I come."

Adjutant Boscawen saluted his superior, and went his way.

"Anne, this is Robin Sandys," remarked Gloster, by way of introduction. Then giving a hand to each, he hurried them through the corridor, and down a broad flight of stairs leading directly to the upper quadrangle.

"You should know, Robin," he went on, "that I am allowed to have St. George's Hall for my drill-room and battle-ground. It is a noble field, fit for any army. Here we are!"

It was, indeed, a noble room that met Robin's bewildered eyes; long and wide, its lofty ceiling decorated with the emblazoned arms of the Knights of the Order of the Garter from its first institution, its walls hung with portraits of a long succession of

English sovereigns, its two music galleries, and the great throne with its background of emblazoned shields. The mullioned windows were set in deep niches, and on the panels between were inscribed the names of knights and crusaders famed in story and in song even from the days of the Black Prince. Truly, it was an inspiring playground.

"Will you go to Mistress Randee, Anne?" said Gloster, hastily. "See! she is in the gallery yonder."

"Nay, if it be as well, I would rather watch the battle from one of the windows," answered the little maiden. "It will be nearer, and I can see better."

"Come on, then," he cried, and with Boscawen's aid the small, golden-haired damsel, in her black cloak and hood, relieved only by a white border, was speedily ensconced in one of the deep niches iike a saint in her shrine.

"As for you, Robin," said the young commander, "climb you up into the window next to Anne, and keep one eye on her while you watch the fight."

Which was speedily done; and the neophyte settled back under his stony canopy with a deep sigh of satisfaction, not forgetting to cast many watchful glances at Anne, who was so near him that he could have touched her by stretching forth his arm.

She smiled at him from beneath her hood. "Dost think any one will be hurt?" she asked, in a voice audible to Robin, but smothered, as to others, by the hubbub of the army. "I was glad to come hither, yet now I would be glad to run away. A battle is a dreadful sight."

"Aye, a real battle," answered Robin, stoutly. "But when all is said, this is only play. Do not be afraid, lady."

"Lady!" she cried, laughing merrily. "I am not a lady yet. Do you take me for a grown woman?"

"Nay. Methinks you are scarcely mine own age. But I must call you something, if I speak to you, — and I would not be overfree."

"Call me Anne," said she. "I am only Anne Gascoyne, goddaughter to the princess."

But here their talk was interrupted by a long roll of the drums, and a clear peal of the bugles. A transformation scene had been going on below. The west gallery had become a battlemented castle with two small cannon — gifts from the King to Gloster — on its ramparts, and the lilies of France, or the semblance thereof, floating from its summit. Just one-half of the duke's small army (for he scorned to take any undue advantage in point of numbers) had changed their nationality, and become Frenchmen under the command of Boscawen, and now swarmed upon the battlements of the beleaguered castle. Boscawen was a discreet youth, and his duties were truly multifarious. In time of peace he was Gloster's adjutant and aide-de-camp. In time of war he was always, by order of her Royal Highness herself, commander of the enemy's forces, — a change of base that must sometimes have been enough to entail mental vertigo.

And now the mimic warfare began. The castle was besieged. Gloster's men rushed to the onset. The vast hall thrilled with the uproar of the toy artillery, the shouts of the gunners, the clashing of broadswords, the ringing of pikes, Gloster's shrill voice in loud command, and the deeper tones of Boscawen. The air was dense with the whiff and smoke of gunpowder, and minute by minute the mêlée grew fiercer. Of course it was foreordained that the castle should yield at last; but Boscawen and his French host were quite too wise to lower their flag until, at least, seemingly compelled to do so. Easy victories were not to Gloster's taste. He was ever in the thickest of the fight, shouting and cheering, his white plume in evidence like that of Henry of Navarre.

"See!" cried Anne. "See! Gloster is half-way up the stairs; he is mounting the battlements! Oh, Robin! Robin!"

At her cry, Robin leaped from his window and was at her side in an instant.

"What is it? What is it?" he asked, though he could scarcely be heard for the din. "Hath aught harmed you?" For her cheek was pale, and the hand that lay upon his shoulder trembled.

"Nay, — what would harm me? The battle is not here, but yonder. But I fear me Peter Bathurst hath wounded Gloster. See!" The little duke had, indeed, ceased from his upward climbing, and was standing half concealed behind one of the guns that his men had captured. But in a moment or two he dashed forward again, and the strife went on, till, amid tumultuous shouts from victors and vanquished alike, Harry Scull tore down the French colors, the French army marched out with all the honors of war, and peace was declared.

But the hall was strewn with the dead and dying. How could it be otherwise after so fierce a battle? Lewis Jenkins, the only historian who makes mention of this fray, and who, a veritable eye-witness, watched it from his vantage-ground in the east gallery, side by side with Mistress Randee, now came down from his perch to see if he could be of any assistance.

"Yes, call the surgeon," said Gloster, wiping the moisture from his forehead, and loosening his sword-belt. "Bid him raise the dead, and succor the wounded."

For, be it known, on the authority of the historian mentioned above, the soldiers of the Duke of Gloster's small army were singularly fortunate. By some occult process inaugurated by their commander, and by him made known to his surgeons, they who fell on his battle-fields were immediately restored to life; or, in case of the merely wounded, to full vigor of lung and limb. This process was called "breathing life into them." Alas! that the knowledge of it should have died with them, and vanished from the earth!

The surgeons began their task, and one by one the fallen rose, saluted, and marched away. It was remembered afterwards that the duke was less absorbed than usual in watching this restoration. Robin had helped Anne descend from her shrine, and the two stood a little apart, the one with a look of tender anxiety in her soft eyes, — for it all seemed so strangely real, — and the other with hand on hip and head erect, smiling at the farce so well carried out. But as the last private departed, Anne gave a little cry, and sprang to Gloster's side.

"Look!" she cried, tearing away the silken scarf he had wrapped about his neck. "See! he *is* wounded! There is blood on the scarf. It is as I said, Robin! Peter Bathurst did it with his pike."

Needless to say, there was a quick stir and commotion, and a running hither and thither. Mistress Randee came flying from her post in the gallery, and Lewis Jenkins swore under his breath, as he examined the wound, which, sooth to say, was a rather long, deep scratch on the side of the neck.

"Now, by my soul," he muttered, "but it shall go hard with that careless varlet! His royal mistress —"

"Hush! hush!" cried Gloster. "Not a word of that! It is not Peter Bathurst's fault. I ran against his pike. Cease your pother, Mistress Randee, and bring hither a strip of plaster. It is nothing! See! it bleeds no longer."

"Aye," wailed Mistress Randee, the housekeeper, drawing some court-plaster from her capacious pocket, "there'll be an end to these fine doings now, I'll warrant me, Master Jenkins. Her Royal Highness —"

"Hush again, I say!" cried Gloster, submitting meekly to the plaster, however. "Her Royal Highness is not to know of this. I tell you it was not Peter Bathurst's fault, and I will not have him blamed. Do you hear? Come hither, Robin! How didst thou like the battle? And as for thee, Mistress Anne, canst thou keep a secret?"

"Nay, I know not," she said. "I fear I may tell it in my dreams, for I was sore afraid."

"If thou dost, thou shalt never see another battle," retorted Gloster. "Thou mayst stick to thine embroidery-frame for all me. No one must tell of this," he went on, turning to the group around him and speaking eagerly. "There's no harm done. Bathurst does not so much as know he touched me. Was I such a baby as to cry out? Lewis, Mistress

Randee, Boscawen, I will not have him disgraced. Promise me you will keep your tongues from wagging."

One by one they gave the pledge demanded by the imperious child, extorting from him, however, a promise of greater prudence in the future.

"Now I must take you back to madam, my mother, as I was bidden," said he. "Come, Anne; come, Robin."

CHAPTER VIII.

AND now a new world opened to Robin; a new day dawned for him. The months that followed were very happy ones. No rose ever unfolded more spontaneously, more rapidly, in the dewy warmth and sweetness of a summer morning, than did he under the stimulus of his new surroundings, and the joy of Gloster's companionship. Every morning, at a stated hour, when certain of the little duke's weightiest duties were over, — those that more especially related to the "getting ready" of which Robin had questioned him, — the latter went to the castle. Every evening, at a stated hour, he returned to his grandmother's cottage.

It may well be doubted whether that stately, handsome prelate, Bishop Burnet of Salisbury, the newly appointed preceptor of the small duke, or John Churchill, Earl of Marlborough, his chief governor, were quite in sympathy with this new whim of her Royal Highness, — for as such the whole court regarded it.

"This boy, Robin, grows to be the very shadow of our young duke," quoth the bishop one day. "I confess I like not these innovations. Yet there seems no harm in the lad. He has good manners, and keeps his place well."

" Aye, as to that," said John of Marlborough, as he rose to take leave after one of their frequent conferences, and stood in the doorway, a splendid figure in purple velvet cloak and full-bottomed periwig, " Aye, as to his manners, my lord bishop — "

The bishop interrupted him suddenly. " But, Marlborough, I tell thee 'tis a sight to see that lad's eyes. I meant not to speak of it, but 'tis an inspiration, man ! "

One may be pardoned for thinking some inspiration must have been needful, both to master and pupil.

For thus wrote Bishop Burnet, long afterwards, of those daily lessons in Windsor, — the curriculum of his royal pupil when less than ten years old :

" He came to understand things relating to religion beyond imagination. I went through geography so often with him that he knew all the maps very particularly. I explained to him the forms of government in every country, with the interests and trades of that country, and what was both good and bad in it. . . . I acquainted him with all the great revolutions that had been in the world, and gave him a copious account of the Greek and Roman histories of Plutarch's Lives, and explained to him the

Gothic constitution and the beneficiary and feudal laws. . . ."

The bishop does not mention the Latin, — then considered perhaps (as, indeed, it long continued to be) the most important part of an English lad's education. But we may be sure that no study of maps and great revolutions crowded out declensions and conjugations and the due repetition of " ad, ante, con, in, inter, ob, præ, post, sub, and super," — or whatever its equivalent may have been in the grammars of that day. And in this, as in much else, Robin, by the express command of the princess, had a full share, to the great delight of Dame Dorothy and Father Hunt.

Meanwhile the drills went on in St. George's Hall, the battles and the skirmishing. Robin became a gallant little soldier, as eager for the fray as the best of them. And when he was promoted on the field, amid the generous shouts of the whole army, who should be first to congratulate him but Anne Gascoyne, a hair's breadth taller, and a trifle more womanly than she was last year? She often watched the battle from afar in the minstrel's gallery, having quite won the young commander's confidence by her reticence as to the escapade of Peter Bathurst.

One night Robin came bounding down the greenwood path from Windsor, announcing that at last he had seen the King.

"We had a grand field day in the upper quadrangle, and his Majesty reviewed the troops."

Dame Dorothy dropped her knitting.

"His Majesty himself! Well, well! I suppose the duke thought it a great honor to have his men do their *devoir* before the King."

"Indeed, and so did we all. It was a grand sight. All the great folk were there, — her Royal Highness and Prince George, my Lord Marlborough, and all the ladies. Yes, — and the little Lady Anne Gascoyne, too, all in white, wearing a new coif set with seed-pearls. I wish you could have seen it, too, granny."

She laughed gently.

"Nay, nay, laddie. It was no place for me in my homespun gown. But tell me about the King. What said he?"

"Oh, he made a fine compliment to the duke, and gave him largess money for his men ; twenty golden guineas to be divided among them according to rank. What think you of that? And he gave two guineas to William Gardner with his own hand, saying he beat the drum equal to the best drummer in the land. A proud lad was William!"

"No doubt, no doubt. Were you near to the King?"

"Aye ; for he asked Gloster some question, — I know not what, — and then he, making obeisance,

took me by the hand and said, 'Your Majesty, it is
my friend, Robin Sandys.'"

Dorothy's eyes flashed.

"And then?"

"Then I made a knee and bowed before him, and
he said something. I know not what. I was dazed,
and there were many eyes upon me. So I drew
back among the lads again, and that was all. But
we are all pledged to the King's service now, I can
tell you that, granny."

"'To the King's service?' How is that?"

King William's grim old heart would, perhaps,
have stirred happily if he could have looked in at the
cottage window just then, and seen by the dancing
firelight the quiet old dame listening absorbed to the
boy's prattle, and the lovely, dark-eyed lad telling his
story with such intense delight and interest.

"You see there is to be another war with France,"
he said, — not heeding his grandmother's interpola-
tion of "Alack! 'tis only the same old war going on,"
— "and we have all put our names to a paper.
Boscawen drew it up, by command of the duke,
as was fitting, for he hath a right clerkly hand. It
read thus:

"'We, your Majesty's faithful subjects, will stand
by you while we have a drop of blood.'

"Then we all set our hands to it. The King must
have been pleased when he read it, don't you think?"

"Surely he ought to have been," said Dame Dorothy. "But who put the duke up to it?"

"No one. 'Twas just his own thought. And there was more. He called for the pen and the ink-horn, and this is what he writ with his own hand. I remember the words, because he bade me put my hand on the paper to keep it steady; and, moreover, he asked me could I tell him if there were two t's in 'dutiful.' This is what he writ:

"'I, your Majesty's most dutiful subject, had rather lose my life in your Majesty's cause than in any man's else; and I hope it will not be long ere you conquer France.'

"Then he signed it, — *Gloster*, and made a fine flourish under the name, — and a big blot. He had a mind to make a fair copy, but there was no time. So he looked at it, frowning, for a minute, and then folded the paper, saying, 'Faith, Robin, let it pass! His Majesty may take it for a big black seal!' But was it not all beautiful, granny?"

"Aye, indeed, beautiful, beautiful," echoed Dame Dorothy, her eyes filling. "He hath a loyal heart, our dear little duke."

CHAPTER IX.

THE days came and went, and season followed
season. The semi-royal household was not always
at Windsor. It flitted, after the fashion of its
kind, to Kensington, to Campden House, to St.
James's, to Whitehall, wherever it pleased, save to
Hampton Court, which was King William's favorite
among the English palaces, and which he had made
as much like one of his beloved Dutch palaces as
circumstances would permit. Here he was accustomed to seclude himself with his alien followers.
Truly, whatever else may be said, and whatever good
undoubtedly accrued to England through the great
revolution of 1688, the manners of those in high
places had not advanced in elegance and outward
refinement since the days of the courtly Stuarts.
The proud English nobles might indulge to excess
in the costly wines of France and Burgundy, and be
drowned, like Clarence, in a butt of Malmsey; but
they certainly were not filled with personal admira-
tion for a king whose particular penchant was for the
gin of Holland.

But, whithersoever the Princess Anne and her

little duke flitted, he at least was always glad to return to Windsor, where Robin was sure to be among the first to greet him. No sooner did the standard of the princess float from the battlements, than he saw it and answered; a blithe, boyish figure racing through the forest glades, eager to welcome him whom his loyal heart called friend and master.

"Windsor is just the dearest spot on earth!" Gloster exclaimed after one of these returns, gazing up at the great gray keep. "I would not like to live where nothing had ever happened. This place is full of stories."

A strange gravity was growing upon him, — the shadow, it may be, of oncoming fate. He was a boy of many moods, and into each one of them Robin entered with entire sympathy. Perhaps the enduring friendship between the two — something that had become far more than ordinary childish love and liking — was chiefly due to this.

"One does not have to explain to Robin," Gloster had confided to his mother one day, somewhat to her mystification. "He always understands."

They were still talking of storied Windsor, as they strayed into St. George's Chapel, and seated themselves in the carved stalls at the right, nearest the chancel.

"Yet 'tis enough to make one sad," said Gloster. "I often think of it, Robin. Castles last, and houses, and even— things," he continued, slowly, as if groping for the one word that would give expression to his thoughts; "but men pass like shadows and are forgotten."

"It is not so," Robin answered, sturdily. "Forgotten? Then why do you love Windsor, for the sake of those who dwelt here so long ago?"

"I? Oh, that's a different matter! So do you. But how many of those who come here to pray ever think of him who lies behind that iron gate?" he went on, pointing to the monument of Edward IV., at the left of the high altar. "King Edward founded this chapel, and yet, even under its very roof, it is as if he had never lived."

Robin looked at his companion earnestly for a moment, and then his eyes turned to the banners of the Knights of the Garter hanging motionless in the still air. Over their heads were the exquisite fan-shaped vaultings of the richly decorated roof, and the whole space was bathed in the many-colored light streaming in through the stained and jewelled windows. His boy-heart thrilled.

"I tell you, great men are remembered whether they be kings or commons," he said. "But what ails you, Gloster? Why do you speak in this way —you who will be a king some day, and have every chance to do the great deeds men are remembered by? I might talk thus, but not you. Oh, I can see it all, Gloster!" he cried, impetuously, a glad light shining in his eyes as he turned them on his companion. "I can see the day when you will be a man and a great king, and as noble a knight as any of these whose arms and shields are in our great hall yonder."

Gloster smiled faintly at his friend's enthusiasm, hesitated for a moment, and then laid his hand on his.

"Robin," he said, "there is something I have wanted to say to you for a long time, — since before we went to Kensington. But bend nearer, for I would not that the serving-men yonder should hear me. I shall never be a great man, nor a king, either. Mark my words!"

Robin started, and his color deepened. "Not be a king!" he cried. "What's to hinder? What did you tell me that first day, so long, long ago, when we sat on the bench by the beehives?"

"Yes, — I remember. But I was hardly more than a baby then. They told me I would be a king when I grew up, God willing, and I believed them. But he does not will it. Nor shall I be a man, either, which is of more account. Mind that you do not speak of this, though; not even to Anne Gascoyne. She can keep a secret as well as any boy, but she would think she must tell my mother."

"But I don't understand! Why do you say this? Gloster, Gloster, what do you mean?"

"Hush, hush! Yonder comes Jenkins with my doublet. Not a word of this — Nay, dear Robin," he continued, as Jenkins withdrew, "be not so cast down. Let me talk freely to you, for there is no one else to whom I can speak."

"But what does it mean? Are you sick unto death, Gloster? What is it?" cried Robin, under his breath.

"Nay — not sick unto death; not that — yet," was the slow answer. "It means that I have never been well and strong like you and the other boys, though I strove to hide it. It grows worse with me, — that's all."

"But does no one know? I cannot bear it! Let me tell, let me tell, Gloster, that something may be done!" and with a brave but futile effort at composure, he sank on his knees by Gloster's side, and laid his cheek upon the hand that still clasped his.

"Oh, there's enough *done!*" said the other, making a wry face, and smiling brightly in spite of the gravity of the subject under discussion. "I have been dosed and physicked with nauseous drugs till I have a qualm in my stomach at the very thought of a bolus. And as for bleeding! — Robin, if you were to prick me with a 'bare bodkin,' as was said in that tragic play of one Will Shakespeare that was played before the court last Michaelmas, be you sure not one drop of blood would follow. They have drained me dry." And here Gloster laughed out so merrily that Robin took heart again, and refused to believe aught was wrong.

" 'Tis all nonsense!" he cried. " You are as well as ever you were. The boluses have cured you, and you do not know it. Come out, now, and let us run races on the terrace! 'Twill stir thy blood, and do thee good, dear — master."

Then with a sudden, overpowering thought of all that had been said, his eyes filled, and he turned away.

" Nay — nay — I do not feel like racing to-night," said the princely boy. " And, Robin, how many times must I tell thee? I am not thy master, but thine own sworn friend. Come out, now, and let us pace the cloister walk before the sun goes down, for I have something pleasanter to tell. If I should not live to be a man, yet one of my dreams has come true. I was made Knight of the Garter while we were at Kensington. King William buttoned the garter with his own hands, and hung the jewel round my neck. I am to be installed on my birthday, and a great chapter will be held here. Now what think you of that ?"

Robin's delight was unbounded.

" Harry Scull told me he heard something of it," he cried. " But he was not sure, and I would not speak of it, knowing you would tell me, if it were so. 'Tis too good to be true."

"But 'tis true, surely."

"Did — did the King strike you with the sword ?"

"Yes, — with the back of it. 'Twas not like Peter Bathurst's pike. It did not wound me. But, Robin," he went on, the laughter dying out of his voice, which was strangely musical, like his mother's, "what is the matter with me ? When I was but a little lad, — only so high, — I longed above all things to be made a Knight of the Garter."

"I know," said Robin, in a low tone. "You spoke of it that first day. And I wondered. I did not know what it meant — then."

"Yes ; I thought it would be a proud thing to have the right to wear the jewel of St. George and the Dragon ! But, some way, I don't seem to care so very much for it now. 'Tis but a bauble ; and I have real dragons of my own to fight. Do you think that's it, Robin ? Don't, don't look at me so, laddie ! It hurts me. You must talk to me, for, as I said, I can speak of this to none but you."

With arms over each other's shoulders, the twain were pacing the long arcade, the bright locks and the dark ones in close proximity. Robin had seen Gloster in many moods, but this was a new one. He seemed suddenly to have grown older ; still the dear, familiar friend and comrade, yet in a way removed from him into some unknown country. Was this the effect of his new knighthood ? Talk to him ?

How could he in this mood? A sudden thought struck him.

"Gloster," he said, in a low, awestruck voice, "tell me, did you keep the vigil?"

For, if he had kept it, what might not have come to him, what growth, what power, in the long, dark night-watches?

"The vigil of arms? Nay, I did not keep it. Very like they thought me too young for fasting and praying and lonely watching by night in the great abbey where there are so many dead folk. There was nothing very serious about it, — only jesting and merrymaking. Here!"—and he pulled a crumpled bit of paper from his pocket. "I brought this to show you, and then came near forgetting it. Read!"

It was a scrap torn from the *Gazette* of that week, containing this chronicle. Robin read it aloud.

Kensington, July 6th. A chapter of the most noble Order of the Garter being held this evening, by the sovereign and eleven knights companions of the said Order, his Highness the Duke of Gloster was elected into this most noble society; and, having been knighted by the sovereign, with the sword of state, was afterward invested with the Garter of George, the two principal ensigns of the Order, with the usual ceremonies.

"Humph! That sounds serious enough, I should think," he said. "Am I to keep this?" and Gloster assenting, he folded the bit of paper carefully, and stowed it away in the sleeve of his jerkin. "But still, — but still, — I wish they had let you keep the vigil, Gloster."

"And why?"

"Oh! I know not that I can tell you, — only it seems noble and fitting, and it has been kept by so many good knights. Perhaps they all kept it, — all those whose arms are in the Hall. Since ever I saw their shields and devices I have wondered what their thoughts were, alone and at midnight, when they kept vigil in the holy places the night before they took their vows. It makes me shiver."

"I understand," said Gloster; "some day, a great way off, when I am not here to see, mayhap you will keep the vigil yourself, Robin. Stranger things have happened."

"I! I keep the vigil of arms?" cried Robin. "I shall never be a knight. I am not a high-born gentleman, as you know right well, Gloster."

"Yet knighthood may find you out. Many a one has been knighted who was not well-born. Come out into the sunshine. It grows chill in here, in spite of the doublet."

They strolled slowly up the hill, rounded the great keep, and, passing through an old Norman gateway, went out upon the North Terrace, and found seats on a stone bench sheltered from the wind in an angle of one of the buttresses. Above them was the hazy blue sky, over which a few white clouds were slowly drifting; below them the winding Thames in its setting of fertile fields and stately forests, all bathed in the golden light of the late afternoon; behind them was the great, historic pile, towered, turreted, battlemented, and gray even in that far day with the storied age of many centuries; and not far off, but beyond the river, rose Eton, half hidden by her encircling trees.

They sat in silence for some minutes, drinking in, as boys will, half unconsciously, the glory of earth and air and sky. At last Gloster turned suddenly, and looked at his companion.

"'Tis a fair sight," he said, with a long-drawn breath. "Robin, did I ever speak to you of Mistress Davies?"

"Never."

"It was she who first taught me of God. Nay," he went on, quietly, as Robin gave an exclamation of surprise, "I do not mean that I had never before heard of my Maker. Mr. Pratt read the lessons duly, and if there chanced to be a story, — how Joseph was cast into the pit, or how the boy David slew Goliath, — I listened; but they meant nothing to me. They were but fairy tales to amuse babies. Sometimes they amused me, and more times they did not. I was a little heathen till I knew Mistress Davies."

"But who was she? Your governess?"

"Oh, no! She was just — Mistress Davies. It was one summer when we were at Twickenham, and lived in some houses that belonged to her. She was an ancient gentlewoman, very old, with white hair and a wrinkled face, but I loved her well."

Robin flecked the dust from the crevice of the buttress against which he leaned, and waited, silently. At length, Gloster went on:

"I must have been about six years old. It was a large estate. All the hedgerows were set with fruit-trees, and I remember how the cherries hung, all richly ripe and red, the night we got there. Mistress Davies ate no meat, it was said, — only fruit and herbs."

"But of what she taught you?"

Gloster smiled. "I was with her a great deal," he said, "for she was kinswoman to Lady Fitzhardinge, who was then my governess. She taught me the Lord's Prayer, and the Creed, and the Ten Commandments, — and much else. Robin, I have never seen Mistress Davies since we left Twickenham that autumn. She must have been well past eighty, and she died soon after. But I have never forgotten; and when you spoke of the vigil of arms, I thought of her words. I did not know what she meant then, when she said, ' Child, I bid thee keep the faith;'

but I know now. If I did not keep the vigil, yet if I live to be a man, — which I doubt, — I will keep the faith, God helping me. I *must* now that I am a knight."

"You would keep it if you were not a knight," said Robin. "Do I not know? What did you say when Mr. Pratt was catechizing the regiment that last Sunday before you went to Kensington?"

"Indeed I don't know," Gloster answered. "I've forgotten all about it."

"I remember, if you do not. Mr. Pratt asked you this, 'How can you, being born a prince, keep yourself from the pomps and vanities of this world?'"

Robin paused, and there was silence between the two lads sitting so long ago on Windsor Terrace.

"Well?" said Gloster, at length, "Well, what then?"

"You answered thus, — and I remember just how you looked, sitting above us all, with the light from the window falling on your head, — 'I will keep God's commandments, and do all I can to walk in his ways.' Don't you remember it now?"

"Yes, now that you remind me of it. But as for the 'pomps and vanities,' truly I like them well enough; and where's the harm? Jewels and pebbles, — where's the difference? The same hand made them. The preachers say many things it is hard to understand, and Mr. Pratt likes a jewelled clasp for his coat for all the catechizing."

Robin laughed as he rose from his seat, and drew his hand along the parapet. "It grows damp, Gloster, see! The dew is falling. 'Tis time you were in."

"Then I will race with you to the third tower. One, — two, — three, — and away!"

"Good-night, good-night," shouted Robin a moment later, looking back and laughing as he touched the goal, while Gloster paused midway.

Lady Marlborough, who was always in the train of the princess, had watched the two lads from her window overlooking the terrace.

"Do but look at them," she said to her kinswoman, Mistress Abigail Hill, then bedchamber woman to the princess. "Do but look at them, sitting there in deep discourse, their heads as close together as two peas in a pod! I tell her Royal Highness it is not fitting her son should be so thick with such as he."

"Ah, indeed! And what says she?"

"She does but laugh, and say it makes the duke happy, and no harm done. 'Tis a pretty pass!"

"Yet he is a good lad, that young one," said Mistress Hill. "He is as well-mannered as any lad about the place, and I heard that my lord bishop said he was as keen for learning as the duke himself, and would be a fine scholar. I see no harm in him."

"You! you!" cried the imperious woman, who would fain have ruled her mistress's household as well as her life. "You! What has that to do with it? I tell you I do not like the lad. 'Tis no honor to the scion of a noble house to be on good terms with Gloster, if his favor must be shared with such a low-born lout as this one. But go you to the princess, now, and be about your business; I'll have no more of your words," and she swept from the room.

Mistress Hill cast angry glances after her overbearing cousin. "'No more of my words!' Hoighty, toighty!" she cried. "How grand we are! But trust me for saying a good word for the poor laddie whenever I get a chance, and a kind word to him, moreover!"

So saying, she ran swiftly down the turret stairs, and intercepted Robin as he was hurrying towards the great gate. "Here, laddie," she said, thrusting a box of comfits into his hand. "See! I brought thee this from London."

CHAPTER X.

It may have been owing to the good offices of
Mistress Hill that the Princess Anne bethought her
of Robin the next day, and of a request of her son's
that had not yet been acted upon.

The morning thereafter, Mat Hansel presented
himself at the door of Dorothy's cottage, at an un-
wontedly early hour. Betty Macthorne was out in
the dewy freshness of the young day, gathering some
watercresses from the margin of a tiny brook that
trickled lazily along behind the paddock.

Mat saw her stooping over among the rushes ; and,
throwing the bridle of his horse over the branch of a
low tree, he speedily joined her.

"Give you good morning, my lass," he said.
"This promises to be a fine day. But verily these be
rare cresses you have here," he added, as he bent to
pull one of the wet sprays. "I have seen none so
fine since I was a bit of a gossoon up in Derbyshire."

"You ride early, Master Hansel," Betty answered,
picking up her basket, giving it a vigorous shake to
rid it of the superfluous moisture, and moving swiftly
towards the cottage. "Yes, we think much of our

cresses. My mistress says they have a wondrous fine flavor."

"But whither away so fast?" quoth the groom. "Sit you here on the stile beside me, lass. There's no need to be in such a hurry. Half an hour is naught, so early in the day."

"Nay, Master Hansel, my mistress is wont to say that if you lose a half-hour in the morning, you may chase it all day, and never catch up with it. Wherefore I must in, and be about my business."

"But stay a moment, Betty," pleaded Mat, as he strode on behind her, the path being narrow. "Tell me now, lass! Wilt thou take a fairing from me, if I buy thee a rare one next fair day?"

"Nay, that I will not," she answered, quickening her pace. "I take no fairings from the lads, be they young or old, — and methinks you are somewhat old, Master Hansel. I give you good morning, and better manners."

But he put out his hand to detain her.

"Nay, now, girl, I tell thee I meant no harm. I like thee well, and would fain be friends with thee if thou wilt, — and I know no better way to begin than by offering thee a fairing, such as 'tis said all lassies love. I am sorry thou art wroth. However, I came not here to say this. I must have speech with thy mistress."

Betty's cheek was the color of the damask roses in the garden.

"I know not that I am wroth," she said, looking at him quietly. "But I like not fine speeches. Sit you here on this settle beside the door, and I will bring my mistress to thee anon."

Dame Dorothy appeared in due time, and Mat rose, cap in hand, to deliver his message, wondering a little in his honest soul why he did so, and why it was that he was always a trifle in awe of Dame Dorothy.

She was to come to the castle the next morning, and repair at once to her Grace's closet, a small, octagon-shaped chamber in one of the turrets.

The princess sat in the deep oriel window, looking out on the beautiful terrace, and afar to the distant hills, when Dorothy entered, escorted by the bedchamber woman.

"Sit thee down, Dorothy," she said; "I have somewhat to say to thee."

"Is aught wrong, my Lady Anne? Is aught wrong with Robin?" the elder woman asked, tremulously.

"With Robin? Oh, no! Yet it is of him I would speak to you. You have heard that Gloster has the garter?"

"Yes, my princess, Robin told me."

"Well, I have more to tell you. Gloster beseeches me that he may be one of his attendants at the procession and banquet of installation."

Dorothy sat with her hands clasped, discreetly silent. If they trembled a little, not even Mistress Hill was aware of it. While Robin had so long been a frequenter of the castle, and the sharer of the young duke's studies as well as of his sports, he had never yet been present on any public occasion, or been in evidence as one of his personal friends. To be sure, there had been that one great day when the King reviewed the boy troops, but then he was but one of many. This was a different thing.

"You say nothing," said the Princess Anne, after a long pause. "I thought this would please you greatly."

Dorothy started as from a brown study. "Please me, my Lady Anne! But what can I say? I have forgotten the ways of courts in all these long years. Yet I do not need to be told that this is a great honor."

The princess laughed. "But for all that, there's many a one would be more wrought up by it. You take all things coolly, nurse. Now listen! Gloster is to have eight young attendants of his very own; four of the elder lads, and four of the younger. Robin is to be one of these last, for so my son wishes, and I see no reason why he should not be allowed to have his own way about it. My Lady Marlborough has had the appointing of seven, and surely Gloster may have the naming of one and not be gainsaid — eh, Mistress Hill?"

For already there was the little rift within the lute, and the placid nature of Anne was beginning to rebel at the overbearing, dictatorial attitude of her lifelong favorite.

"Methinks, as your Royal Highness permits young Churchill to be one of the duke's attendants, my fair cousin hath no cause of complaint," said Mistress Hill, screwing up her embroidery-frame. "But, as we all know right well, her ladyship is hard to please. She saith — "

Breaking off suddenly, as if dismayed at her own audacity, she toyed with her silks for a moment. Then, pursing her lips, she added, meekly, "But I have no right to meddle with these matters."

"Aye, — but what said she? This is my affair, not hers. What said my Lady Marlborough? I bid you speak."

"It is not I who should tell it, seeing she is my own kin, but heaven knows I must speak if your Grace bids me! She says she is not sure she will permit her son, my young Lord Churchill, to attend the duke; that 'tis no such mighty honor, as things are going."

"Is that the way the wind blows?" said the princess, with a light laugh. "Nathless, I know my Lady Marlborough right well. Whoever else may or may not march in the procession as one of the duke's attendants, be you sure young Churchill will be there!   His mother would not miss it for a new coronet.   But now about Robin.   He must have fitting apparel.   Send him to Mistress Hill's chamber at noon on the morrow, Dorothy, and she will see that he is properly fitted out."

"Indeed, thou art most generous and thoughtful, my Lady Anne," Dame Dorothy answered, after a moment, rising as she spoke.   "But, truly, there is no need of this.   I have means enow to procure for the lad whatever is needful, if I may but know what your Grace wishes.   A bit of camlet for a jerkin, and mayhap an ell or so of velvet, — surely I can compass that much for the nonce, and not pinch myself, either."

"Nay, but he must have a full page's suit of fine white camlet, slashed, and a short cloak of scarlet velvet, and — let me see!   What else?   Oh! — a broad hat of French felt, well cocked and looped with silver.   What say'st thou to a periwig, nurse?" she added, with a laughing glance at Dorothy's grave face.   "Dost thou think he will need one?"

"Verily, no, I do not!" she answered, hastily. "The good God hath given the child such a periwig as no barber ever made.   Beseech your Grace to let it alone, nor meddle with his work!"

"Very well, if you say so, — I doubt, myself, if Monsieur Davillier could furnish him a better set of curls.   Nurse Dorothy, if thou must have a finger in this pie, thou shalt make him a shirt of good Holland, with fine plaited ruffles, a little open at the throat, — thus, — and a pair of clocked hosen. But as for the rest, — send him hither, as I said, and he shall be fitted at my cost, by the court tailor, that he may flaunt his fine feathers with the best of them. See to it, Mistress Hill."

"Aye, your Highness," said the woman, whose name has descended to a race of Abigails, "and I shall do your Highness's bidding all the more gladly that it is a pretty lad and a civil, God bless him ! He hath always a little bow and a smile for me when I chance to meet him in court or corridor. The tailor shall do well, if I have aught to say about it."

"No doubt, no doubt," interrupted the princess. " Now fare thee well for a week, Nurse Dorothy, and be sure thou dost have the shirt and hosen ready in due season."

Dorothy was just disappearing when the princess called her back.

"Wait a moment," she said. "You will want to see the procession, surely, if Robin is to be in it. Stay, — I have it ! Can you climb two or three flights of crooked stairs, think you ? Then go you to the third story of the great tower, and tell the keeper it is my will that he give you a seat in a window overlooking both courts."

Windsor was early astir when the great day came.

The summer morning dawned gloriously, with just enough of the soft English haze to temper the glowing sunshine, and add new beauty to whatever it enfolded. A light breeze stirred the treetops, and in it a thousand flags were flying. They floated from every housetop, and from half the windows of the village, while the castle itself was alive with them, glowing masses of color streaming from every turret, tower, and pinnacle. The whole place was swept and garnished, but the decorators were still at work, giving the last touches to wreaths and garlands, the hanging of rich tapestries, and the emblazoning of heraldic devices on arch and doorway, wall and entablature.

If the small duke in whose honor all this splendor was evolved had, as he said, a liking for pomps and vanities, it must surely have been gratified that day. All the noble Knights of the Garter were there, each with his splendid retinue of esquires and pages, one vying with another in the magnificence of his appointments. Plumes waved, jewels gleamed, and banners bearing proudly the escutcheons and armorial devices of the noblest names in England were borne aloft in glittering array. Trumpets sounded, bugles called, and silver flutes and hautboys filled the air with their melodious murmurs. St. George's Chapel, beautiful and impressive always, was magnificent beyond description when, in festive array, it was made ready to receive its throng of stately guests.

Should one rather say its throng of worshippers? Nay, — for though there were prayers and the rolling thunders of the organ, sublime ritual and the pomp of lofty ceremonial observance, yet it was all to enhance a splendid pageant, rather than for any purpose of religious worship.

The knights were seated in their carven stalls, with their gorgeous banners drooping over them, outwardly decorous, yet inwardly a trifle amused by the thought of Gloster's youth, and somewhat inclined to wonder as to how he might carry himself under his new honors.

"They be rather weighty for such young shoulders," said his Grace the Earl of Dorset, to his neighbor, the Duke of Northumberland. " Nathless, my lord bishop saith he is wondrous wise for his years, and hath great understanding."

" Surely, surely," answered Northumberland, with a shrug ` of the shoulders, and a shrewd smile. "Hath not my lord bishop the honor of being his preceptor? But hark! I hear the trumpets. Now must we to the door to receive him."

For Gloster's own father, — Prince George of Denmark, — with the Dukes of Norfolk, Northumberland, Southampton, Shrewsbury, and Devonshire, and the Earls of Dorset and Rochester, were

to be his knights companions that day. Four of
them attended him from his apartments in the
castle to the door of the chapel. There the other
four received him, and joined the procession in its
slow progress up the nave.

What wonder that the hum of voices ceased at
the sound of the trumpets, and every eye in that
assemblage of England's best and greatest turned
expectantly towards the west? First came the
heralds, two by two, in cloth of gold; then an
escort of the Queen's guards, followed by sundry
high dignitaries of Church and State; then the eight
knights companions; and then — the cynosure of
all eyes — the duke himself, walking alone, and
a little in advance of his eight young attendants,
who were resplendent in scarlet and white. At the
choir gates the uninitiated withdrew, and awaited
without the reappearance of the duke and the garter knights.

Gloster himself wore a suit of white velvet embroidered with seed-pearls, and literally blazing with jewels, — even the buttons being great brilliants. Anne
cared little for sparkling baubles, and seldom wore
them, but on this occasion she lavished them unspar-
ingly on the costume of her son. From his shoulder
hung a cloak of azure blue velvet, the color of the
order, richly wrought with gold; and around his neck
he wore the magnificent collar and jewel of St. George

and the Dragon, that was the personal gift of his Majesty, the King.

We may not follow him within the choir, where he was duly installed in knightly state. But we have the word of an eye-witness that he bore himself with such grave dignity, that his blue eyes took in the unwonted scene with so much quiet assurance, and such keen appreciation of its meaning and its beauty, that he received the highest praise from all present. The Marquis of Normandy bore instant word to his mother that "the young duke could not have carried himself better if he had been four times as old."

Yet little did the spectators, little did the knights companions, little did any, save Robin, know what grave and unworldly thoughts were his in that splendid hour. Little did they dream that he was thinking, behind that boyish brow of his, less of the scene around him, with all its brilliant show, and stately pageantry, than of some lonely vigil of arms wherein the bravest neophyte of all might gain new strength to keep the faith. Little did they think that, while he rejoiced, as a boy might, that "one of his dreams had come true," he was yet looking soberly into the future, and, with a chastened spirit, foreseeing a shadow there. Was it, indeed, the shadow feared of man?

Then came the marshalling of the procession again, and the stately march to St. George's Hall, where tables were spread for the grand banquet. If the procession to the chapel was imposing, this was doubly so, for to it was now added the magnificent array of garter knights, before each of whom was borne his banner, resplendent with all the heraldic colors. Many of them were just from fields of battle and conquest, — seamed and scarred veterans, their brows newly crowned with the garlands of victory. Some there were who had not yet received, and perhaps never would receive, the much coveted garter. But they wore their fresh laurels proudly, and the populace made themselves hoarse with their cries of, " A Marlborough ! A Marlborough !" " A Villiers ! A Villiers !" "A Mohun ! A Mohun !" alternating with their shouts for Gloster and St. George.

Every balcony swarmed, every window was thronged. On every inch of vantage - ground, every handsbreadth of space, human beings crushed and crowded. High up in her tower, Dame Dorothy watched the mêlée below, and congratulated herself that she was out of it. It seemed to her afterwards that, of all the glorious show, she saw but one thing, — the slight figure of Robin in his unwonted bravery of apparel, and the rapt and radiant eyes with which he watched every movement of Gloster. To all appearance, he was utterly unconscious of himself, lost in the occasion and its meaning.

More than one eye was bent upon him curiously, for it was well known to all about the castle that this was, so to speak, his first appearance, his début.

"*Bon Dieu!*" cried a young gallant, just a little too old to have been chosen one of the duke's attendants, and consequently removed from the danger of jealousy. Having lately returned from France, he was fain to adorn his speech with fine French oaths. "*Bon Dieu!* do but look at the lad! 'Tis an old saying that fine feathers make fine birds, but truly he wears his as if they grew on his own back. He thinks of them no more than the mavis of its red wing."

It was true. Neither overbold, nor overshy, he had the grace born of utter forgetfulness of self, and entire absorption in the thought of another. What did it matter that he, who had worn cloth of frieze, to-day wore cloth of gold? His princess had ordered it, — to do honor to Gloster. It was not his affair; he had only to wear it as he was bidden. Neither was it for his own glory that he had a place in the procession assigned him. Gloster had so willed it, for his own pleasure.

Mistress Hill had joined Dorothy in the tower window. It was very narrow, so narrow that it had quite escaped notice and consequent capture, yet it was so placed that it commanded the whole distance from the chapel to the hall.

"We are lucky to be up here," said she, settling herself contentedly on a high stool. "My faith! how they crowd and jostle each other down there! See now, Dame Dorothy! Here comes the procession of her Royal Highness. Body o' me, but 'tis a splendid sight! Look! look! for here comes the princess herself! That blue brocade she hath on came from the tailor's but last week. See! it hath a tremendous full skirt, well in the fashion, and a long, pointed body that becomes her rarely. It is fastened down the front with double clasps of rubies. Dost mark the strings of great pearls looped for shoulder knots? I fastened them with mine own hands, and it was well done, if I do say it. Her Highness cares not much for finery of that sort, but I besought her to remember it was all for the duke's honor, and to put on of her best."

"Her Grace looks well," Dorothy remarked, quietly. "I have dressed her myself before now."

"Ha!—and now comes my Lady Marlborough, fine as a fiddle, and proud as a peacock, dressed from top to toe in rose colored velvet, with rare lace of Flanders, and a diamond necklace. It is well my lord hath a good income these days. Be it fair or foul, he needs it!"

"Her ladyship hath splendid hair and complexion, and a fine figure of her own," quoth her companion. "It is said the princess doth love her dearly."

"Aye, — aye! Every cat hath its day. She is a cousin of mine own, and I knew her well long before she was my lady. The airs of her, — to threat she would not allow young Churchill to walk in the procession, forsooth! But the princess getteth to know her fairly well. He was there all the same, — didst thou not see? But there goes a sweet lady, — she in silver brocade, with a gray overmantle, and a long, flowing veil. It is the Viscountess of Armandale. Is she not lovely?"

And thus she went on as the slow procession passed beneath the window.

"Is the little lady, Anne Gascoyne, she that is goddaughter to her Highness, within sight?" asked Dorothy.

"Nay; I do not see her. Mayhap the princess thinks her too young for such — Ah! but there she is, just turning the corner. Dost thou not see? Bend but a little farther forward. 'Tis the little maid in a white taffeta gown, and wrought muslin cloak of fine needlework. See! she hath silver ribbons in her hair, and carrieth a little fan."

"I see her," said Dame Dorothy, leaning forward and following her with her eyes. "She seemeth a sweet little maiden."

"Seeing there are none here but just we twain," she went on, peering down from her high niche, "I would I had made bold to bring my good lass, Betty

Macthorne, with me. But I was afeard she might be in the way, and when we passed the great gate, I bade her shift for herself."

"Never you mind," remarked her companion. "Betty is a sprightly lass, and a comely. Some young gallant has her in tow, no doubt, which will please her better than being up here with two old women."

If Dame Dorothy could have looked directly beneath her window just then, she would have seen Betty Macthorne perched on a narrow ledge of masonry, with one foot on a projecting stone. And had her ears been keen enough, she might have heard Mat Hansel's voice.

"Put thy hand on my shoulder, lass. It will make thee feel less shaky, and keep thee from falling,— though, to be sure, I should catch thee if thou wert to fall, and it would be small matter."

"Nay," said Betty, "there's no need. I am not wont to fall. This ledge is broad enow, and if it were not, I have a steady head, Master Hansel."

Mat shrugged the rejected shoulder. "Good faith, so thou hast, as I know to my cost! Betty, thou art prickly as a chestnut burr. Wilt thou never let me know if there be a sweet kernel within?"

"It takes sharp frosts to open the chestnut burrs," she said, laughing merrily, "and this is but midsummer. If thou shouldst tear them open now, thou wouldst find the nuts green and bitter enow, take my word for it," and she settled herself more firmly on her narrow seat.

"Then I will wait till the frosts come," he answered, with a gruff tenderness that brought the swift color to her cheeks, "though methinks thou didst flout me once for being too old already. But tell me one thing, lass. Thou hast no other sweetheart?"

"No other? I have none at all. What have I to do with sweethearts? I am in no haste to wed. Leave me alone, Mat Hansel! Yet be not wroth with me, either, for truly it was good of thee to put me up here where I could see the grand procession, and our Master Robin in it! But let me down now, and I will wait by the gate for my mistress. She will be going, presently."

With a quick spring, she was on her feet, eluding the arms outstretched to receive her, but letting her hand rest in Mat's for an instant, with a glance that went far to repay him for all her flouting.

The long pageant was over at last, and quiet settled down on moonlit Windsor.

CHAPTER XI.

Unintentionally, no doubt, on the part of his instructors, — for it is well known that both his Majesty, the reigning sovereign, and Prince George, desired above all things that the heir to the throne should be bold, bluff, and warlike, — Gloster's whole training had been such as to intensify and strengthen one side of his nature: the side that was thrown into a mood of exaltation by the unchildlike experiences through which he had passed. When he was only four or five years old, a Knight of the Garter seemed to him to have reached the supreme height of earthly glory. His very playground — St. George's Hall — was dignified, one might almost say sanctified, by majestic, shadowy presences that swayed his heart and his imagination. The vigil of arms, with all its deep, poetic meaning, was something as real and vivid to him as a boat race, or a cricket match, to the lads of to-day.

History, for the most part, grandly ignores the small figure that for so brief a moment flitted across the stage, holding the eyes and hearts of the English nation. But Bishop Burnet tells us he was mature and thoughtful beyond his years; and the Welsh usher, who was almost his sole chronicler, gives the same impression in even stronger terms.

Yet, he was singularly reticent. It was only to Robin — and, perhaps, in a much slighter degree to Anne Gascoyne — that this phase of his being ever betrayed itself.

Let it not be imagined, however, that because of these graver thoughts and emotions, Gloster had put away childish things, or that the thought of death was ever present. Often he forgot it for weeks together, and looked forward to a long and brilliant life. He was still a boy, with boyish loves and likings. Still the drills went on in St. George's Hall, the sham battles, the mimic warfare, with all its fire and fury. For all this seeming play was but a part of Gloster's education. Warfare was the chief business of kings in those days; and St. George's Hall was the training-school of the young commander and his men-at-arms.

As the summer days went on, and the crisp autumnal weather brought in the pomp and splendor of the dying year, Robin almost forgot that he had ever heard Gloster's confession of weakness and weariness. The duke seemed to him as well as ever, as ready for work or play, as deeply interested in all that related to the life of the castle. Wherever there was most going on, there was he, eager, alert, always well to the front, and ever in the heart of things.

Since the events narrated in the last chapter, there had been a distinct, though perhaps undefined change in Robin's position. Until then, Dame Dorothy had scrupulously avoided taking anything whatever for granted.

No gentlewoman in the land was more dainty than she in all the essential refinements of life, — its sweetness, its purity, its cleanliness. But Robin's little jerkin of brown frieze, made after precisely the same fashion of that he wore the day the Princess Anne first summoned him to the castle, had never been exchanged for anything a whit finer, or more costly. Possibly she may have been a trifle more lavish in the matter of shoes and hosen, or taken a shade more pains in the clear-starching and getting up of the fine linen collars in which she took just pride, they being her own handiwork from carding to hemstitching. But that was all.

Now, however, since the boy had appeared in the duke's train as one of his self-chosen attendants, on what he justly accounted the proudest day of his life, something more seemed due. So after consultation with Mistress Hill, and not a little of her connivance in the way of patterns and borderings, Dorothy had made for him a little page's suit of dark, rich cloth, handsome, yet plain and serviceable withal. And as human nature was much the same then as now, it must be confessed this new departure not only added greatly to Robin's peace of mind and body, but to the consideration with which he was treated by grooms and lackeys, to say nothing of their betters.

More and more, as the days went by, did Windsor, lifting its imposing front, its great round keep, and its battlemented towers, high above the village sleeping at its feet; Windsor, with its many fair terraces and gardens, its sheltered pleasaunces, its parks, and its far-stretching forest, capture the hearts, and fire the imaginations of the two boys; more and more did its historic associations appeal to them. Aye, and to Anne Gascoyne as well. A strong tie of friendliness and good-fellowship had grown up between the three children; and she was often allowed to break away from the thraldom of the embroidery-frame, and wander far afield with them in the fair, sunlit lands of fancy and romance wherein they loved to stray.

"Little Lady," Anne was called by both the boys.

"Call me Anne," she had said to Robin, on the day of their first meeting. But a certain quaint, knightly deference, or courtesy, that was ingrained in the boy's nature, forbade such freedom, and he had compromised on "Little Lady." Whereat Gloster had laughed at first, and then, seeing its exquisite fitness, had himself adopted it.

There was many an old servitor about the place to whose magical words the three young people listened spellbound. But perhaps of all the stories and legends that had been handed down from father to son through many generations, — chronicles of the older time, that grew richer in coloring, and more deeply dyed in glamour and mystery with each repetition, — none took stronger hold of them than that of James I. of Scotland, and his long captivity of nineteen years. To them it was the romance of romances, this tale of the strong love that united the captive prince to brave Prince Hal and his three brothers, John of Bedford, Thomas of Clarence, and Humphrey of Gloucester. They roamed with the lads through the sunlit glades of Windsor Forest when, clad in suits of Lincoln green, they twanged their bowstrings, and sounded their silver horns right merrily. They hailed James as knight and troubadour when he fell in love with fair Joan Beaufort ; and fully believed that the madrigals he sang in her honor were as musical as the notes of Windsor nightingales.

One dark, rainy afternoon in early spring, — the spring after that July day when Gloster was installed as Knight of the Garter, — when the parks were dripping, and the terraces impracticable, he presented himself at the door of his mother's chamber.

"How now?" said the princess, with a welcoming smile. "Are lessons over thus early? What hath the bishop taught you this morning?" and she made room for him to sit beside her.

Gloster shook his head ruefully.

"Oh!—maps, and fortifications, and a long string of Persian kings. I like learning about our England better. But no matter about that now, madam, I am tired of it all! May we have Little Lady this morning?"

"'We?'—who are 'we?'—the whole army?"

"Nay, madam,—only Robin. It rains so hard I bade him tarry awhile and wait for fair weather. We are going to tell stories in the little library. Anne is good at story-telling. May she come, madam?".

The princess assented, and Anne being summoned, off they went, hand in hand, in pursuit of Robin, who was waiting without.

The little library, so-called, was a small room in one of the towers, east of St. George's Hall, and communicated with it by means of a narrow corridor which led, also, to the duke's apartments. It was plainly furnished, but bright and comfortable; and, being seldom frequented by the older inmates of the castle, had become a kind of neutral ground, so to speak, of which Robin had perfect freedom and where he felt as much at home as in his grand-

GLOSTER, ROBIN, AND LITTLE LADY IN THE LIBRARY.

mother's cottage. It was in fact his Windsor home. Thither, then, they went — the three of them — for an hour of story-telling.

"Now sit you here, Little Lady," said Gloster, "here in the window, and we will sit at your feet."

She shivered, with a glance at the dripping panes, and the flood of rain without.

"Nay," she answered, "it is cold up there. Let us draw the settle closer to the chimney. Robin shall kindle a fire. There are logs enough, and a basket of pine-knots that will make a fine blaze."

"And here be flint and tinder," said Robin, with his head in a cupboard where he was rummaging. "You shall have your blaze in a trice, Little Lady."

The fire was speedily leaping and sparkling in the broad fireplace. Meanwhile Gloster's head and shoulders were in the big cupboard.

"Ho!" he cried, "here be four russet apples, and a bag of chestnuts that must have been left over from last Hallowe'en! We will roast them and have a feast after the story-telling. There you are, Little Lady, with the blaze in front of you and the settle at your back. On with your story!"

"We might put the apples down to roast, meanwhile," said Anne, on housewifely cares intent. "But not too near — there, like that! Push the big brand further back, Robin, and bury the chestnuts in the hot ashes."

But when they had arranged the apples and chestnuts to their satisfaction, a new thought occurred to Gloster.

"Let us have a play!" he exclaimed. "A play —or a pantomime—of Prince Hal and King James. I will be the prince, and you, Robin, shall be the king."

Robin was silent.

"And I?" asked Little Lady, tremulously. This was a new departure.

"You?—Let me see! Why, you will be Joan Beaufort, of course, and King James will fall in love with you, and watch you from the corridor, with gloomy eyes and his arms folded thus," — suiting the action to the word, — "while you pace back and forth in the pleasaunce. Come, Robin, throw this mantle over your shoulder thus, like the picture in the old chronicle, — the one with the mandolin, —do you remember?"

"And there's the mandolin hanging on the wall," cried Little Lady, clasping her hands softly in sudden, self-forgetful ecstasy, "and here's a ribbon for your neck. 'Tis only black, when it should be red or blue, but 'twill serve to hold the mandolin."

"The black is more fitting, since James was a prisoner," said Robin, gravely. "Gloster, let us change parts. Be you the king, if we must play this play, and let me be Hal."

"Now tell me why, if thou canst?" was the quick retort. "Nay,—let me have my way, and be Hal of England. Come now, Anne. You are the beautiful Lady Joan—"

"But,—what must I do?" she interrupted, with a little gasp.

"Do? How can I tell you? 'Tis easy enough. You have only to be beautiful and gracious, as a lovely lady should. And when Robin—James, I mean—makes love to you, you must answer fittingly. That is all. You know how."

But Anne shook her head in dire distress and perplexity, and Robin perceived that her tears were very near the surface.

"Only the good God can make one beautiful," she said, her lip trembling, "and I know not how to be 'gracious,' nor in what words to answer 'fittingly.' I like not this play, Gloster!"

"Nor do I," echoed Robin, coming gallantly to the rescue. "No lady in all the land is more beautiful and lovely than our Little Lady here. But— but—"

"Then let her flout you, and scorn you, if she knows not how to be gracious," said Gloster. "I'll warrant me Lady Joan did not cry, 'Thanks, my lord,' and make a low curtsey the first time King James tossed her a flower. Let her flout you! That's easy enough, surely."

"Nay, but that would be harder than to be gracious," cried Anne, fairly in tears now, to the great discomfiture of both lads, and absolutely refusing to play Joan to Robin's James. There is no telling how the unwonted dispute might have ended had not a messenger from the princess presented himself at that moment, with a demand for Gloster's immediate presence in the chamber of her Royal Highness. The King had arrived at Windsor, and must be received with all due observance.

"And the apples are just roasted to a turn!" exclaimed the duke, as he lingered for a moment, gazing at the bed of glowing coals, before which the red-brown beauties were swelling and puffing, and exhaling a spicy fragrance as of summer orchards. "And the chestnuts are popping! But it cannot be helped. I must haste to mine uncle. Eat them, you two; and then, Robin, go you up to the Hall, if you will, and see if I did not leave my lance there yesterday."

With a quick nod, he was out of sight, only to come dashing back again the moment after.

"If you find the lance," he called from the doorway, "just bring it down and leave it here, where I can get it to-morrow," and away he flew again.

The two he left behind him lingered but a moment or two over the apples and chestnuts.

"Now you must find the lance," said Anne, "for

the Hall will soon be dark," and they sped up the stairs and through the corridor into St. George's Hall.

One side of the lofty, spacious room was already in deep shadow, but the other was bright with the rays of the afternoon sun. For the rain had ceased, the dripping boughs were set with jewels, the birds were singing in a mad ecstasy, and all nature was jubilant. Robin found the lance, after a prolonged search, safely stowed away in an angle of the carved oak throne at the east end of the hall. He busied himself silently for a few moments, polishing it on the sleeve of his jerkin, after the manner of boys, and then turned in pursuit of Anne. At first he did not see her, and thought she had left the room. But presently he saw her, a quaint little figure in a black silk hood and cape, standing far down the hall with the sunlight full upon her upturned face. She was gazing at the full-length portrait of James II., which hung there then, as now.

Robin watched her silently, vaguely realizing in that boyish heart of his how fair and sweet and true she was, yet feeling, too, in his keen sense of the infinite distance between them, that, in spite of the gentle comradeship permitted him, she was yet as far removed from him as any star.

But presently he saw that tears were streaming down her face; and before he could reach her side in a quick rush of questioning sympathy, she had leaned her head against the wall beneath the picture, and was sobbing under her breath.

"Dear Little Lady," he cried, half beside himself with fear and sorrow, and laying his hand upon her shoulder for an instant with a pitying touch, "what is it? What has happened to grieve you thus? Tell me, Little Lady!"

"Nothing has happened," she answered, looking at him through her tears, and struggling for composure. "Nothing new has happened. Only — I was thinking, Robin! There are so many things that trouble and perplex me. Mayhap if I were older and wiser I could understand."

"But what is it? I never saw you thus before. Why do you weep, if nothing has happened?"

"Oh! I know not that I can make it clear to you," she said, with a long-drawn breath. "There is so much one cannot understand. The princess is always kind to me. She would fain do her whole duty by her godchild. And yet, Robin, yet," — and the small maiden sprang up with eager, flashing eyes, to gaze again at the portrait of King James, — "Robin, does it not seem hard and strange that my father should have been slain for loving hers?"

Robin returned her tearful gaze, awestruck and dumb. This was all new to him. He had never heard the story of Little Lady. Gossip of one sort and another was rife about the court. But certain subjects were tabooed, or, at least, mentioned only under one's breath. He drew back, and studied the picture silently, as if the dumb lips could solve the mystery if they would.

"It does indeed seem hard," he said, softly, with his eyes on the canvas. "He looks like a king. Do you know, Little Lady, I never really saw that portrait until this minute? It is strange, is it not? But I have never been in this hall until now, except in Gloster's company, and —"

He hesitated, and Anne caught up the word.

"And in his presence you could not look at the picture of James II. I know that, and understand. If you had looked at it as you are looking now, Gloster might have asked troublesome questions. Robin, do you think he knows?"

"As to that I cannot answer, Little Lady. I only know that, before I was admitted to the castle, I was told, both by the princess and my grandmother, that I was never to speak to Gloster of his grandfather, James II., nor of the little prince, his uncle, who is but a few months older than he. Of course I have obeyed. He knows the early history of England well, and I have often heard Bishop Burnet catechize him thereon. But not of these later matters. Yet he is wise, and methinks he knows more than they would have him."

Anne looked soberly and thoughtfully at the semblance of the exiled king. Her tears were dried, though their traces yet remained.

"It is my belief that he knows the whole story," she said, in a low whisper, as if fearing that the very walls had ears. "Or, at least, that he knows all that we know. How could they think to keep it from him? I, too, was told that there were many things of which I was never to speak to Gloster, and I never have spoken of them. But he must know, Robin, he must know."

"His very silence makes me sure of it," said Robin. "I have often thought about it. If he did not know, he would ask questions, as he does about everything else that is not clear to him."

"But what if he does know?" asked Anne. "Does it make him unhappy?"

Robin shook his head. "Nay, I think not. He knows no king but King William, and he has been taught that he owes him allegiance. He has a loyal heart, has Gloster; and he believes in the King and in her Royal Highness. He does not grieve, whether he understands or no."

For a few silent minutes, they paced back and forth, and then Robin paused beneath one of the great windows. "Sit here, dear Little Lady," he said, taking Anne's hand gently, and leading her to a low seat that ran along the wall. "Sit here, and tell me about yourself. Who was your father? Was he slain in battle? 'Tis a glorious death."

"Nay, not in battle," she answered, her color coming and going, and her lips quivering. "I do not remember him well. I was but a little child. But he was slain on Tower Hill, where so many good and great men have died before and since."

Robin was silent. What was there to say in response to such a statement? Yet he must give some token of his wordless sympathy, and leaning forward, he lifted the black ribbon of her sash as it fluttered near him, and raised it to his lips.

"I know now why you wear no gay colors like other maidens," he said.

Anne lifted her eyes gratefully. "My father was Lord Frederick Gascoyne," she went on after awhile. "You have heard of Lord Preston, and of young Mr. Ashton? It was soon after the battle of the Boyne. There was a conspiracy, so it was charged, — a plan for the restoration of King James. It may have been true, and it may not. How should I know? But they were beheaded, all of them. It is a hard thing to think of. I dream of it in the night, and cry out in my sleep."

"And a harder to speak of, Little Lady," cried Robin, remorsefully. "I did but think your noble father died in battle, — not that he —"

"Was murdered," said Anne, quietly, for her

emotion had spent itself. "But we will not talk of it any more. We must go down now. The sun is getting low."

But as they retraced their steps to the little library, with the lance, Anne went on with her story.

"My mother died very soon," she said. "My father's awful death killed her. The Princess Anne was my godmother, as you know, and when I was left desolate she did not forget her vow to watch over me, but took me to be one of her own maidens. Truly, Robin, I am grateful for all her watchful care. And yet, — Robin, Robin, is it not hard and strange that my father should have died for loving hers too well ?"

CHAPTER XII.

ENGLAND was never fairer than she was that
summer. It may have been with a different beauty
from that of to-day, for two centuries have done
their chiselling work since then, adding many a fine
touch of grace and exquisite finish to what must
have been beautiful always. But nature, not art,
has to do with the making of her tender blue-gray
skies, a flush with the glory of dawn, or sunset; with
her countless wild flowers starring every field, croft,
and roadside; with the rich luxuriance and riotous
tangle of her ivys, trailing and climbing here, there,
and everywhere; with her stately trees, and the love-
liness of rose and fern and thorn and countless forms
of forest undergrowth ; her sleeping lakes, her flashing streams, and over all the wondrous magic of
sunlight and shadow on her green hills and valleys.
These she must have had always, — and perhaps with
a stronger, fresher, and more vivid beauty than now,
even before the Norman Conqueror first cast adoring
eyes upon her, and seized her in his iron clasp.

Be that as it may, she was very fair that year.
Strife and dissension were abroad in the land. The

seeds of sectarian and political bitterness, sown so long ago, and watered by blood and tears, were continually springing up in most unexpected places, and could only be kept down by continual care and watchfulness. Smouldering fires burned in Scotland, and on all the Irish coast, ready at any moment to burst into flame. The Welsh marches were uneasy. A dream of peace had for a time bridged over the chasm of war with her hereditary enemy, France; and by the treaty of Ryswyk, Le Grand Monarque had acknowledged William III. as King of England. But this peace was no mighty structure of stone, against which wild floods might dash and tempests beat, leaving it still unharmed. It was but a drawbridge over a moat. At any moment it might be raised, the portcullis be dropped, the trumpets sound, and war begin again.

The life of her whom Dame Dorothy loved to call my Lady Anne Stuart, cannot have been altogether a happy one. No doubt her strong Protestantism was a salve to her conscience. Yet she had been an undaughterly daughter, an unsisterly sister; and she would have been less than human if the thought of the sad exiles at St. Germain had not often troubled her in the night watches. If we admit that the dethronement of James II. was legal, we admit also that Anne was her sister Mary's lawful successor. She had yielded her right to the throne to Mary's husband, and he had slighted and scorned her, treating her often with less consideration than he bestowed on his own lackeys.

But notwithstanding all the jars and discord from which her gentle, submissive, affectionate nature shrank, and the self-effacement which, learned early and practised for years, must yet have been a sore trial to the proud nature of a Stuart, the year of which we write must have been one of the happiest she ever knew. She was acknowledged heir to the throne, and mother of the heir presumptive. She was treated at last as became her position; for William had learned beyond a peradventure that such was the will of the English nation. If there were intrigues at home and abroad, there was peace and quietness in her own little domestic circle. Prince George may have been dull and humdrum, but he was a devoted husband, loyal and true in an age of disloyalty. It may well be believed that Anne, who was by no means a brilliant woman herself, was far happier with him than she would have been with many a man of greater calibre. Her son, who was her idol, seemed to be outgrowing the frailty and the frequent illnesses of his early childhood, and at last she was beginning to look forward to the future without fear or dread.

But out of a clear sky there fell a thunderbolt into this atmosphere of peace and calm. Gloster's birth-

day had fallen upon a hot day late in July. It had
been kept with all the usual festivities. There
had been a review of the boy troops, the fiercest
of mock battles, with the thunder of cannon, the roll
of drums, and the fanfare of trumpets. To crown
all, there was a grand banquet in Gloster's own
presence-chamber, whereat he presided with all due
ceremony, the victors in the day's sports being
graded on either side of him, in the due order of
their achievements.

Robin was far down the hall; for though he had
won a small victory with the long-bow which had
made him the possessor of a silver arrow, — a pretty
toy at which he took frequent happy glances, wondering if he might venture to lay it, in knightly
fashion, at the feet of Little Lady, — he had not
achieved the highest honors. As to the arrow, he
would ask Gloster's advice on the morrow, being
not now within easy speaking distance. So he con-
tented himself with watching his friend, as he sat at
the head of the table dispensing smiles to right and
left, — a little flushed, perhaps, with the heat and
excitement of the day, but triumphant and happy,
and with eyes that were like twin stars.

Suddenly there was an outcry, followed by as sudden a hush. The music ceased with a discordant
clang as the startled musicians lowered their instruments and leaned aghast from the little gallery, and

the attendants rushed forward just in time to save Gloster from falling headlong. He had risen from his chair, and, raising his glass, had just bidden his guests drink to the King's health, when the slender crystal fell from his nerveless fingers, shattered into a thousand fragments, and he stood swaying to and fro irresolutely, white and trembling.

He was borne quickly to an inner chamber amid smothered exclamations of fear and sorrow, while the boys huddled together in one corner of the room, a silent, awestruck group, until young Mr. Boscawen, who had been lately promoted and was now one of the grooms of the bedchamber, appeared with an anxious face, told them the duke was very ill, and bade them depart with all silence and despatch.

Robin lingered on the terrace for two hours under the lighted windows of the chamber where Gloster lay, hoping for further tidings ; but none came, and with a heavy heart he went home through the moonlit forest. He had almost forgotten the conversation of so many months ago, when Gloster had confided to him his own fears and anxieties ; or, if he chanced to remember it, he had believed, without any attempt to reason it out, that it was only a phase of the exalted, uplifted mood into which Gloster had been thrown by the circumstances of the hour.

But now, as he hurried homeward through the long-drawn, shadowy aisles, half sick and faint with the burden of sudden grief and terror, it all came back to him, and he wondered if his friend and comrade had been wiser and more far-sighted than he thought.

Dame Dorothy met him at the door of the cottage.

"Thou art late, sweetheart," she said, drawing him in. "Betty Macthorne has been abed and asleep for full two hours while I waited up for thee. It is not well for thee to be out so long past midnight, child. Young eyes — but what ails thee? Hast thou seen a ghost that thou art so pale, or hast thou eaten too many sweets?" she went on, hurriedly, as he dropped wearily on the settle, and leaned his head on its wooden arm. "Art thou ill? Child, surely thou hast not been looking too deeply into the wine-cup, after all my teachings?"

"I have drank nothing, granny," he answered, with a faint smile. "Only one small cup of sack, and that not of the strongest. Never fear but that Master Randee looked out for that. But we have had a sore fright, I can tell thee. Gloster was carried to his chamber in a dead faint, and was not out of it when I left, three hours after. He is very ill."

Dorothy's face changed, but she answered lightly, her hand resting tenderly upon Robin's bowed head, and giving it a little shake as she spoke.

"'Tis a pity he should have fainted and broken up the feast. But fret not about it. He is over-tired with all the merry-making, and I make no doubt the heat went to his head; for the day has been so hot that the very birds hid themselves from the sun. But go you to your bed now, Robin, and to-morrow morning you shall run up to the castle right early. I'll warrant me, you'll find the duke — God bless him! — as bright as a new sixpenny bit, after a night's rest."

The cottage, notwithstanding the late hours it had kept, was astir early next morning; and after a hurried breakfast, Robin hastened to the castle. Mat Hansel was leaning against the Norman gateway north of the keep, with the shadow of unwonted disturbance on his honest face. Robin looked at him eagerly, but silently. He had not the heart to ask a question, but Mat answered to the mute appeal.

"No better, — no better, my young master," he said. "The leeches have been with him all night, so Master Boscawen tells me, quarrelling as to whether they should bleed him or no; and now a post has been sent for Doctor Radcliffe."

"Could I see him, do you think?" asked Robin. "Or would they but let me stay in the anteroom, where possibly I could do some service?"

Mat shook his head. "That I cannot say, Master Robin. But here come Mistress Randee and Mistress Hill on their way up from matins. By my troth, women are always pious when there's trouble to the fore; do you mind that? What with fasting and praying — "

But here the near approach of the two women brought his discourse to a swift close, and he saluted them with an air queerly compounded of deference and good-comradeship.

"By your leave, ladies, but young Master Robin here was asking about the duke," he said. "Mayhap you can give him later tidings than have come to my ears."

Mistress Randee, who was weeping, passed on her way through the upper court, unheeding this appeal; but Mistress Hill stopped, throwing up both hands. "I fear me he is worse," she cried. "When he came out from the swoon he was distraught, and knew none of those about him, not even his mother. He babbles of this and that in words that have no meaning, and whispers, whispers, when he is not talking wildly, and tossing about in the burning fever that consumes him. Ah, may the saints help him!"

"Do you think they would let me be near him? I would be very still, very calm and quiet," said Robin, in proof of which he was trembling from head to foot.

"Come with me to my chamber," answered Mistress Hill, "and I will see what can be done. I can say thou hast a good headpiece of thine own, and might be handy to run of errands. But I fear me for our little duke, child! The leeches shake their heads, purse their lips, look wise, and say nothing. Bishop Burnet hath said prayers twice already, and my Lord Marlborough hath been summoned."

Three or four days dragged on wearily. The castle was as still as a charnel-house. Even in the quadrangles the servants and retainers moved softly, and spake under their breath. Robin and Anne Gascoyne met occasionally in corridor and anteroom, and gravely saluted each other in whispers, with furtive glances at the closed door behind which their young prince was fighting a losing fight with death.

"Let the lad stay," the princess had said, when Mistress Hill made her little plea for Robin. "Let him keep without in the anteroom, if it will be any comfort to him. Surely we all need comfort, and Gloster loved him, — nay, loves him, — poor child."

Already she found herself using the past tense, — this poor princess, — and caught her words up for correction, like a schoolgirl.

So he watched and waited, hearkening with ears sharpened by love and anxiety to the incoherent murmurs that reached him now and then, the wanderings of a mind distraught. Once he heard his own name called sharply, "Robin! Robin!" and sprang to his feet in quick response, only to sink down again in blank despair when the return-tide of recollection swept over him. Twice, when Gloster slept, he was permitted to steal into the room, and, half hidden by the heavy draperies of the bed, look down upon him. Small comfort was there in that, so changed was he, flushed with fever, with parched lips, and unfamiliar lines drawn deeply about the mouth and eyes, and across the fair, upturned forehead. Robin drew back behind the arras to hide the tears that, boylike, he was ashamed to shed.

But he was of service; that was one consolation. No feet so swift as his to do the bidding of the nurses, to carry messages, or to run of errands. And once the princess came through the room, and seeing him withdrawn in a far corner, she beckoned him to come near, spoke to him tenderly, and letting her white hand rest for an instant on his shoulder, bade him be of good cheer. He could have knelt and worshipped her then.

It was the afternoon of the sixth day, when, after a quieter sleep than usual, Gloster awoke in no pain, and, for the first time since his illness, to perfect consciousness. Young Boscawen, who, by virtue of his office, had entrance to the sick-room, came forth with a beaming face.

"He is better, he is better!" he cried, in a whisper, while clapping his hands noiselessly. "Robin, we may all take heart of hope now.   His Grace knew me, and thanked me for looping back the curtain."

But the older ones made no comments.

Just as the sun was dropping behind the Eton elms, and all the gray turrets and lovely green terraces were aflush with sunset light, Gloster turned his head slightly, and looked at his mother, who was holding his hand.

"Madam," he said, "I want Robin.   Is he within call?   I dreamed he was here last night."

In a moment Robin knelt by the bedside, raining tears — how could he help it, poor lad? — tears and kisses upon the wasted hand that clasped his so feebly.

"You remember what I told you, Robin?   My words have come true, just as my dream did," Gloster said, smiling faintly.   "Mamma!"

"Yes, my son."

"You will take care of Robin?   He is my last gift to you."

"Nay, nay!" she cried.   "God helping me, I will.   But you are better, Gloster.   Surely you are better, and you shall have Robin for your own squire yet, and ride off to the wars together."

He shook his head, smiling faintly.   "Stay you here, Robin; but I am tired now and would fain sleep," he said.   And then the weak voice sank into silence.

Presently he roused himself, as with an effort.

" Did you win the silver arrow, Robin ? I forget."

" Yes, I won it, Gloster."

" That is well. Is — Little Lady — roasting — the chestnuts ? Tell her — But I forget what I would say. Good night, Robin ; " and he slept.

At midnight the great bell tolled solemnly ; and when the winds of early dawn sighed through the tree-tops, every flag and pennant in Windsor and in London drooped mournfully at half-mast, and all the people knew that he whom they had called so proudly the hope of Protestant England, was no longer a child of earth.

CHAPTER XIII.

Worn out with grief and excitement, Robin slept late that morning. The tolling bells did not disturb him, though their deep-toned, solemn voices pealed forth from every church tower and steeple, blending in one rich, melodious harmony, till all the fair sunlit land seemed full of sweet, sad music. Neither did he heed the sounds of ordinary morning life, the lowing of the dun cow, the singing of the early birds, the rippling of the little brook behind the paddock, or the nearer clatter of pots and pans, as Betty Macthorne spread the table, and made ready the breakfast.

Once or twice Dame Dorothy stole softly in to look at him as he lay with one arm thrown over his head, his dark hair clinging closely to his forehead in short, crisp curls, and his brown cheek flushed with sleep. Once, as she bent over him, he smiled as if in a happy dream. She had not the heart to waken him.

But in that age, as in ours, the merciful commonplaces of life entered into the deepest sanctuary of

grief, — to console as well as to disturb. Whoever
dies, be he king or peasant, the survivors must clothe
themselves, and eat and drink, and attend to the
petty details of daily living. It is little that suns
rise and set, and stars wheel on in their courses.
But the beds must be made ready, and the tables
laid, and the food prepared and eaten. The sowing
and the reaping, the buying and the selling, the
building up and the tearing down, all must go on.

So the sun was not high in the heavens when
Robin came out of his chamber, clothed and in his
right mind after the stupendous event of yesterday,
— stupendous to his thought, and (though he did
not think of this) in what might be its consequences
to him.

His grandmother was sitting on the settle outside
the door, in the shadow of an overhanging vine.
"'Tis a fair morning, child," she said, beckoning him
to her side. "Sun never shone on a fairer. Come
sit thee down here in the sweet fresh air, and thou
shalt have thy breakfast. I ate mine an hour ago,
but thou wert sleeping well, and I would not waken
thee. Art thou hungry?"

He shook his head.

"Nay, but thou must eat, dear heart. Here
comes Betty with thy porridge, which is rarely good
this morning, and a new-laid egg, and the end of the
wheaten loaf. Mayhap thou wouldst relish a bit of

the veal pasty I made yesterday, with plenty of parsley and marjoram?"

And thus she chattered away while the lad tasted this and that to please her, but ate little. Betty fluttered in and out anxiously, and at last brought, held carefully in both hands, a little bowl of red glass with two quaint twisted handles. It was filled with a dark, amber-colored substance.

"'Tis but a morsel of that rare conserve that was sent thee from beyond the seas, as thou didst tell me, mistress," she said, apologetically. "It is sweet, and hath a flavor of wild honey with a dash of wine. Taste it, Master Robin. There's a chance 'twill do thee good."

"Nay, Betty. Put it by, and let me have it for supper. But now, — wilt thou go with me to the castle, granny?"

"Not to-day," she answered, after a moment's hesitation. "Why wilt thou go, lad? Thou canst do no good, and it will only vex thee."

But Robin persisted, and was soon slowly making his way through the forest in the direction of the great gray keep.

The sun was hot. The leaves hung motionless. There was an oppressive stillness in the air, — a benumbing quality, so he fancied, that deadened all emotion. Some strange influence emanated from earth and tree and flower. There was no joyousness in the clear blue sky, and none in his own heart. Yet he thought of Gloster without a conscious pang or a tear. All things seemed unreal and phantasmal, and he felt like one moving in a dream.

Slowly he wandered up Castle Hill, and instead of entering the upper ward and going straight to the little library, as was his custom, he turned aside to the South Terrace. Leaning over the stone balustrade, he looked down on the fair gardens at his left, all aglow with color that summer morning, and filling the air almost to faintness with perfume. A little figure was moving gracefully here and there among the lilies and roses.

As he watched her, Little Lady looked up, and beckoned him to join her. But he had never frequented the gardens. In fact, he had never entered them except once or twice under Gloster's immediate guidance.

"Come down to me! I need you!" she cried, imperiously, as he shook his head by way of denial. "Come!"

He hesitated a moment, and then, descending the long flight of steps, stood before her, cap in hand.

"Cover thyself, and carry these," she said, laying a great sheaf of lilies across his outstretched arms. "I have more to cut. They are for — him."

Robin followed her from bed to bed, and through the bosky shrubbery, while she added to the fragrant spoil he carried, but neither spoke. Ordinary topics seemed forbidden ; and with the curious reticence of young souls, they shrank from the one theme that was yet all-engrossing to them both. What was there to be said? The realm of silence was too near. Its shadow was too all-pervading.

Leaving the gardens at length by the steps leading up to the East Terrace, Little Lady led the way to the nearest tower, and from thence turned her steps in the direction of Gloster's own suite of rooms.

"Come on!" she said, as Robin hung back, overpowered by a strange dread of he knew not what ; and he obeyed meekly.

Her own hands held a basket overflowing with violets, fresh and dewy from the deep recesses of the shrubbery. Reaching the door of the presence-chamber, which Robin had not entered since the fatal night of the banquet, she unlocked it with a key that hung from her girdle, and drew aside the tapestry swaying beyond it.

"He lies here," she whispered ; "follow me!"

For a moment, in the semi-darkness, Robin could see nothing ; but as he waited his vision cleared. He was familiar with the room, a large, oblong chamber, roofed and panelled in carved oak. He had played there many a time. Yet, as his eye swept down its long length, he doubted its identity,

— or his own, — so changed, so altered did it seem. Across the upper end of the apartment was a dais, raised by three steps. Here the walls, windows, and ceiling were heavily draped with fine black baize, fold on fold, studded with silver stars. In the middle of the dais was a light and graceful canopy of black and silver; and beneath it, on a low catafalque, lay all that was mortal of William, fifth Duke of Gloster. Great waxen candles burned in silver sconces, shedding a sombre light on velvet pall, on escutcheon, shield, and banner.

At the head and foot of the bier, erect and motionless as so many carven statues, stood four soldiers in the full uniform of the Queen's Guards, that still bore some slight traces of ancient armor. Beyond it, two dignitaries of the Church, in black gowns and scarlet hoods, paced slowly back and forth.

Robin caught his breath quickly, as the beautiful, sad picture revealed itself, and it was with difficulty that he restrained himself from crying out. Little Lady had seen it all before, and in some degree grown familiar with it. Quickly, but silently, she glided down the long room, and, after a little delay, Robin followed at a slower pace through the half darkness, bearing his burden of roses and lilies.

As Anne reached the steps of the dais, she paused a moment, making her obeisance as one who approaches an altar. The silent guards saluted as the two drew near, and the pacing priests stayed their monotonous march to see what was going on. Robin stood motionless, almost without breathing, while his companion took the flowers from him, one by one, and laid them, with no definite attempt at arrangement, wherever there was room on the white pillow and the pulseless breast, and even slipped one pure lily into the half-shut hand. But when, at last, she lifted the basket of violets, and let them fall in a full, fragrant, purple shower on the still form of him whom they had both loved so deeply, he sank on his knees with a low cry, and buried his face in the folds of the velvet pall.

Then there was not a heaving of a sigh, nor a quiver of his frame. He lay as one dead.

Anne looked at him for a moment, and then — enacting already the woman's part of consoler — she knelt beside him, and took his cold hand in hers.

"Come away, come away with me, Robin," she whispered. "Come out of this dread place into the sunshine, and let me try to give you comfort. Come, Robin!"

But he did not move; and presently Anne, in a sudden panic, flew to the smaller of the two clergymen, who still stood watching the scene with grave, sympathetic faces, and grasped his robe.

"Come and speak to him, dear Doctor Ken," she sobbed. "You will know what to say! He will hearken to you, but he will not take heed to me. Come and speak to him, dear sir!"

And Thomas Ken, the saintly man who had sacrificed to his sense of duty, not only his bishopric, but all hopes of worldly preferment, yet who loved the Princess Anne and had hastened to her in her grief, took Little Lady's small hand in his own, and led her back to the bier.

"The peace of our Lord Christ be with thee, my son," he said, stooping over the bowed form.

As if the strong, thrilling, tender voice had had power to call his soul back from some far country, the boy lifted his head, looked into the kind yet masterful face that bent over him, and answered in the common words of the ritual, — "And with thy spirit."

Ken, touched beyond measure by this unexpected response, raised the lad to his feet, and led him and Anne to a seat at the other end of the room. Here, for a full hour, he gave of the opulent riches of his mind and heart to the comforting and strengthening of those two young grieving souls. What he said to them may not be repeated here. But when, giving them the blessing they knelt to receive, he bade them go forth calmly, with hearts uplifted from the shadow of death, they obeyed him, feeling that an angel had been with them.

"Who may the lad be?" Ken asked of his companion, who was one of the chaplains of the castle, as he returned to the dais. "Is he of the blood royal?"

"Bah, no!" was the answer. "'Tis but a village lad who hath been allowed to be much with the young duke, and to have a share in many of his lessons. A kind of David and Jonathan affair. It may go hard with him, now that the duke hath gone, poor lad! No wonder that he weeps."

"Thinking he hath lost his best friend? It is hard. But I tell thee he hath a rare nature, that lad, if Thomas Ken be any judge of such matters. And he hath known much of boys, first and last."

But just then a summons from the princess called Doctor Ken from his long watch in the presence-chamber.

On the night of the fourth of August, 1700, a solemn torchlight procession wound its slow way from Windsor to London. In the odorous, dewy, starry darkness, it passed on silently, with not even the sound of soft music to direct its steps, through the Little Park and Old Windsor, by Staines and Brentford, by the side of the flowing river, and under the majestic trees of Richmond, that turned to quivering gold as the rays of the passing torches fell upon their leaves; raised aloft on a stately bier, with sable plumes and trailing banners and all the paraphernalia of mourning, was the body of the young prince, that it might lie in state in Westminster ere its burial in the mighty Abbey, — that crowded sepulchre of kings where sleep so many of England's noblest sons.

The procession was in charge of the Duke of Marlborough, and was conducted, no doubt, with all due observance of form and precedent. But none of those with whom this story has most to do went on this midnight journey, — not even the princess. They were all waiting at the great gate, however; all but the poor mother, who watched the sad pageant from her turret chamber.

Little Lady was there, in charge of Mistress Randee, with an uplifted look on her small face. "I cannot shed one tear," she said to Robin, who stood at a little distance with Dame Dorothy. "It is all so beautiful and solemn."

There was a look of exaltation on his face, too, as he turned it towards her in response. "Aye," he answered, "and so noble. Little Lady, doth it not seem to you that he is keeping the vigil to-night, up there in the darkness? I would, oh, I would I were with him!" he cried, in a sudden burst of boyish emotion.

Anne put forth her hand under cover of her cloak, and touched his arm. "Hush!" she said. "Dost thou not remember what the good Bishop Ken said to us? Have peace!"

He drew a little nearer, comforted by the light pressure of her hand. "Little Lady," he whispered.

"What, Robin?"

"Is it all over? Is everything changed? Will you still speak to me sometimes, if we should chance to meet?"

"Speak to you? Why should I not? Is what over, Robin?"

But he said no more, for just then the procession they had been watching from afar came down the hill, and they stood breathless as it passed by and wound its slow way through the gates.

As it disappeared from sight, the group of sad-faced women, of whom Mistress Randee was one, turned back to the castle; and Dame Dorothy, slipping her arm into Robin's, — for he was now taller than she, — said, "Take me home, laddie! I am weary with standing so long on my old legs, and it must be that you are tired, too. Come home, and rest thee."

CHAPTER XIV.

Royal etiquette in the seventeenth century demanded that, in case of a death, the family should at once seek other quarters, leaving the house where it had occurred to the mute occupancy of the dead, and in control of the officials having charge of the funeral.

But the Princess Anne refused to yield to the mandates of custom in this matter, and pertinaciously remained at Windsor, in spite of all entreaties to the contrary. She had attended her dying child with the utmost tenderness, but with a composure that astonished all beholders. As one chronicler remarks, " She gave way to no violent bursts of agony, and never wept, but seemed occupied with high and awful thoughts."

What those thoughts were, in an age when a stern belief in the retributive justice of God, and in temporal judgments, was thoroughly in accord with all accepted theology, may readily be imagined. In that hour of her stony grief, her heart turned to her exiled father in a passion of remorseful tenderness. To advance the interests of her own son, she had branded, or had stood idly by and allowed others to brand, his son — her young brother — with the stigma of illegitimacy. Now the object of all this cruel, sinuous policy was but dust. She had sinned for naught, and God had punished her.

With an expression on her face that was never forgotten by those who saw it, she rose from the bed where lay the body of her dead child, retired to her own chamber, dismissed her attendants, and locked the door. They who prepared her son for his burial had not yet completed their task when she poured out her whole heart, with its burden of grief and penitence, in a letter to her father, telling him of her bereavement, beseeching his forgiveness, and begging for his sympathy. This letter she sent by an express, but with the utmost secrecy, to St. Germain; so that King James II. was probably the first person outside the kingdom to be informed of the death of his grandson.

As for William III., he seems to have been torn by conflicting passions. He was in Holland at the time of Gloster's death, at his favorite palace of Loo, and was speedily informed of the event by Lord Marlborough. But August and September passed, and October was almost half gone, before he condescended to take the least notice of the loss of his heir. Meanwhile, of course, no court mourning had been ordered.

At this distance of time it is perhaps easier to discern the reason for this than it was then. The perspective is better. It is not possible to believe that his Majesty of England was so devoid of the common instincts of humanity as to have felt no sorrow at the death of the princely child he had made his heir, and whom in his saner moments he had seemed to regard with affection. But he was in one of the long fits of silent moroseness that were a part of his mental endowment. He had in some way become aware of the fact that the Princess Anne was in communication with her father. Her only son was dead. Her ambition had been for him rather than for herself. What was more natural than that her lonely heart should turn to her nearest living relatives, — her father, brother, and sister in France?

However, in October, when Gloster had lain in his grave more than two months, his Majesty wrote thus from Loo: "I do not think it necessary to employ many words in expressing my surprise and grief at the death of the Duke of Gloster. It is so great a loss to me, as well as to all England, that it pierces my heart with affliction."

Dame Dorothy, whose skill in lace-making made her a rare mender of the choicer tissues of Flanders and Venice, was often summoned to the castle to repair a torn flounce, a frayed veil, or a fine purfle. The day after this letter from his Majesty was received, she was in the bedchamber of the princess, looking critically at a fragile web, somewhat the worse for wear and tear.

"'Tis a bad rent," she said, holding it up to the light. "Bad, indeed, my Lady Anne. But methinks it is not past mending. I will do the best I can, if your Grace chooses to trust me. Shall I take it home with me, madam?"

"Nay, you may as well do it here," answered the princess. "Take the basket over to the oriel yonder, where the light is good. Your eyes are marvellous, Dorothy, but you need good sunlight for such fine work."

"Yes, my lady. My eyes are not what they once were, though they have stood the strain of well-nigh seventy years fairly well, thank God! But my basket and I would be more out of the way in the inner room. The light is good enow;" and she glanced in at the door of the smaller chamber adjoining.

The princess hesitated a moment, and then pointed to the oriel. "It is better there," she said; "and, if it were not, I like to see you sitting in that window. I am troubled and lonely this morning, Dorothy. I would you could take me in your arms, and rock me on your breast, as you did when I was a little child."

"I wish I could, dear my lady," she answered, raising to her lips the hem of the princess's flowing black sleeve, "for I understand, though I say little.

I have learned in my long life that death and sorrow are no respecters of persons."

"Aye, they are not. Neither are mean jealousy, and hatred, and spiteful revenge. Dorothy, my heart is sore for Gloster, yet sometimes I am glad he is out of it all."

To this, Dorothy's only answer was a mute glance of sympathy. Presently the princess went on, her voice trembling :

"Dorothy, the King has ordered that the salaries of Gloster's servants should be stopped at the date of his death. Yet it was not till yesterday that he gave token of being aware of it, and the court has not yet gone into mourning. But it shall not be! It shall not be!" she cried, wringing her hands. "I will pawn my jewels, if need be, but they shall every one be paid their full year's wage, and those who have been long in service shall be pensioned. I cannot bear this, Dorothy! It would have broken Gloster's heart, and it breaks mine. Ah, *mea culpa, mea culpa!*" she moaned, turning to the window, and gazing out over the autumnal woods with eyes that saw not.

Dorothy did not know the meaning of the Latin words, but she did know the meaning of the moan. Yet it was several minutes before she remarked, with her eyes fixed on the flower she was restoring, "But, surely, Parliament, my lady —"

"Parliament!" interrupted Anne. "Parliament placed in the King's hands, for the support of the Duke of Gloster's establishment, a yearly sum thrice as large as he has ever expended. It has gone to swell his own coffers. But the servants shall be paid, if from my own privy purse. They loved the young duke,—God bless them!—and they shall not be turned off empty-handed, as if they had been but breaking stones on the highway."

The small foot of the princess beat a nervous tattoo on the Indian rug as she spoke. Presently she changed the subject.

"Dorothy, tell me of Robin. I have not seen him for many weeks. God forgive me, but I have scarcely thought of the lad,—and I promised Gloster I would care for him."

"Your Grace has had much else to think of. It is not strange," said the old woman. "Robin is well, but he is very sad. The loss of the young prince lies heavy on his heart; and he misses the old life, no doubt,—both the work and the play. But he will get over it in time, my lady. Youth forgets."

The princess sat for some minutes lost in thought. It was Dame Dorothy who at last broke the silence that fell between them.

"My Lady Anne?"

"Yes, Dorothy."

"As thou knowest, I am not poor. I have enow

for his small needs and for my own. And there is Father Hunt. He will look after him now and then, and give me counsel if needs be. Fret not thyself about Robin, dear my lady!"

"Nay, but I promised, I promised!" cried the princess. "It was the last thing Gloster asked of me; and if it were not, I care for the lad myself. But I must take time to think, for the way is not clear to me. Trust me, Dorothy, for I shall keep my word."

"My princess, art thou not a child of the House of Stuart? I would trust thee with my heart's blood, if need be," said Dorothy, in a low voice that was yet thrilling in its intensity. "I meant only this. Thou hast many cares already, and the times are strange and troublous. I would not add so much as a feather's weight to thy burden," and Dorothy dropped her work, letting her hands fall idly in her lap as she bent her tender blue-gray eyes on the face of her lady.

"The House of Stuart is ill-fated. Death and disaster follow the race," said Anne, with a long-drawn sigh. "Bloody deaths, exile, woe upon woe. I have had my share in bringing them about, and in return William tramples upon me, crushing my heart. It is God's will. So he punishes me."

The Stuarts, as well as the Plantagenets, were a superstitious race. Perhaps it was not strange that, in this hour of her desolation, the daughter of James II. should have regarded William III. as the instrument of God's vengeance. Dorothy rose quietly and folded her work. "Nay, my lady," she said, "we are not overwise as to God's will. Be not too sure as to his punishments, or the purpose of the sorrows he permitteth. Is it your Grace's wish that I come to-morrow and finish this?"

"Yes; and then we will talk further as to Robin. I must think."

The next day Dame Dorothy sat in the oriel window again, patiently plying her needle. She had brought pillow and bobbins also, and leaf and flower grew fair again under the skill of her deft fingers. There was much coming and going that morning.

Sarah of Marlborough, a stately, splendid figure, far more queenly than her Royal Highness, swept in and out imperiously, never deigning so much as a glance at the quiet figure in the oriel. Her star was in the ascendant just then. The death of the Duke of Gloster had greatly lessened the worldly importance of the Princess Anne, even in her own household; and her ungrateful favorite was by no means the last to make her aware of this fact. Yet, in spite of her cruel insolence, Anne could not forget the friendship that had been the one romance of her life.

Whether Lady Marlborough ever had any real

love for Anne may well be doubted in the light of subsequent events. But Anne's for her cannot be disputed. She bore with her haughty favorite, condoning and overlooking until forgiveness ceased to be a virtue.

The day was far spent before the princess found a moment for her conference with Dame Dorothy.

"Put by the work," she said, when they were at last alone. "If the rent be not mended, come again to-morrow. Dorothy, I must leave Robin to you for awhile. I promised Gloster that I would care for his future, and the promise is sacred. But the time is not yet. I cannot plan even for myself. Next week we leave Windsor, — and go back to St. James's, where I was such a proud and happy mother only last May! Heigh-ho! 'Tis a strange, sad world, as full of ups and downs as the merry-go-round at Bartholomew's Fair. I would I might stay at Windsor, where my son drew his last breath. But I am but a puppet now, and must move as the string is pulled, whether I will or no."

"Fret not about Robin, dear Lady Anne," Dorothy answered. "As I said yesterday, he is well off with me; and if he be a little downcast at times, it is no marvel. But he hath many books, — thanks to your Grace, —and he hath the forest for hunting and fishing, and Father Hunt, to whom he can go for a man's counsel. Lads like not always to be shut in with women.   Robin will do well for awhile, my lady; and, to speak truth, I would not choose London for him till he is older, even in thine own court.   'Tis a place full of peril, God knows."

Anne mused for a few minutes, with her finger on her lip, then turned, smiling more brightly than for many days.   "We must not make a milksop of the lad," she said, "nor a bookworm, as the soldiers call the scholars.   Learning is well enough in its place; but 'tis a stirring world.   Mat Hansel knows the points of a good steed.   He shall choose for him the best saddle-horse in the mews; and do you mind that he rides and shoots and does not sit pothering over dry books all day.   For what I think is this, Dorothy: the lad should have a place in some brave gentleman's household.   That is better than the court for him at his age.   But I cannot manage it now.   My heart is dull and heavy, and the future is uncertain.   Let him bide as he is for awhile."

"That is just what I would have chosen for him, madam," said Dorothy, her eyes kindling, "a place in a brave gentleman's household.   But there is no need of haste in the matter, God be praised.   Look, my lady!   Mistress Hill waits to do her office."

"Go, then, and send Robin to me on Monday next.   I would fain speak with him before we go up to London.   Dorothy!"

The old woman turned, and curtseyed.

"Let not your Father Hunt make a Papist of the lad! That would ruin all."

"Never fear, never fear, my lady. Father Hunt is wise and honorable. He hath his own faith, but he meddles not with that of others. Yet I would to God, madam, we were all of one faith in this poor, distracted land, and worshipped him without all these fierce quarrels. What doth the great God up in heaven care whether we be called Papists or Protestants, if we do but serve him under either name? But Father Hunt will not harm Robin."

"See to it that he doth not," retorted the princess, laughing at Dorothy's vehemence. "Fare thee well. Send the lad to me as I bade you, at three o'clock on Monday."

CHAPTER XV.

FOR three or four happy years Windsor had been closely associated with the princely boy who loved it, and for whose sake, chiefly, his mother, while often living elsewhere, had yet made it her own favorite home.

But now, all was changed. With the disappearance of the bright, alert figure that had been always in evidence, scaling the ramparts, climbing the towers, racing over the terraces, wandering in forest and garden, or drilling his "men," silence and desolation seemed to settle down on the great castle and its environs.

Robin seldom went up the hill, though he was always sure of a welcome from Mistress Randee. Heretofore, when the household had been away for weeks and months at a time, absence had seemed nothing. Soon the flags would be flying again, and the old life renewed. But now, every gray stone in Windsor spoke to him of the unreturning dead. He grew strangely quiet and reticent. All the boyish zest had gone out of life, and it fell flat and insipid.

Dame Dorothy did not tell him what was in store for him in the matter of the horse, rightly thinking that the sudden surprise and pleasure might rouse him from the lethargy into which he had fallen. Two or three days passed, and then Mat Hansel, nothing loath, led a beautiful bay filly to Dame Dorothy's door. "All saddled, all bridled, all fit for the fight," she pawed the ground with her one pretty white foot, and champed the bit, as if eager to greet and acknowledge her lord and master.

Mat knocked with the handle of his whip, and Betty Macthorne opened the door, — the upper half of it, — and stood leaning upon the lower half, with her plump arms crossed.

"Oh! Is it you, Master Hansel? What will you? My mistress is out of an errand."

"I came not to see the mistress this time," he answered, fastening his horse to the paling. "By your leave, I will come in and wait. I have a small matter of business with the young Master Robin, but faith! if he be not in either, I will make shift to bear it. Betty," he continued, trying to slip his arm about her waist as he pressed past her, "I grow older every day. See! I have brought thee a gray hair the barber plucked out yesterday. Wilt thou have it put in a gold locket?"

She eluded his clasp, laughing lightly. "Oh, Master Hansel, wilt thou never forget that gibe?

Thou art too old for a playfellow, and not old enough to inspire reverence, for all thy one gray hair. That's how the matter stands."

"I am old enough, and young enough to love thee, lass! Believe thou that!"

But here his love-making was suddenly cut short by the appearance of Dame Dorothy and Robin. The former had seen the filly tethered at the gate, but she held her peace, merely remarking, "The head groom, Mat Hansel, must be within."

Mat was, on the whole, rather a favorite with the mistress of the cottage; all the more of one, perhaps, because, with the common obliviousness of approaching age, she did not realize that Betty had outgrown her childhood, and was old enough to have suitors. He rose and saluted her respectfully.

"Sit thee down, sit thee down, Master Hansel. 'Tis a fine evening. Art thou out for a ride in the cool of the day? It is wondrous warm for the season."

"Aye, so they say. 'Tis always either too hot or too cold for the season, as I was saying to one of the maids this morning. But I have something to show to the young master, if he will come to the door. Saw you ever a finer filly than that, my young sir? Look at her legs! Look at her feet! And that well-turned head! 'Tis the finest that ever sat on shoulders. Tell me now, is she not a beauty?"

Robin walked round the pretty creature, gravely commenting and admiring; wondering, too, a little, if the truth must be told, at Mat's unwonted enthusiasm, which was all explained when he loosened the bridle, and put it in the boy's hand. "Take her, Master Robin," he cried. "She is yours. The princess bade me bring her."

Never was bewilderment greater than Robin's, as he stood for a moment, looking from Mat to the filly, and from the filly to Mat. "Mine!" he exclaimed. "Mine! It cannot be! The princess would have told me if—"

"But she told me," Mat interrupted, taking a silk handkerchief from his jerkin, and polishing the mare's glossy coat. "She is yours, fast enough, sir, and much pleasure may you have of her."

"The princess told me you were to have a horse," said Dorothy, smiling happily. "The filly is truly yours, Robin,—a gift from her Grace. Master Hansel is to teach you how to take care of her, and you are to be in the saddle half the day. Hear you that?"

Robin's wonder and delight, when he at last realized his good fortune, was unbounded. The possession of any horse would have pleased him; but the sole ownership of this beautiful, perfectly appointed little creature was too much. He threw both arms about her neck, and kissed the forehead she bent towards him as if seeking his caress.

"Oh, you beauty, you darling!" he cried, his eyes dancing, and his cheeks aglow as they had not been for many a long day. "What is her name, Mat? What shall we call her? She must have a name!"

"Sure, and she has a name already," quoth Mat, stroking her sleek sides. "Soh! Soh! my lady!— Yes, she has a name; a queer, outlandish one, to my thinking. But it is better than none, and, may-hap, better than a new one. It goes like this,— Fan-u-el-la. Heard you ever before such a name as that for a pretty young beastie, my master?"

Robin stood in a brown study, trying to capture some fleeting memory, while a puzzled look stole over his face.

"Oh, I know! I know!" he shouted, clapping his hands. "She is named after Cœur-de-Lion's war-horse Fanuelle, who was slain by the Saracens at Ascalon! Fanuella! Who named her, I wonder? But it must have been Gloster," he said, his voice falling, as he turned towards his grandmother. "It must have been Gloster. He was always pondering over those old stories, and trying to make them live again. Did not his Grace name her, Mat?"

"Very like, very like, though I don't just know.

It was one of the other grooms had charge of her. But she was being trained for the duke's riding, and very like he had the naming of her. I would have called her 'Lady,' myself, she is such a dainty piece, or, mayhap, 'Whitefoot,' for she weareth a white stocking. But I am glad if the name she hath suits your ear, my young master."

"I would have no other," he answered; and then there followed a long discussion as to her care and keeping. There was a warm, well-aired stall in the cow-shed, to which Robin led Mat rather tremulously. "It is not so fine as the stables at Windsor," he said, with a doubtful air. Would this dainty new friend be content in such humble quarters?

"Not so fine, but just as comfortable," answered Mat. "Never you fear about that. Keep her well rubbed down, and give her pure water and a warm mash, with a quantum of oats as she needs, and she will do as well here as in the castle mews. As for the currying, I'll come down and lend a hand myself, now and again, till you get used to it."

From that day forth, Fanuella became Robin's close friend and unfailing ally. There was no more morbid brooding and listlessness. The two became known to the whole country-side, as they scampered over it, racing up hill and down dale with entire sympathy and good-comradeship. And if there be any better comrade for a growing boy than a sweet-tempered, spirited, intelligent horse, this chronicler has yet to hear of it.

When Robin made his appearance at the appointed hour on Monday, Mistress Hill gave him instant admission. It was the first time he had been in the immediate presence of the princess since the day that he knelt by Gloster's bedside. Just what passed between them no one ever knew. But when he left the green and silver chamber, his eyes were wet with tears, and there hung about his neck a slender gold chain, from which was suspended a miniature of Gloster.

Mistress Hill met him on the way out, and laid a detaining hand on his shoulder.

"We are going away in a day or so, my poor lad," she said, "and mayhap thou mayst not be on the hill again ere then. Wouldst thou not like to say good-by to the little Lady Anne Gascoyne? I saw her not long ago loitering by herself in the pleasaunce, near the great rose-arbor."

Robin hesitated, — but the temptation was too great. In a moment he was bounding through the shrubbery.

They did not say much. Both felt instinctively that they met on a different footing from ever before. He who had been at once friend, playfellow, and chaperon, was no longer with them. Little Lady, in the innocence of her heart, had said, "Why not?"

when Robin, on the night of the funeral march, and in the stress of many vague, half-defined emotions, had spoken of their future meetings. But he, young as he was, was wise enough to know that all appearance of anything like clandestine meetings must be avoided, — for her sake.

For a few moments they paced up and down the alley side by side, while Robin showed her the miniature, and they spoke tenderly of their lost friend. Then he took the little silver arrow from his sleeve.

"It may be long ere we meet again, Little Lady," he said. "Perhaps we may never meet, for the world is very wide, and I know not what is .before me. Wilt thou take this little token, which is the best I have to give thee, and keep it to remind thee now and again of thine old playfellow?"

Little Lady took the arrow from his hand, and kissed it reverently. "I saw Gloster give it to you that last bright day," she answered. "I will wear it for his sake, — and for yours."

CHAPTER XVI.

THE King was still at Loo. The princess was at the palace of St. James. She had not yet recovered from the shock of her son's death ; but royal personages have little time to weep. In her case, to her natural motherly grief was added the sting of fallen fortunes. Even a more obtuse woman than she could not have failed to perceive the change in her importance to the nation, now that she had no longer an heir.

But she had her little court, nevertheless,—a few faithful adherents, and more than the usual proportion of trimmers, time-servers, and hangers-on, who were waiting to see whether the winds would blow east or west. One evening several different groups were assembled in her drawing-room. She herself was at cards, with a number of her ladies and gentlemen about her, — some playing, and some looking on.

In one corner two ecclesiastics were absorbed in a game of chess, their earnest, thoughtful faces bending over the board, while a young gallant of the court, with well-curled periwig and plenty of furbelows, leaned against the casement, twirling his jewelled cane as he watched the moves, and gave much sage advice, to the evident discomfiture of his elders. At last one of them looked up, with a slight frown.

"By your leave, my young lord," he said, stroking his chin gravely with his left hand, "methinks we can manage this play better if left to our own devices. Chess brooks not so much interference."

My young lord shrugged his shoulders, as he turned on his heel. "As you please, reverend sirs. Have your will, have your will! But, I assure you, I know the noble game at which you are dabbling right well, having had much practice both at Paris and at The Hague. That last move was not according to rule, nor was the one you were about to make. But, — as you please, —as you please!"

The first speaker looked after him with a half smile, and then slowly and deliberately made the move just scouted.

"Beshrew me! but these young cocks crow loud," he said, taking up his pawn. "And they who have once roosted on foreign palings crow loudest of all — Paris and The Hague, forsooth!"

Two or three pages were flitting about on hospitable cares intent. A pair of lovers were half hidden in the embrasure of one of the heavily curtained windows. In another, alone, with an unopened book on her knee, a small maiden watched the scene with grave, untroubled eyes. She wore a silver arrow in her hair.

Far down the room, and quite apart from its other occupants, two men had possession of a high-backed settle, and conversed in subdued tones.

" Her Royal Highness hath a sad face to-night, Sir Francis," said the elder of the twain, " in spite of the smiles she dispenses. Faith ! there is cause enough."

"Yes, my lord. She lost much when the young duke passed."

" Ah, but I meant not that, solely, though God knows it must have wrung her heart. Have you heard the latest rumor ? "

"Whether it be the latest, or no, is more than mortal man can tell, my lord," replied Sir Francis. "They fly in swarms. But I have heard the one current to-day with the coffee-house politicians — to the effect that his Majesty thinks of taking unto himself a second queen. Is it to that your lordship refers ? "

" Yes. But I doubt if there be a word of truth in it. Two years ago the king coquetted somewhat with the German princess you wot of, but it amounted to nothing. I believe not that he cares for marriage at his age. Its coming up again now is but a straw to show the way o' the wind, that's all."

Sir Francis lowered his voice still more. " There

are those — and their name is many, if not legion —
who assert that his Majesty would marry, or adopt
the young Prince of Wales, or do any other improb-
able thing, if so he could divert the succession from
her Royal Highness yonder. 'Tis even said he will
use every endeavor — if other schemes fail — to
place either the Electress Sophia or her son George
of Hanover on the throne as his immediate successor,
in spite of Parliament or people."

The older man played with the crimson tassel of
the cushion against which he leaned for a full minute
before he answered, in the same low tone: "His
Majesty will not succeed. I am no politician, as you
well know ; neither do I pose as a statesman. But
I can read the signs of the times as well as another
man. The Princess Anne is loved by the people.
Moreover, I know the noble Electress Sophia well.
She will stoop to no base intrigue, and she is loyal to
the House of Stuart, at least in so far as this. She
maintains that before the lapse of the crown even to
herself, or to her son, the young son of James II. has
the right as a free agent to make his own choice, —
to choose for himself whether he will renounce his
Catholicism or his kingdom. But the chance will
not be offered him. Take my word for it, Sir
Francis, her Royal Highness is predestined queen of
this realm."

"Yet 'tis said she is herself in communication

with the late king, her father; and that, as is but natural, now that she has no direct heir, she has stronger leanings towards her nearest of kin, than towards her far-off cousins of Hanover. What think you of that, my lord?"

"That her Royal Highness is ever strongly moved by the influence of the moment. Just now, when her heart is torn by the death of her son, it turns, no doubt, to her father. But it will not last. You will see, my friend; you will see. Prince George is a greater power than men think, and he has unbounded influence with his wife. As he thinks, so thinks she, in the long run. He makes no show of his religion, and raises no war-cry of Protestantism. Yet he is a stern, uncompromising Protestant. Neither does he yet despair of having a child of his own to inherit the crown. He will not encourage the princess in any leaning towards her brother. Mark that!"

"'Tis a pretty boy," said Sir Francis, with a sigh. "Now that our little duke hath gone, I feel like crying with the Moor, 'Oh, the pity of it, Iago!' A pretty boy, and a princely; generous and kindly withal, emptying his little purse unprompted at any cry of distress. Heigh-ho! 'Tis a queer world this! Shall we go up yonder and make our adieux, my lord? I see the game is ended."

Whether the impulse of affection that led the

Princess Anne to reopen communication with her father would have been short-lived or no, it is not for us to say. Fate settled that question in so far as the king himself was concerned. He died in less than six months, sending from his death-bed his forgiveness and blessing to his daughter, and charging her to make reparation for the cruel wrong done her brother.

When the news reached London, public curiosity was greatly excited. What notice would his Majesty, King William, take of the event? How would the princess carry herself? Would she wear weeds? Would the court go into mourning?

These questions and their like were on all tongues. It is a queer commentary on royal political squabbles, that William not only wrapped himself in sable in token of his great grief at the loss of the uncle and father-in-law he had driven from the throne, but clad his footmen and his coaches in the same sombre hue.

As for Anne, — she might have been Cordelia herself. St. James's was hung with black. At church and chapel the princess appeared in all the paraphernalia of deepest woe. The court, though not expressly ordered to do so, quickly followed the royal example, and all England mourned in sackcloth and ashes for its deposed monarch, James II.

Events moved rapidly. Six months passed; and

then the stumbling of a pony in Ranger's Park brought on the fatal illness of William III. On the 28th of February, 1702, in a message to Parliament urging expedition in the passage of a bill for the attainder of young James Stuart, he alludes to the mishap that had befallen himself in the breaking of his collar-bone. Early in March he was seized with cramps, and danger became imminent. Anne sent a kindly message entreating permission to visit him. A short, peremptory " No! " was the only answer vouchsafed by the dying King. In a day or two he breathed his last.

" Ah, then and there was hurrying to and fro! " Ecclesiastics and courtiers ran mad races with each other from that death-bed, in their strife to be the first to carry the news to Anne. It was a dazzlingly bright Sunday morning. Bells clanged from all the steeples, calling to morning prayer, but clanged in vain. Whig and Tory, Jacobite and Republican, alike rushed to the presence-chamber at St. James's, to do homage to her Majesty, Queen Anne.

There were, in fact, very many in the kingdom, who, while they had been strong partisans of James during his lifetime, now felt that the only hope of the country lay in the peaceful succession of his daughter. There were others who, like her uncle, Lord Clarendon, sought her presence in the vain hope of persuading her to remember and obey her father's dying injunction as to his son, her brother. There were those who had avoided her levees for months, while waiting the turn of the tide, who now shouted themselves hoarse with cries of "God save Queen Anne!"

Both houses of Parliament met, Sunday or no Sunday, and after the due speech-making was over, went to St. James's with addresses of congratulation. Anne's chief accomplishments were her knack at writing pretty little notes and making graceful little speeches. My lords were charmed with her grace and dignity. She had a certain sweetness of voice that was remarkable even in her childhood, and she had been well trained in the use of it. All through her life she retained the power of swaying an audience by this subtile charm of voice and manner, which often stood her in good stead where brilliant intellect and rare wit might have failed her.

But notwithstanding this almost unseemly haste to greet her, the new Queen was not crowned till April. Then in the glorious abbey, with magnificent array of velvet and ermine and jewels, with all stately ceremonies, splendor of ritual, organ thunders and rolling music, the crown was placed upon her brow, and the coronation ring upon her finger, wedding her to her people. She was girt with the sword of St. Edward, the vows were taken, the blessing given, — and Anne Stuart was Queen of England.

She was now thirty-seven, in the very midsummer of her womanhood. Too large in person, she yet retained much of the simple beauty of her girlhood, her fresh English coloring, her wealth of softly curling hair, — brown, with a glint of gold in it, — and the perfectly moulded hands and arms, that were said to be the most beautiful in all Europe. The people loved her, — all the more, perhaps, because she was neither learned nor brilliant, but merely a simple, kindly woman whom they could understand. So they greeted her with loud acclaims, rejoicing that the sun shone on her coronation day; and regarding it, after the literally stormy weather of the preceding reign, as a favorable augury for which it was meet to thank God and take heart of grace. They called her then, as they called her always, "Our good Queen Anne."

Perhaps it was due to this kindly, unaffected nature of hers that a little group from Windsor might have been seen that day in the abbey, if one had happened to look closely in a somewhat unusual place. High up in the triforium, half hidden behind one of the clustered columns overlooking the stalls in the choir, were three people looking eagerly down on the surging pageant below. Mistress Randee was there in her very best gown of crimson padusoy, with a black mantle over it, and Dame Dorothy Sandys in the purple petticoat and gray cloak she always wore on grand occasions. Behind them stood Robin, a tall, handsome stripling with dark hair and eyes, and cheeks browned by sun and wind.

"Lady Anne Gascoyne must be somewhere down there," quoth Mistress Randee. "I wish we could but get a glimpse of her. Oh, no, not with the great folks in the procession!" — this was said in answer to a remark of Dame Dorothy's. "She is too young for that, and her Majesty doth not believe in putting her forward. But, nathless, I make no doubt she is here somewhere, if we could but get our eyes on her."

"I see her," said Robin, his face set gravely, but his color deepening. "She is in the south aisle, leaning against the third column. Look, granny! Canst thou not see her?"

The old woman peered down vainly, and so did Mistress Randee. "Nay!" exclaimed the latter, drawing back impatiently, "I see her not, nor do I believe you do. Who should know her in this crowd if I do not?" she continued, bridling, "I, who have had charge of her many and many a time!"

"But I tell you she is down there, and I see her," repeated Robin. "Look again! There, — close by the third column. She wears a petticoat of some rose-colored stuff, with a white mantle looped over it. Look! She is bending forward at this minute."

"'Tis she herself, truly!" cried Mistress Randee,

recovering her good temper. "'Tis no wonder I did not know her in that pink brocade, — she who would wear nothing but black and white. Methinks her Majesty hath bade her put away her little whimseys! 'Stuff!' Robin, thou hast an eye for the points of a lady's costume, no doubt, — but that petticoat is of rare substance, and your 'mantle' is no mantle, but a full gown of white taffeta, worked with silver."

"And look thou!" said the elder woman. "She hath a silver arrow to match it in her hair. Robin, at this distance 'tis much like the one you won at the archery games."

"Aye, 'tis somewhat like it," he answered; and presently there was a shifting of the scenes, like the dissolving colors of the kaleidoscope. Little Lady with her rose-colored petticoat and her silver arrow was lost in the vast throng making its way to the great west door.

Early in June the Queen removed to Windsor. It was her first visit, save for a day's hunting now and then, since the death of Gloster. No doubt her new royalty, with all its unaccustomed splendors and responsibilities, deadened somewhat her sense of loss. Yet she was a woman, a childless mother, she who had so gloried in her son. Her heart must have ached under its purple and fine linen.

It gave her great pleasure that many noblemen who had steadfastly refused to visit the court of

William and Mary, or to take the oath of allegiance to them, had come to do her homage as the days went by. One of these was Lord Weymouth of Longleat. An honored guest at Windsor, he sat in the Queen's chamber one morning right glad, it may well be believed, to feel himself once more at peace with the powers above him.

The two were alone, save for two or three silent figures at the other end of the long room, quite out of hearing. The Queen and her new adherent had also been silent for some minutes, Anne apparently pondering some question of absorbing interest. At length she looked up with a smile.

"My lord?"

"Your Majesty."

"I have a favor to ask of you in honor of our new compact. Will you grant it?"

It is, perhaps, not strange that Lord Weymouth should have hesitated for a barely perceptible instant. One never knew in those troublous days what might not be required of one. Then he said, quietly:

"Your Majesty's new liege will do whatever is asked of him that is not at odds with his own honor. Command me, madam."

"Nay, nay, my Lord Weymouth, take it not so seriously," said Anne, laughing. "You are all wondrous sensitive about your honor! Think you I do not know that song of one Lovelace, 'I could not

love thee, dear, so much, loved I not honor more?'
Never fear aught I shall ask of you! But, seriously
on my own part, it is because I trust your honor and
have faith in it, that I would have you do me a
favor."

"Which is granted before it is named," was
Weymouth's answer, as, rising, he drew nearer to the
Queen, and bent his knee in graceful, courtier-like
fashion. "Your Majesty has but to speak, and it is
done."

"Then be seated again, my lord, and let me lay
the matter before you. Have you room in your
household for a young lad whose advancement I
have at heart?"

"Room can be made, if it be your Majesty's wish,
whether it be there already, or no. I will do it right
gladly, madam. Do I know the lad?"

"You have never seen him, my lord. His name
is Robin Sandys. He is grandson of an old nurse of
mine, — a faithful, loyal heart, and a woman of rare
character. This lad was much with my son for some
years. He was his favorite companion in his studies
and his sports, and was greatly loved by him. For
this reason, as well as for his own sake, I would place
him in your charge that he may have proper training
in all that is befitting. When he is older, I shall
take him to my own service. But he is young for
court life as yet."

"He was one of the Duke of Gloster's 'men,' your Majesty?"

They both smiled. "Yes. He held high rank in that small army, I believe. The lad does well whatever is required of him, my lord. He will not shame you."

Lord Weymouth looked up suddenly. "Your Majesty, I had quite forgotten the circumstance. But this must be the lad of whom my dear friend, the former bishop of Bath and Wells, spoke to me after his return from Windsor. Your Majesty may remember that he came hither to offer condolence on the occasion of that death for which all England mourned. He found a young boy grieving at the duke's bier, and had some talk with him."

"It must have been he," said Anne, with a long sigh. "'Condolence!' Yes, the good bishop did not forget me in my sorrow. But he comes not now to offer his allegiance. I would he were not so obdurate and wrong-headed. Can you not persuade him to better manners, my lord? I like not that conforming dissenter to whom my sister gave Doctor Ken's bishopric. And I am told that while he holds the see with all its benefits, Doctor Ken does all the work."

"Which may not be wholly Bishop Kidder's fault, your Majesty," said Lord Weymouth. "As for the work, — the people will have it so. The see is Doctor Ken's spiritually, though he is deprived of its temporal dignities. He and his old white horse, almost as infirm as he, are well known in all the hills and dales of Somerset. Your Majesty's kind heart would ache, if it could but know all this good man suffers from illness and poverty."

"But it need not be! It need not be!" cried Anne. "If the proud, wilful man will but take the oath of allegiance, he may have Bath and Wells back again before he sleeps. It is easy enough to manage Kidder. He shall have Carlisle. Oh, my lord, I have loved the good bishop ever since I was a young maiden at my sister's court in Holland. I would fain have been crowned at his hands. Why will he not be reasonable?"

Lord Weymouth was silent for a moment, looking thoughtfully downward.

"Then, — have I your Majesty's permission to speak plainly in behalf of my friend?" he said. "I am an old man, and if I speak at all, I cannot mince my words."

"Say your say, my lord. I can forgive anything but treason, — which I do not fear from you."

"Your Majesty need not," he answered, quietly. "As I am permitted to speak, I will tell the story as I understand it, — I, who know the man so well. Thomas Ken refused to read the Declaration of Indulgence to please James II., because he saw in it peril to both Church and State. For that contumacy he was sent to the Tower. Yet when James was dethroned, he refused to take the oath of allegiance to his successors. And why? Your pardon, my Queen. Shall I go on with the story?"

"Yes, yes," she said. "Tell me why the man is so obstinate. And for the nonce, I pray you drop 'your Majesty' and all that, and speak to me as man to woman. Go on, my lord."

"I thank you, madam. My friend had been sent to the Tower by James. But what had that to do with the oath of allegiance by which he had sworn fealty to him and his throne forever? It did not absolve him. He could not take, — mark me, I say *he* could not, — I speak now for no other man, but from the standpoint of Thomas Ken's conscience, — he could not take the oath to William and Mary while your honored father was living. The fact that he was in involuntary exile did not alter the matter. He was still, in Ken's eyes, the King, and so entitled to his fealty."

"But he is not living now," cried Anne, "yet the obstinate man will not swear troth to *me*. Explain that, if you can!"

"Easily, madam, if I may. His old master, James II., is indeed dead. But that master has a son. The oath of allegiance to your Majesty is preceded by the oath of abjuration which deprives that son —

your brother — of his every right to throne, title, and estate; and, so Ken thinks, repeats the verdict of illegitimacy that has been so thoroughly disproven. For myself I see the matter differently, thank God! and have been able to take every oath required right gladly from a loyal heart. He knows this and rejoices, for he loves your Majesty. But with all my heart do I honor Thomas Ken for that he is what he is, a true and stainless man who will not turn a hair's breadth from what he believes to be right, though the heavens fall and crush him."

"Enough, enough, my lord," said Anne, half mollified, half angry. "You have indeed used plain speech, but as I gave you full leave, I cannot retract now. Nathless, I may not do away with test oaths and abjurations for the sake of any obstinate old man in Christendom. I would he were not so set, but he must needs go his own gait."

His lordship made a deep reverence. "I beg your Majesty to remember I spoke only from Thomas Ken's standpoint. I, too, wish from my heart he could accept present conditions as I, and so many others who loved your Majesty's honored father, are content to do. But, — we are not all cast in the same mould, madam."

"Well, well! He would always have his own way. You remember how he refused to give shelter to Mistress Nelly Gwyn, and all the pother he made

when my uncle Charles brought her to Winchester?
But no more of this. My lord, when go you to
Longleat?"

"To-morrow, if it please your Majesty. Or later,
if such be your will."

"Pray let it be the day thereafter, if it will not put
you to inconvenience," said the Queen. "But now of
the lad. I will command his attendance at once.
Ho, Margery!"

She gave an order to one of her women. Then
waving her hand in token of dismissal, she continued,
"Adieu, my lord, for the present. The lad will
be here in two hours' time, — that is, if he be not off
scouring the country on his good mare, Fanuella."

"He rides, then, your Majesty?"

"So well that horse and rider are one. Again
adieu, my lord."

Dame Dorothy's cottage was in a tremor of suppressed excitement that night. One might have
fancied the very rafters shook and the walls trembled, as they surely would if ever inanimate objects
thrilled in unison with human emotions. There
was an added dignity in Dorothy's bearing, as
she gave Betty minute directions as to the clearstarching and fluting of Master Robin's ruffles.
For was he not to ride Fanuella on the next day but
one, in the train of my Lord of Weymouth?

This same cottage has changed, somewhat, in the

years that have passed since we first saw it. Another room has been added at the left, with a small bay window looking towards the sunset. There is a rug on the stone floor. There are some low book-shelves on one side the bay, and a chest of drawers with brass handles on the other ; and opposite is a brick fireplace, with curious black fire-dogs, and a table and chair near it. There are chintz curtains at the window ; and on the north is an alcove similarly curtained, with a narrow bed in it. These changes and furnishings have been achieved so slowly that they have hardly been noted ; and the vines that veiled the old building have taken the new part in their embrace. It is the same low, unpretentious cottage, gray without, and grown a trifle broader and more roomy. That is all.

This room is Master Robin's own. Here are centred all his most prized belongings, — his books, which are by no means so numerous as Dame Dorothy thinks them, his bows and arrows and fishing tackle, and that rare and precious thing, a gun. Truth to tell, though Fanuella is not present in person, yet is she well represented. On a hook over the high mantel-shelf hangs her saddle, with a riding-whip dangling hard by.

That night Dame Dorothy came to him as he sat by the low fire, after Betty had gone to bed and the house was still. His eyes were brooding and thoughtful, and he did not speak as he put out his hand and clasped a fold of her gown. She stooped and kissed him.

"So! Thou art to fly abroad and see the world, art thou? Trying thy wings while I stay here in the old nest and keep watch for thee," she said, drawing a chair to his side. "Tell me about it, laddie. What said the good Lord of Weymouth? Could I have had my pick of all the noblemen in England, I would have chosen him for thy patron and master. What said he? Was he gracious to thee?"

"Aye, gracious enough. And yet hardly that, either. Why should he be? He does not know me. He did but say that it was the Queen's will I should be of his household for a time, and that she assured him he would find me dutiful and well mannered. He seems grave and stately, yet gentle withal."

"And her Majesty, — what said she?"

"That I was to do Lord Weymouth's bidding in all things, even as I would do hers when in her service. Then she bade me show my lord the likeness of Gloster I wore about my neck; but when she saw it, she gave an exceedingly bitter cry. I turned my eyes away, that I might not see her face."

"And what else?"

"Little save that she bade me remember I had been Gloster's friend, and to so bear myself as to do him honor. Then my lord spoke to me of Fanuella, asking if she were fit to carry me for the two or three days' journey to Longleat. I made answer that she could go like the wind to the ends of the earth if need be, whereat he smiled; but nathless Mat Hansel is to look her over to-morrow and see if she be in good condition. The Queen said whatever was needful would be provided for me at the journey's end, and that you were to take no thought about it. Granny, tell me! What is the life to which I am going? I almost shrink from it. 'Tis a great change."

"'Twill not be unlike the life you have seen at the castle, save that you are older and will be more a part of it. Never fear! 'Tis what I have always craved for you, laddie. You are to look forward and not backward. The Queen — God bless her! — has kept her promise to the duke, and all is well. In two or three years' time you will come back to me, a brave and gallant gentleman, my Robin."

But the lad's eyes roved tenderly about the tranquil room that seemed, in the flickering firelight, a very haven of peace. He had often chafed under the bonds of that very quietude. He had longed, ever since Gloster died, for a larger life, a wider world. Now that the door of his cage was opened, he shrank from freedom. It is a common experience.

They talked late that night, — talked as mother

and son talk in their hours of closest, tenderest communion. It mattered not that the lad had learned from books much of which the woman had never dreamed; that names, and things, aye, and thoughts, were familiar to him of which she had absolutely no knowledge. It is character, not attainment, that tells in all the crises of life. She had lived; he had only dreamed. They met on the same plane.

The next day was a busy one, crowded with the bustle of preparation. And at dawn of the following morning, Robin and Fanuella joined the train that wound slowly through the woods and lanes of Windsor, on their way to the great thoroughfare that led to Somersetshire.

CHAPTER XVII.

It was four o'clock on a Sunday afternoon, — the
Sunday after Robin's departure. Mat Hansel leaned
against the door-post of the gray cottage, twirling
between his fingers a gray-green sprig of rosemary
he had plucked as he came through the small garden.
The pungent odor of the crushed leaves filled the
room.

Dame Dorothy, in fresh white cap and kerchief,
was shelling peas for supper. They were talking of
Robin, as was but natural.

"He hath had fine weather for the journey, God
be praised," said Mat. "Neither too hot, nor too
cold, and not a cloud in the sky these three days.
I'll warrant me that little mare Fanuella hath carried
him well. There was naught in my lord's train
could hold a candle to her, if I do say it. That
black stallion his lordship rode hath something
wrong in the near hind leg, and is too heavy for
a long pull, moreover. And as for the other horses,
— well, — I say nothing. It's not my affair, I thank
the good Lord!"

Dame Dorothy laughed. "You men who have dealings with four-footed beasts do always be bragging about your own, and decrying those of others," she said. "But no doubt Fanuella played her part well. She's a good creature and a dainty, lifting her feet as if the ground were not good enough for her tread, yet fond of petting as any baby. She was always begging me for barley sugar."

"Yet she is high-spirited, withal," quoth Mat. "He had best not try to mount her who hath not the reins well in hand. And she hath good sense, too, — not a bad thing in man or beast. Good even to you, Mistress Betty."

For just here Betty came in for the peas, which were surrendered to her with a caution as to the cooking thereof.

"Be thou sure the water boils when they are put in the pot," said Dorothy. "Else you can spoil the best peas that ever grew. And put in no mint, my lass. I can't abide it."

Betty was about to vanish with the pan, throwing a laughing glance at Mat, for she had received that same caution about the peas ever since she could remember, when he stepped forward, tossing away his sprig of rosemary.

"By your leave, Dame Sandys, but can Mistress Betty be spared to go with me to even-song in the chapel, — if she will?"

"Aye, if you will bring her back in due season. A good lass keeps early hours. But, — 'Mistress Betty,' forsooth! Thou art over particular, Master Hansel. Betty is but a child."

He looked from one to the other, Betty standing meanwhile with downcast eyes, holding her pan of peas dangerously aslant.

"A well-grown one," he said, stooping to pick up half a dozen green globules that had rolled to his feet. "A very well-grown child. She is taller than thou art, Dame Dorothy, and comes well up to my shoulder. Wilt thou go to even-song, lass?"

Betty nodded assent, and ran off, while her mistress made Master Hansel understand that he was to return after service and share the peas.

"Leave them on the dresser, Betty," she called after her. "I will put them over the fire myself when it is time."

Even-song was over, and Betty and her cavalier were slowly straying homeward, down the long forest path. "It is early yet," said Mat. "See! the sun is not down and will not be for an hour. Sit here on this tree-trunk beside me, lass. I have somewhat to say to thee."

He was graver than usual; and after one quick glance at his face, Betty obeyed him, without one of the gibes and flings with which she was accustomed to give spice to their intercourse. But for some minutes they sat in silence, somewhat to Betty's discomfiture.

"Well, — what hast thou to say?" she remarked, at last. "It is not worth while to sit here mooning. The peas will be overdone."

He turned to her suddenly, covering with his broad, brown hand hers lying idly on her knee. "Betty, — wilt thou marry me, my lass? I have not asked thee plainly before, because I could never get thee to listen to reason. But now, here goes! Wilt thou marry me? Tell me, lass?"

She sat beside him silently, her head turned slightly away from him, her cheeks glowing.

"Speak to me, lass," he continued, placing his hand on her shoulder with a masterful touch, and compelling her to turn towards him. "Wilt thou marry me?"

She shook her head, but did not draw away from him.

"Why not? Surely thou dost care for me, Betty? With all thy flouting and jeering, I believe that. Dost thou not, my lass?"

His arm stole around her waist. She did not repulse him. Betty was crying. Never was man more amazed than Mat.

"Why, lass! why, Betty! what is ill with thee? Why dost thou cry? I will hold thee fast now that for the first time I have my arms about thee, till thou dost let me see thy heart. Speak, lass! Wilt thou not marry me when the late harvest apples are ripe? I will have a little cot all ready for thee."

But again she shook her head. Mat withdrew his arm. He was not the Strephon to woo an unwilling Chloe.

"We are at odds, I see," he said, rising. "Never mind, lass. 'Tis not thy fault. But I must take thee home as I promised Dame Sandys."

Betty put out her hand, "Nay, Master Hansel," she sobbed, and he reseated himself, his face brightening.

"Say 'Mat'! Away with your 'Master Hansels'! Say 'Mat'!"

"Mat, then! I — I did not mean —"

His arm stole back to its old position, and he drew her head to a resting-place on his shoulder. "You do care for me, lass?"

"Yes, mayhap, just a little," she faltered.

"That's enough, that's enough to begin with!" cried Mat, exultantly. "Never mind about the 'little'! I will make it much before the year dies. Kiss me, lass!"

But Betty turned her tear-stained face away from him, and with a brave effort at composure compelled herself to speak coherently. "Nay, nay, I like you well enow, Master — well — Mat, if you must have it so.　But I will marry no man at present.　I will not leave my mistress."

"Phew!　Phew!　Thy mistress!　Here's a coil. What has she to do with it, good woman though she be?　Art thou bond-slave to her?"

"Yes, in this thing.　Hear me, Mat Hansel!" and she bent her clear, steadfast blue eyes full upon him.　"I was a bond-slave to every ill a little maid might know in cruel city streets, until she found me out, drew me forth, and called me hers.　I was in rags and she clothed me.　There was none to give me bite of bread or sup of water, and she fed me.　I was beaten and ill bested, and she gave me care and watching, and almost a mother's love.　I will leave Dame Dorothy for no man, Mat Hansel, now that she is old and needs care herself.　Believe thou that."

Mat was silent.　He could understand this.

"Thou art a true-hearted lass," he said.　"It shall be as thou sayest, — for a time.　Only, — tell me one thing, I do beseech thee.　Dost thou love me?"

She lifted her brimming eyes to his face.

"Yes, Mat, — I love thee, — but I will not wed thee."

"Not now.　Say that, Betty!　Say 'I will not wed thee now, Mat.'"

She repeated the words mechanically, emphasizing the "now" as he did.

"Then I will wait," he said, gravely.　"I will wait

till thou canst, till thou wilt," and he kissed her, for the first time, as reverently as ever knight kissed lady's hand. "But I cannot stay here in constant sight of thee, my girl, with naught to put thee out of my head, from dawn to dew fall. I must away. It was this I meant to tell thee, — that if thou couldst not wed me, I would even ride with the army in Flanders, or in Spain, where English hearts are needed. When I come back, thou wilt give me another answer, mayhap."

This announcement did not startle Betty, as it might a maiden of to-day. War was the normal condition of things, peace the abnormal. Men were always going off to the wars, and for the most part, so it seemed to her, coming safely back again. It meant adventure, prowess, the chance of advancement, seeing the world. It was wise for a man to test his powers, and try his luck.

She put her hand in his, after a long silence, — "Thou art very good to me," she said, quietly; "and thou wilt be a brave soldier. When thou dost come back, — why then — why then — "

He caught up her words —

"Why then we shall see! But the kiss, lass! Give me the kiss of troth before I take thee home to the gray cottage. Be not so chary! I tell thee, my girl, the touch of thy lips will be a safeguard against the wiles of the French damsels across the water, which, they tell me, be many.   Give it me!"

Her eyes flashed with somewhat of the old laughing fire, as she lifted them.

"Take it then, if thou must have it," she said. "But I tell thee, Mat Hansel, if thou dost need a guard against the wiles of other maidens, be they French or English, no touch of my lips will save thee.   Be thou sure of that!"

They sauntered slowly back to the gray cottage. Dame Dorothy saw nothing, heard nothing, suspected nothing.   Why should Betty disturb her peace?

So Mat Hansel went off to the wars.

CHAPTER XVIII

It was in July that Robin Sandys first saw the imposing façade of Longleat House lifting itself above the wide reaches of level turf surrounding the great gray pile, that was at once a palace and a home. Therein is England blest, that she can make homes of cottages and palaces alike. She has learned the art.

It is now a brilliant July morning of the third summer thereafter. The whole place is astir. The great lawns are being newly shaven, swept, and garnished, as it were, till not a withered leaf or a dry twig mars the perfection of their long reaches of emerald velvet. The wide gardens and shrubberies are ablaze with light and color. Gay parterres glowing like jewels, and cool, shadowy closes where the dewy freshness of the early day still lingers, alike invite the wandering feet. Every path has been freshly rolled. The very lake has been rejuvenated by the removal of every yellow leaf and unsightly root, and the water-lilies dotting its surface are as white as the swans reflected on its bosom.

Inside the noble mansion, an army of men and

women are striving to make still fairer that which
was superlatively beautiful before. Rare tapestries
were being hung; from antique chests, carved, iron-
bound, and black with age, half-forgotten treasures
are being exhumed, — yellow laces, rich creations of
Eastern looms, costly fabrics and embroideries, the
spoil of altar and of shrine. In one suite of rooms,
the most magnificent of all, the ceilings are being
freshly decorated, and on every panel appears the
royal crest, and the A. R. of Anne Regina.

For her Majesty is coming to Longleat!

Queen Anne was not so fond of making royal
progresses and going a-visiting as was her great
predecessor, Elizabeth. But she did sometimes visit
her great nobles.

This morning, in one of the outer courts, near the
stables, a number of young men and lads, with two
or three older men who looked as if they had seen
service, were turning over, and examining critically,
a pile of ancient armor. Not by any means so
dowered with antiquity in that day as in this of
ours; but even then armor had been falling into dis-
use for more than one generation, and the younger
men were full of curiosity and exclamations.

"Look at that, now!" cried one of them, holding
up a great helmet of dull brass, with the visor closed.
"What think you of that for a head-piece, Robin
Sandys?"

"That I would not care to wear it on a hot day like this," he answered, "nor that heavy breastplate, either. But see! It hath been thrust through with a spear, for all its thickness, and there are blood stains on it. Some brave man wore it to his death."

"Never mind, never mind, Robbie," said the other, flippantly. "There's no call for a long face. 'Tis but what the thing was made for. But look, now! Here's a dainty bit of steel, — chain mail as light and flexible as a lady's necklace. By'r lady, but it takes on a wondrous fine polish, too," and he rubbed it vigorously with his sleeve. "What say you, Martin Howe? Shall I wear this when we tilt before the Queen?"

Martin Howe was one of the older men. He lifted the delicate, tinkling mass of metal, testing its weight, before he answered:

"That's as it pleases you. But I should advise you youngsters to try nothing heavier. Little you know of tilts and tournaments. Woe's me, but the times have changed since I was young! There's no strength in men's arms, now that musket and blunderbuss have taken the place of pike and broadsword. I remember well when I was but a small lad myself how John of Brentford met Mark Winthrop in the lists, and wore — "

"Ah, shut thy mouth, Martin Howe!" cried the

irreverent youth, whose name was Ralph Montague, "we've heard that old saw a thousand times. To-day was never half as good as yesterday since the world was made, if we take your word for it. I tell thee John of Brentford was no braver, nor a whit more knightly, than our good Lord of Weymouth, if he did wear weight of armor fit to crush him. More fool he, say I! Still, if we are to tilt for her Majesty's pleasure, we must make ourselves as fine as may be, and I mean to deck myself out in this bit of splendor. Look now, Robin. What say you to this shirt of mail with pointed greaves to match it? 'Tis of blue Milan steel finely wrought, and seems lighter than some. Or that fluted thing over yonder, with the pass guards for the neck? 'Tis a pretty bit of finery. What think you of that?"

"'Finery?' 'A pretty bit?' God save us!" exclaimed another of the elders. "Boy, dost thou think life was but a farce when these were worn? God save us from the folly of youth, again say I!"

Robin, meanwhile, paying slight attention to this stream of words, had been bending over the pile, scrutinizing each piece carefully. He had quite lost the remark of the last speaker.

"That 'fluted thing?' Speak not so lightly of it, Ralph Montague. 'Tis the very perfection of armor, such as Harry Richmond wore on Bosworth field. Look! its counterpart is in the armory, labelled duly. But I'll none of it, — grand as it is. 'Twould weigh me down. I will but take this shirt of mail with the pointed greaves, and mayhap something for a head-piece. But here comes Gaffer Ambrose. Give him room, lads," he added, as an aged man approached with tottering footsteps. "Here's a high-backed stool for him. Sit thee down, Gaffer."

The man, who was evidently very old, wore a long brown surcoat, reaching nearly to his feet, and a red cap, not unlike a Turkish fez, with a long tassel. Giving a groan, he lowered himself slowly into the seat offered, grasping his staff with both hands, and looked about inquiringly, his eyes blinking in the sunshine.

"Gaffer can tell you what's what," said one of the older men, who was yet a youth as compared with Gaffer. "He knows all about the old armor. Dost thou not, Gaffer?"

"Hey? — know about w-h-a-t?" and he curved his hand around his right ear, and leaned forward, listening intently.

"Why, about all this old truck the lads have brought down from the lofts," was the answer. "They don't know a greave from an arm-piece."

"Speak for yourself," cried Ralph. "Wisdom wasn't born with you. I know a hawk from a hand-saw, if I am but twenty years old. But what's this, Gaffer? How did a man ever wear it?" and he held up a bit of embossed steel, curiously shaped and moulded.

Gaffer rose slowly and approached the pile of armor, leaning heavily on his staff.

"That! That was for the steed, not for the rider, man! 'Tis but a head-piece for a horse. And here's another like unto it, only it hath wings at the side. No man ever wore that."

He tottered back to his seat, while a sarcastic laugh rose from the ranks of the older men, augmented now by twos and threes.

"Dost know a hawk from a hand-saw, Master Montague, and wilt thou wear a horse's head-piece when thou dost tilt before the Queen?" asked one of them, giving him a punch in the side, which was returned with interest.

But a new thought had made its way into Gaffer's clouded brain. "I am very old," he said, "older than the oldest of you. I can remember when James I. was king. I was chief armorer here when my lord went out to fight at Naseby—"

"'Twas this lord's father, rest his soul," interpolated one of the bystanders, by way of explanation.

"Aye, aye, I reckon we all know that," remarked Ralph. "Go on, Gaffer."

"I helped him on with his hauberk that day, and fastened his greaves. Ah, he was a man!"

He shook his head slowly, and the bystanders

waited on his moods. Old Gaffer was, by virtue of his years, honored and deferred to by the whole household.

"Aye, and after that, when Raglan was besieged, I was sent to the help of the old marquis. My Lord Herbert of Somerset, he was there, too. There was a white horse in the court that spouted water up to the sky. There was a black moat that was bewitched, and would rise up and drown folk unawares; and there were strange doings with fire and water, — marvels on marvels. There were those who said my Lord Herbert was in league with the devil. Verily, I know not, — but 'twas a strange, unearthly place, that Raglan castle."

"But about the armor," said Robin, to bring the old man back from his wandering. "Saw you ever this before?" And he held up something from the heap. It did not matter what.

"That? Let me have it, lad! It looks like the dragon that was on my lord's helmet. Give it here!"

He turned it over critically, then tossed it back. "'Tis not the same," he said. Then straightening himself up, with a sudden flame as of blue fire in his eyes, he cried out:

"What means this, my men? I am chief armorer. I have charge of all the armor of this house. Every bit of mail passes through my hands. At my lord's bidding I put it in order, and set it up in the armory at the end of the great hall, — piece by piece, in the manner it was worn.   I did it with my own hands; and now, here it is in all this coil, covered with rust, and tossed about by, ploughboys and lackeys.   'Tis pitiful!"

His voice sank to a mere whisper; his eyes grew dim and lustreless again, and he covered his face with his wrinkled hands, sobbing like a child.

Both Robin and Ralph sprang to his side, supporting him tenderly.   "Nay, nay, Gaffer," said the former.   "'Tis not as you think.   Look up, and let me tell thee.   This is not the armor from the great armory.   'Tis but some odd pieces from the loft that you did not think worth the setting up.   Look you, now!   There's hardly a full suit here; but my lord said we were to furbish up what we liked for the Queen's tournament."

 "The Queen?   What Queen?"

"Why, our own good Queen Anne, who comes here to-morrow."

The old man shook his head.   "The Queen's name is Henrietta Maria," he said.   "She is a French woman, and a papist, and 'tis thought she leads King Charles astray."

Then, looking around with a bewildered air, he put his hand to his forehead.   "I am so old," he continued.   "I am distraught; I lose my wits. Charles I., — is he King now, lads?"

ROBIN AND LORD WEYMOUTH.

The older men had slipped away, one by one, when Gaffer Ambrose's wits began to wander, leaving him to the ministrations of the younger ones. They looked at each other significantly, lifting him to his feet.

"Here's your staff, Gaffer," said Robin. "You are tired, that's all. Come now to the buttery for a bowl of broth, and when you have had an hour's rest, you shall come out again and tell us tales of the old wars that shall make every hair in our heads to stand on end. Come, now! First one foot and then the other!" And they led him away forgetful of the present, and babbling happily of dead kings and coats of mail.

Returning to the court, the young squires resumed their investigations. Before noon all who were to take part in the mock tournament were well fitted out, and smiths and armorers were at work, mending, restoring, and polishing.

That night, Robin, as was his custom, took the sleeping-cup to my Lord Weymouth in his chamber. He was in velvet dressing-gown and slippers, reclining in a large armchair with wings. The light from a hanging lamp fell full upon his iron-gray hair, and a letter with a great red seal from which he was reading.

"Put it on the table," he said, as Robin presented the cup, "and wait awhile. I have somewhat to say to you when I have read this letter."

Robin withdrew to the window and looked off across the park to the wooded hills in the distance. It was still light without, with the lingering twilight glow. Through an opening in the woods he caught a glimpse of the radiant sunset sky, slowly changing to purple and pale gray.

"'Heaven's Gate,' our good Doctor Ken calls that gap," thought Robin, his eye following afar the flight of a rook, dark against the sky. "It is well named."

"Come hither, lad," said Lord Weymouth, folding the letter and laying it beside the agate cup that held the sleeping-draught. "The Queen defers her coming for a day, thus arriving, not on the morrow as we thought, but on the day after. Whereat I am not sorry, as it gives more time for preparation. The place must be in full regalia for the reception of her Majesty, my lad," and my lord smiled as he motioned Robin to a low seat at his feet.

"Everything is in good trim, my lord," was the answer. "The men have outdone themselves. There's not so much as a leaf out of place, from lodge to turret."

"And how about the tournament? Is all going well? 'Tis but a merry farce, of course; less for the pleasure of the Queen than for the amusement of the younger ladies of her train. Yet still I would have my young squires at their best."

"They will be, my lord, they will be. There has

been naught going on to-day but practising at arms, the fitting and trying on of mail, and the comparing of head-pieces."

"And are the armorers doing their part well, that all may be fair and seemly? How long hast thou been of my household, Robin?" he asked, suddenly changing the subject.

"It will be three years when Tuesday comes, since I first saw Longleat. 'Twas a happy day for me, my lord."

"And you have been my secretary for a full twelvemonth, and, in a way, chief of the younger squires, also. Not an easy part, either, this last," Lord Weymouth went on, with a twinkle in his eyes. "Somewhat like being Head of the Schoolhouse at Rugby, — eh, Robin?"

"Nay, I know nothing of that, my lord, never having been at a great school. As for my being, as you are pleased to say, chief of the squires, it so happened that the oldest of the young men who were already here left your service soon after I entered it, leaving me somewhat in advance of those that came after. It was no desert of mine, I do assure you, sir. I did but know the ways of Longleat better than later comers."

His lordship laughed.

"Is that it? Very well, — state the case as best pleases you. But — I have watched; I have seen.

You have ruled your small court well and wisely, Robin. I shall miss thee, my lad, when the Queen calls thee hence," and he laid his hand kindly on the strong young arm beside him.

Robin, greatly moved by this unlooked-for praise and unwonted show of feeling on the part of his grave lord, dropped on one knee, and kissed the hand that had caressed him.

"My master, my master!" he cried. "Thou hast been like a father to me. I would I could show thee my love and gratitude, but thou canst never know it."

"I do know it," was the answer. "Thou art a good lad, Robin. But now to business — to business! On the day after to-morrow the Queen comes, and I ride to Frome to meet her. Let my gentlemen and men-at-arms be ready to act as escort. See that all is as it should be. Now go, — for the hour grows late. But send hither to me the Master of Horse. I must confer with him before I sleep."

As Robin left the room with a low obeisance, Lord Weymouth looked after him with a lingering gaze. Then sinking back in his chair with a long-drawn breath, he said to himself, musingly, after the manner of men who are much alone, as was he in spite of his large household, for he had neither wife nor child living: "Strange how my heart goes out to that youngster! Never since my own son fell at Sedgemoor have I so loved any of the youths about me. 'Grandson of an old nurse of mine?' So said the Queen that day. Yet seems he 'native here and to the manner born.'"

There was a knock at the door, and Hubert Langley, Master of Horse, entered.

CHAPTER XIX.

OF all the busy folk at Longleat on the morrow, none were busier than the young gentlemen who were to take part in the mock tournament. Such trying on and fitting of armor, rubbed and polished to the last degree, such strutting in the borrowed plumes of dead heroes, had not been seen for many a day. Six gentlemen in the service of a neighboring nobleman, Lord Hargrave, were to tilt with six of Lord Weymouth's. For the whole country was alive to the honor and glory of this visit from her Majesty, and every lord and gentleman within its limits had been bidden to Longleat.

There was to be a grand banquet; there was to be a merry masque, with lovely ladies in fanciful disguises; there was to be dancing on the lawn by moonlight and torchlight, and the treading of minuets in the great hall by the blaze of a thousand waxen candles set in silver sconces; there was to be an archery contest in the green glades of the park, and athletic sports on the tilting ground, with an award of prizes, — and, to crown all, there was to be the grand tournament for which all were preparing.

No wonder that not only Longleat, but all Somerset-shire, was in a whirl of excitement.

The Queen was to sleep at Westbury, — about ten miles from Frome ; and it had been announced that, to avoid the heat of the July day, she would start from thence as soon after sunrise as might be, reaching Frome by ten o'clock.

So the sun was hardly above the hills when the great stable court at Longleat was astir. Horses were being groomed and saddled, accoutrements were receiving the final perfecting touches, and grooms and pages were darting hither and thither on a hundred different errands. There were few to look idly on, for in kitchen and buttery, hall and chamber, corridor and closet, heads, hands, and eyes were busy. Only Gaffer Ambrose had crept out of his quiet nest, and sat on a bench in the sunshine.

The talk of the Queen's visit had indeed reached him, where he dwelt afar, like the murmur of the sea. In a vague way he felt the stir and tension in the air. But that was all. If he comprehended that the Queen was coming, he disapproved, shaking his old head slowly. Henrietta Maria was a papist, and she led King Charles astray.

Lord Weymouth's black stallion was champing the bit, and making passes at the groom who held him. Robin, in a riding suit of dark purple with a glint of gold here and there, broad collar and cuffs of fine white holland, wide-brimmed hat of black felt, cocked, and fastened with rosettes of velvet, and high, yellow Cordovan boots, was whispering in the ear of Fanuella, who bent her head towards him, listening wisely.

"You must carry thyself well, my lady," he was saying. "Thou knowest thou wert given me by our good Queen, and she will surely mark thy paces. And who knows —"

But at that moment my lord appeared, the order to mount was given, and in less time than it takes to tell it, an imposing cavalcade was filing out at the great gate.

Robin rode at Lord Weymouth's left hand, his heart in a tumult of expectation and dread. Not that he feared the Queen. She had always been kind to him; she would be kind now. Lord Weymouth's approval was an assurance of hers.

But who would be in her Majesty's train? Would Little Lady be one of the younger ladies of whom his lord had spoken, and for whose amusement they were to tilt? He would have asked if he had dared. But this morning Lord Weymouth, who often talked with him freely and companionably, rode on silently, absorbed in thought, or in a critical mood watched the riding and carriage of his train. Robin could not summon courage to speak.

For three years he had not heard her name, save

once or twice in some stray mention of the court. He had had no glimpse of her since that Coronation day in the abbey when she wore his arrow in her hair. She was his Little Lady no longer, but the Lady Anne Gascoyne, the brightest star in her Majesty's galaxy. For there could be no doubt as to that! Did she ever think of him? Did she still remember the old *camaraderie*, the story-telling in the little library, the apple-roastings, the chestnut-tings, all the simple, kindly, honest good-fellowship when Gloster lived and was the friend of both? Would she greet him kindly now in her beautiful maidenhood? Would she smile on him, and perhaps even give him her white hand to kiss?

But if she did, what could ever come of it? Who and what was he, that he should aspire to the favor and friendship of the Lady Anne Gascoyne? He was no beggar. He did not think of himself even as the protégé of the Queen. As Lord Weymouth's secretary and favorite his position in that household was well assured, and was never questioned. For a long time now, he had been put in quiet, unremarked possession of an allowance, or stipend, amply suffi-cient for his needs. And the wage was well earned. He knew that. He was no mere pensioner, living on his lord's bounty. As for his birth, no one at Longleat, save Lord Weymouth, knew aught of it, or ever gave it a thought. There were plenty of young men all over the kingdom, who, for various reasons, political or otherwise, held similar positions to his own in noble households; though few of the number, it must be added, had good command of the pen as well as of the steed and the sword.

But when it came to thoughts of love and marriage, it was quite another matter. Truth to say, of marriage Robin did not think; nor had he thought consciously of love, save as a bright fantasy. Youth dreams and wonders long before it thinks.

Frome is now a modern little town, with commonplace little shops as its chief points of interest. Little is left of its old importance save the noble church beside which, under the chancel window, Thomas Ken lies buried. But two hundred years ago its streets had not lost their picturesque setting, — the quaint old houses and antique architecture of an elder day. The town was at its best that morning, as Lord Weymouth and his brilliant train rode through to meet the Queen just on its farther limits. Royal progresses, royal entrances, royal processions, have been often described. But let no one think of Anne as a second stately Elizabeth, in green velvet riding-habit, and cap with floating plume, guiding a superb milk-white charger with imperial grace and dignity. Nor was Lord Weymouth, as he bent his knee in salutation, a Leicester

in "cloth of gold, blazing with jewels." The days
of such splendid pageantry were over. But he was
a noble English gentleman, suitably apparelled; and
the Queen was in a grand open carriage, drawn by
four fine horses, as became her age and state.

The dust of the highway was annoying in spite
of a sharp shower in the night. After due salutation, a movement of Lord Weymouth's hand sent
his whole train, Robin included, galloping to the
rear, that the Queen might not be discommoded;
and he alone rode by her side from Frome to
Longleat. It was a relief, indeed, to pass from
the heat outside into the cool green stillness and
shadowy recesses of the great park; and as they
went on and on through the vast, silent, perfectly
kept spaces, and at length caught sight of the
stately Elizabethan mansion, with its many square
bays, its Doric columns, its multitude of domes and
turrets surrounding the line of the almost horizontal
roof, its many statues standing out in strong relief
against the sky, together with its vast dimensions
and massive dignity, her Majesty gave an exclamation of delight.

"Surely my nobles do house themselves well!"
she cried. "My Lord Weymouth, you have a palace
wherein to receive your Queen."

He bowed low in the saddle, as, tossing the reins
to a groom, he sprang from his horse, and assisted

her to alight. "It is, indeed, a palace while your Majesty honors its roof," he said. "Welcome to Longleat, my Queen!"

He would have conducted her at once to the suite of apartments prepared for her, but it pleased her Majesty's fancy to linger for awhile in the lofty, spacious, vaulted hall with its noble staircase.

"Nay, my lord," she entreated, "I will sit here for a moment, if I may, and look about me. Truly, as I said before, thou art well housed. I had no thought that Longleat was so grand. Who may have built it, my lord?"

Falling in with her mood, Lord Weymouth went on for five minutes, telling her of its Italian architect, John of Padua, and of sundry legends of love and crime connected with the vast edifice. Meanwhile, her younger ladies flitted quietly hither and thither like a flock of bright-winged birds, perching on window-seat and staircase, and peering out of windows with pretty half-smothered exclamations of wonder and delight, while the older ones stood gravely by, awaiting somewhat impatiently their mistress's pleasure.

Lady Marlborough was first to speak.

"Methinks you are flushed and tired, madam, and it would be wise to seek some rest before listening longer to my Lord Weymouth's romancing," she said, making him a half-mocking curtsey, but smiling withal. She had no mind to quarrel with her stately host.

"I beg pardon," he said, bowing low. "I beg pardon if my romancing was out of season. But — grant me one moment, Lady Marlborough. I have your Majesty's permission?"

Queen Anne nodded. "Indeed I am in no haste to go to bed, my lord," she answered. "What will you?"

Lord Weymouth had just caught sight of Robin standing without, while Fanuella was being led away to her stall, and with one swift gesture beckoned him to his side. Then, taking his hand, he led him forward without a word, but smiling.

The tall, lithe, handsome youth knelt at the Queen's feet, with downcast eyes and arms folded on his breast, perfectly quiet in outward bearing, though, to his amazement and indignation equally, his heart was thundering in his ears. What ailed it? he thought, contemptuously. He had not been abashed in the Queen's presence when he was but a child. Why should he tremble now? This was no time for philosophizing; but had he only known it, it was partly due to Lady Marlborough's cool, critical gaze bent steadfastly upon him now, with the same hint of displeasure and dislike that he had so often felt in Windsor; and partly to the happier fact that, in one swift, all-embracing glance, as he entered the hall, he had caught a glimpse of Little Lady in a bevy of maidens who were leaning over the balustrade and looking down on him from the first landing.

It is, perhaps, not strange that for a moment Queen Anne did not recognize him. He had changed greatly in this period of rapid transition between boyhood and early manhood. As he knelt, his head was bent low, and his rich, dark curls, worn rather long, after the manner of the cavaliers, — for Lord Weymouth did not approve of wigs for the young men of his household, — half hid the brown cheeks on which the color was slowly deepening. Anne looked inquiringly at Lord Weymouth, and smilingly at the kneeling figure before her.

"'Tis a goodly youth," she said. "Here, I give him my hand to kiss, though you have not yet vouchsafed to give me his name, my lord. But, nathless, — Robin! Is it thou?"

The lad lifted his eyes to her face, and as she met their full, wide, undaunted gaze, she knew him, and her face changed. For a moment she saw two childish figures at her feet. Gloster was present in that ancient hall. As Robin took her hand, reverently, and bent his head over it, her fingers closed over his and she raised him to his feet.

"Faith! but I did not know the lad, so changed and grown is he!" she cried. "Why, he is as tall as you, my Lord Weymouth, and he hath the air and bearing of a man. I give you joy of your handiwork. Truly I beg pardon for calling thee 'lad,' Master Sandys," — and she smiled on him with upturned face as he towered above her.

All this had passed in a moment's space. Then Lady Marlborough swept forward.

"Come, come, madam!" she said. "'Tis time you were in your chamber, if you care to be fit to be seen at the fête this evening. And the Lord knows we all need rest after this long drive. Let us to our rooms, please you, my Lord Weymouth, without more delay."

And her Majesty meekly obeyed her imperious monitress.

Shall the truth be told? It has been said already that Queen Anne was swayed, even more than most women, by circumstances and the strongest present influence. Her life was full of engrossing interests; from war and politics, to the quarrels of her women. If it was not strange that she did not at once recognize Robin after the lapse of three critical years, so neither must it be considered strange that during those years she had hardly thought of him. Even the shadow of Gloster had grown dim in the whirl of other interests; and Gloster's friend was to her, after all is said, only the shadow of a shade.

She had kept her promise to Gloster, by placing Robin where he was, — in the path of promotion.

Having done this, except when on her rare pilgrimages to Windsor an occasional glimpse of Dame Dorothy may have recalled him to her mind, she straightway forgot all about him.

Yet now she was honestly delighted to find that he amply justified, in the beauty and promise of his splendid young manhood, the friendship of her son, as well as her own goodly share in furthering it. And this was not strange, either.

"On my life, I have not seen a finer or more comely gallant than this same Robin Sandys, for many a day," she said, after reaching the magnificent room that had been set apart as her presence-chamber, — with its canopied dais, and its splendid ceiling newly decorated, in her honor, with her own crest and initials. "Verily, my Lord Weymouth hath made a man of him, and I do thank my stars that I sent him to such a fine place. We must have him up at court ere while, — eh, my Lady Marlborough?"

"It seems to me he is fairly well off where he is," said Lady Marlborough. "I see no need of haste in the matter of his further advancement. To speak the truth, madam, I always thought him a forward lad, somewhat in the way of his betters. But very like your Majesty would do well to make him gentleman of the bedchamber, or mayhap privy councillor, in place of my Lord Rochester," she flouted. "I have naught to say about it, thank the Lord! Mistress Hill, make you her Majesty comfortable, if you can, while I go to take some rest. Where be all those young damsels we be cumbered with bestowed? So silly they be, as if no one of them had ever seen a fine place before this! Yet for my own sake I would have them fit themselves to make a decent appearance this night."

CHAPTER XX.

Longleat was in a blaze of glory that night. Even by day the windows and bays of the magnificent pile seemed countless as the sands of the sea. Now every triple and quadruple casement was set with a living, palpitating jewel from which rays of light streamed far across the wide spaces of the pleasaunce, and down the leafy avenues that encircled it. Not only the façade, but every side of the great, almost square, edifice, whose walls enclosed acres of space, was lighted up till there was not a hint of night or darkness anywhere. No hint of night ; yet overhead the full, round moon soared upward and onward through a cloudless, dark blue sky, its majestic splendor dwarfing man's highest endeavor.

All Somersetshire, and many of the rank and fashion from adjacent counties were there, and the scene, both without and within, was gay and beautiful beyond description. Naturally its magnificence culminated in the presence-chamber where, on the raised dais, Queen Anne sat enthroned, with her group of ladies about her, while below thronged the beauty and gallantry of the southern half of her kingdom.

Robin stood in the corridor without, leaning against the doorway. Ostensibly he was watching the gay scene within the chamber. In reality he had eyes but for one figure, — that of a slight young girl, in a robe of glistening white brocade, with a string of pearls clasped closely about her throat, who stood quietly behind the Queen.

Up came Ralph Montague to join him, in a great flurry of excitement. " Look, Robin," he cried, pulling him by the sleeve, "tell me, is the knot of my laced kerchief straight? I caught it on Wat Bradshaw's sleeve button, and tore a great rent in the border, — worse the luck! Doth it show to shame me?"

Robin looked him over from head to foot, with a slight smile, noting the fair hair curled and powdered, the crimson velvet coat faced with white satin, the long, embroidered waistcoat of white and silver, the black knee-breeches, the silken hose, and the dainty shoes with their sparkling buckles. He carried his cocked hat under his arm, and wore a short sword with a jewelled hilt.

"You are as fine as a peacock, Ralph," he said, "and as trim and trig as a newly rigged ship. Never fear for you when fine dressing is in question."

"But you? Are you fine enough?" his companion

asked, anxiously, — for they were good, true friends,
these two, though not overdemonstrative about it.
"Let me see!   Purple velvet coat and breeches,
white waistcoat, lace ruffles, white silk stockings.
Yes, you'll do, though that waistcoat would have
borne a trifle more embroidery.   You're always
chary of finery, Robbie, my lad.   Are we gentlemen
to be presented to her Majesty, — do you know?"

"Her Majesty was pleased to speak to me this
morning," said Robin, tranquilly.   "I was often at
Windsor, when a child."

The peculiar relation that had led to Robin's present position was not known at Longleat, Lord Weymouth having wisely considered that if he were
known, in the household, as in any sense a protégé
of the Queen, it might work to his disadvantage.

"Phew!" exclaimed Ralph.   "You have been
close-mouthed about it.   Is she gracious, her Majesty?   But look there, Robin, quick!   Do you see
her, — that young demoiselle in white, standing at
this minute just behind my Lady Marlborough?   I
marked her this morning straying by herself in the
privy pleasaunce.   By the soul of Venus, but she is
the fairest maiden my eyes ever rested on!   Her
hair is like spun gold.   I must compass her acquaintance in some way, and strive for the honor of a dance
with her.   Think you my lord would present me if I
were to muster courage to ask him, — eh, Robin?"

But before Robin could answer, some one touched Ralph on the arm, and he was lost in the gay, swirling crowd, leaving his companion with a pang at his heart that was half joy, half sudden terror. Yes, — his Little Lady was indeed fair, fairer even than in his dreams of her. And her fairness, her sweetness, charmed other eyes than his.

He turned again to watch the scene upon the dais, as one looks at a fair picture. But, as he looked, it dissolved. The Queen dismissed the younger ladies with a smiling word, and a wave of her hand, and one by one they withdrew.

The great picture-gallery, where hung the portraits of the Lords of Bath, from the founder of the house, Sir John Thynne, to that of Lord Weymouth himself, was on the same side of the house with the suite of rooms set apart for the Queen and her retinue. Five minutes afterwards, Robin, suddenly remembering a wish his lord had expressed as to the rehanging of a picture, went thither to see if the matter had been attended to. The long, stately room was brilliantly lighted, as was all the rest of the house. But it was quite deserted. Who cared for dead beauties? The living were stronger magnets, — warm, glowing flesh and blood, palpitating with life and joy. Art was at a discount when compared with the attractions of the ballroom, the banqueting-hall, and the presence-chamber, to say nothing of the lawns and gardens where colored lamps gleamed in the soft, still air, and the moon shone overhead.

Robin was no ascetic, and no saint. He was fond of song and dance, of fun and merriment, and of the good things, even the splendors of life. If he scorned all that was ignoble, if he was not given overmuch to the wine-cup, it was, perhaps, more a matter of taste and refinement than because he had deliberately reasoned the matter out. What we call goodness is as apt as otherwise to be a matter of fortunate temperament rather than of stern principle.

But to-night he was in no mood for gaiety. The viols entreated in vain, and the twanging of the stringed instruments stirred him no more than the humming of so many bees. He threw himself down on one of the settles ranged against the crimson wall, and his thoughts went on a far flight backward, — to his early childhood, and his grandmother's fairy tales of kings' houses; to his boyhood, and Gloster's faithful, unchanging love, and all he owed to it; to the days that had followed in the gray cottage, and the still forest, — and then turned, with a great longing, to Dame Dorothy. How good she was, how true, how noble in all real nobleness, and as sweet and pure as any fine lady in the land! Yet at that moment he was conscious, as he had never been before, that he loved Little Lady, — nay, — the Lady

Anne Gascoyne, — and that he had loved her always. When the heart once awakens, its doors fly open wide, and all loves, if they be holy, enter in ; the old and the new dwelling together in perfect harmony.

Just then, a slender figure in white glided out of the half darkness of a corridor that led from the Queen's apartments to an entrance at the upper end of the long gallery, lifted the arras, and looked timidly in. Robin's heart gave one great throb, and then stood still, as Lady Anne, seeing no one, let the tapestry sweep back, and, leaning against the casement of the wide, mullioned window, looked soberly out on the gay pleasaunce and the white moon overhead.

She thought she was alone. She had neither seen nor heard him. Should he stir? Should he speak? Or should he steal softly away, and leave her to her maiden meditations?

Before he had answered these questions it was too late. She turned, and came slowly down the gallery, glancing here and there at a portrait, and paused at length, midway, with dropped hands folded lightly, and uplifted eyes, before that of a beautiful woman in the bloom of her youth.

Robin, partly hidden by the shadow of a great banner that hung above his head, was still unseen, — but now he rose quietly, and stepped forward into the light. "Little Lady!" he cried, under his breath, "Little Lady!" For, in her near presence, he had forgotten time and distance, — all, save their old companionship.

She gave a little start, a look of inquiry. Then her face grew radiant, and she came swiftly towards him, with outstretched hands. "Robin!" she said, and that was all; while he, dropping on one knee, after the graceful, reverent fashion of his day, kissed them both, and then rose, trembling.

She, as is the manner of women, be they old or young, was the first to recover herself.

"Fie on you, for a lazy renegade," she cried, with the little imperious air he so well remembered. She had always been in the habit of laying down the law in trifles, both to him and Gloster. "Why are you mooning here in this dull place? You should be playing the gallant in the ballroom, or leading the dance on the greensward. I thought better things of you."

Robin led her to the seat he had deserted. "Then you have thought of me, Little Lady? You have not forgotten me? Tell me that, I pray you, for truly there has not been a day — nay, hardly an hour — since we parted that I have not thought of you, and with a great longing to see your face once more. Tell me, Little Lady," and he again bent his knee at her side, "tell me you have remembered the old days?"

She turned her face slightly away from him, but

did not withdraw the hand he had taken. "Yes, I have remembered," she said, softly. "See!" and she drew from its hiding-place, in the thick coils of her hair, the little silver arrow. "See! It has been precious to me as part of the old life. The Queen bade me keep it out of sight, if I must wear it; but I have worn it always."

"The Queen!" for this startling reminder overpowered for the moment the thought of her remembrance. "The Queen, say you?"

"Nay, she did not know you gave it to me. It was not that. It was only that as I grew older she bade me wear finer things, as befitted one of her train."

Something in her voice moved him. He gazed earnestly on her half-averted face, and a memory of their talk, long ago, under the portrait of the king in St. George's Hall, came to him. "Little Lady," he whispered, "tell me, for the sake of the old days. Are you happy?"

She did not answer directly. "I like not this court life," she said. "I would I could fly away from it and see it no more, nor be a part of it."

"But, are you not happy? Surely the Queen loves you!"

She hesitated a moment. "Her Majesty is kind to me," she said. "She does her duty to her godchild, whose father was slain for loving hers. Oh,

yes.   She will do her full duty, and see that I make
a fine marriage some day.   The Queen's goddaughter will have a reasonable dowry given her, no doubt,
wherewith to buy a husband; and then all will be
well, and her father's shade will sleep."

She spoke bitterly, scornfully, but her eyes were
heavy with unshed tears.   Robin realized at last what
he had known without fully realizing before, that it
was by a woman's side he knelt, and his own manhood responded.   Yet there was the little silver
arrow, and her hand lay trembling in his own.   He
bent his head and touched his lips to both.

"Lady Anne," he said, "thou hast done me much
grace to keep this poor trifle.   But tell me, Lady
Anne, — "

"Nay, call me not 'Lady Anne,' but 'Little
Lady,'" she cried.   "I hear enough of Lady Anne
other where.   But, — what wilt thou?"

"Would they wed you to one for whom you do
not care?   And are you indeed weary of the court?"

"Yes, and yes, — to both questions," she answered.
"It is all a tangled maze, strife and treachery, jealousy and ill-will; and I, who have no father's house
to turn to, as have the other maidens, I weary of it
beyond all telling.   And there is no door of escape
save one," she added, with a sudden turn of the head
and a quick breath.   "But now no more of this, — of
me.   Tell me of yourself, Robin!   Sit here, and let

us pretend for a moment that we are again children, telling stories in the little library."

Yielding at once to her mood, he told her, painting the picture with a few bold, rapid strokes, the story of his life since they parted; a life at once quiet, yet stirring; uneventful outwardly, yet full of growth and development. Unconsciously to him, it was a self-revelation. Its telling brought the smiles back to her lips, the color to her cheeks. Then she rose. They had been together but twenty flying minutes.

"I must needs go, I shall be called for," she said. "Will you take me to the ballroom, Master Sandys? I wonder are you not going to ask for the honor of a dance with me?" and she swept him a low curtsey.

"If I may, if I dare!" he cried, exultingly. "But, — Little Lady!"

"Well?"

"You know we have a tournament to-morrow, and tilt before the Queen?"

"Yes, so I have heard."

"I would it were a real joust, a real tourneying, Lady, that I might be your champion, and challenge one you wot of, — thus avowing myself your true knight before all the world."

She looked at him with laughing eyes.

"I doubt if you could overthrow him in the lists, Master Robin. Thou art taller than he by three good inches; but nathless, he is stouter than thou

art, and much thine elder both in years and dignities.
Be not rash ! "

"But, — Little Lady ? "

"Well ? " she said, again.

"If it were a true fight, if it were a real tourney,
wouldst thou choose me for thine own true knight,
and bid me do battle for thee ? Speak, Little Lady !
On my knees I do beseech thee."

She hesitated for a moment with downcast eyes,
her color coming and going. Was this real, or was
it play, like the mock tournament itself ? — or like
the semblance of love-making into which Gloster
would have beguiled them, in the old days of James
and Joan ? But her hand fell slowly on his shoulder as he knelt, like the touch of the sword in the
accolade.

" Yes," she said, in a voice that could have reached
no ear but his, " Yes. If this were a real tourney I
would choose thee for mine own true knight."

He sprang to his feet, as one ennobled.

" And if I won the fight ? "

" Then thou shouldst have a knight's guerdon,"
she answered.

Was this real, or was it play ? He, too, asked the
question secretly of his own heart and hers. He
had been borne on by the spirit within him almost
without his own volition. He had said more than in
a saner moment he would have dared to say. Was

he in a dream, or no ?   Yet he went on, bowing low again as he raised her hand to his lips.

"Give me a favor to wear to-morrow, then," he said. "Lady Anne, give me leave to dream awhile !"

On a loose thread of gold she wore a tiny Eastern amulet. "Here," she said, slipping it from her wrist. "Take it for good luck ! And now keep me not another minute, but take me to the ballroom straightway."

Was there ever such a dance as that ? Was there ever such bewildering music ? Was earth ever before so full of light and joy and melody, the glory of existence, the delight and splendor of being ? Even when forced by certain unwritten laws, cogent then as now, to resign Little Lady to Ralph Montague and to seek another partner for himself, Robin still trod on air and moved as one on wings.

A dais and canopied chair had been prepared for the Queen in the splendid ballroom ; and thither she had repaired, attended by Lord Weymouth. Lady Anne was dancing with young Montague, who was evidently enchanted with his fair partner. Her Majesty watched the stately mazes of the minuet with pleased eyes.

"Lady Anne dances well," she said. "Ah ! it is good to be young and lithe and supple, my lord. I was fond of the dance once myself," and the woman within her gave a sigh for the lost youth.

Lord Weymouth bowed.

"The Lady Anne? Is she the daughter of Gascoyne of Ashtonwold, madam?"

"Yes," said the Queen, curtly, "and my god-daughter."

She said no more, and Lord Weymouth resumed his silent observations. The shadow of the dead father had always come between Anne and her name-child, in spite of every outward observance, and it always would.

But presently she turned to her companion with a smile.

"Twould be a matter of prudence not to leave the lady exposed too long to the wiles of your young gallants here, my lord. See how they hover about her! Lord Dalkieth has asked her hand of me; and as I have sanctioned his suit, they are, in a way, betrothed."

"The old lord, your Majesty? He must be very greatly her senior. And is the fair demoiselle propitiously inclined?"

"One can never prophesy as to a girl's whims," the Queen answered, evasively. "She knows very well that I approve his suit. He will take better care of her, belike, than a younger man," she added, laughing. "My Lord Weymouth, I find the heat oppressive. Shall we return to my presence-chamber?"

Lord Weymouth escorted her Majesty to the door of her chamber and retired.

"Another sacrifice," he said to himself, frowning slightly as he turned thoughtfully away. "'Tis a pity, — for 'tis a rarely sweet maiden."

CHAPTER XXI.

AND now the great day had come, — the day of the tournament. Everything was in order, the tilting ground made ready, the lists set. The morning had been spent quietly, though more than one pair of would-be knights had stolen away to some secluded corner of the park for practice and consultation. Only Armorer Smith was in demand. If he were not busy at his forge, bending and plying and fastening rivets, he was busy answering questions, — for who understood better than he the weighty problems of the hour? Even Gaffer Ambrose deferred to him — sometimes — as to the relative weight of lances, or the right adjustment of shields. Gaffer, leaning with clasped hands on his staff, gazed idly at the anvil and watched the heavy strokes of the hammer. Why all this pother and excitement? How could the Queen be an honored guest at Longleat? He shook his old head, and tottered back to his quarters. They were very wise, these young folk, — but he knew. Henrietta Maria is a papist, and she leads King Charles astray.

The ladies were in their chambers. Lord Weymouth wandered somewhat restlessly from point to point, his thoughts busy, his eye on everything, his hand on the reins.

Dinner was over. Guests from far and near were assembling, and it was almost time for the tourney. Lord Weymouth, on the terrace, was bowing low over the hand of a stately dowager in velvet and diamonds, when a rider came clattering up the drive at full speed, sprang from his horse, and gave one quick glance to right and left.

"This for my Lord of Weymouth," he said, doffing his cap and presenting a letter.

My lord's face changed as he glanced hurriedly at the seal and the superscription, — "For the hand of the noble Lord Weymouth. Haste — post-haste!"

"Give this man food and rest. Take his horse to the stables," he said, tossing him a gold piece. "Your pardon, friends and neighbors. I will be with you again anon," — and he withdrew to his closet.

Some minutes later his bell rang violently. "Find Master Sandys, and send him hither at once," said he, as the summons was answered.

The lackey hesitated and stammered. "Sir, — sir, — I beg my lord's pardon, — but Master Sandys is making ready for the tourney. He is arming himself at this instant."

"Never mind that. Make no delay. Send him hither."

When Robin entered the closet a few moments later, having waited only to throw a long cloak over his shirt of blue Milan steel and the crimson juppon embroidered with the Weymouth crest, his lord, who was pacing the room, approached him hurriedly with outstretched hands.

"Robin," he said, huskily, "Robin, I am in sore trouble and perplexity. I must put thee to the test, my lad. Wilt thou help me?"

His face was pallid, his hand trembled as Robin kissed it, saying only, "With my life, if need be, my lord. What wilt thou have me do?"

"Ride to Southampton before the tide goes out, — 'twill be less than five hours, — and place this packet in hands of Master Sampson, captain of the ship *Falcon* lying there. She weighs anchor to-night at ebb-tide. Bid him make all speed to France, and deliver the papers as directed herein. He will understand, and will obey without parley. Canst thou do it, Robin?"

"There's not a moment to lose, my lord, but I will do it if man can. Fanuella has speed and endurance. We can but try. Hast thou any further commands for me?"

"Only this. Stop at the sign of the Dolphin, near the quay. Here, — put this in thy pouch. 'Twill more than pay thy keep. Ah, but thou hast on thy mail! I had forgotten —"

"My lord, my lord, think not now of that! Only

tell me how to serve thee best and, God helping me, I will do it. Shall I say aught else to the captain?"

"Nothing but what I have told thee. He knows my crest and seal. Robin, my honor, mayhap my life, is in thy hands. I have a foe who seeks to compass my ruin. I know not but —"

"Nay, nay, my dear lord," cried Robin. "Do but tell me one thing to give me courage. Wilt thou be safe if I do this thing?"

"I think so. I trust so."

"Then," dropping on one knee, "give me your blessing and let me go. We do but lose time, and the way is long."

"The Lord give thee strength and courage; the Lord bless thee and keep thee," said his master, solemnly. "Now fare thee well — and see thou speak to no man of thy mission."

But as Robin sprang to his feet, Lord Weymouth flung his arms around his neck, strained him to his breast, and kissed him twice on the cheek, crying again, "God help thee, my boy. Now go!"

In a moment, as it were, Robin had flown to his chamber, torn off his gewgaws, donned his riding suit, and was in the stable court. Fanuella, pawing and prancing, turned her head as she heard his step, and greeted him with a neigh. She was richly caparisoned, with splendid housings, and embroidered saddle-cloth. The amazed grooms stared as, bidding them make all haste, he began to unbuckle her gay trappings.

"Quick!" he cried. "Bring hither my lightest, strongest saddle, and see you that the girth be sound, and the stirrups right."

With a sure hand, and a quick eye, he himself tested every strap and buckle. Then, vaulting into the saddle, he shot out of the court, like an arrow from the bow. The amazement of the grooms deepened into awe as they watched his flight.

"By the great sword of Gideon," exclaimed the elder of the twain, who boasted that in his youth he had been in Cromwell's stables, "here's a fine coil! But now, Master Sandys was all agog for tilting, having been challenged, as the say is, by Lord Hargrave's nevvy. Now there he goes shooting off on a wild tangent. Hath he lost his stomach for the fight, think you, Jock? or is the tourney off?"

But it was not off. Just then there was a distant bugle call, and Jock and Hobbs scurried away to peep through the palings, and get a glimpse of the tilting ground.

Robin, too, heard the bugle, as under cover of the hedge he swept around the corner, and dashed by the shortest cut through the park to the highroad. It would be idle to say that at the sound his heart did not sink like lead. He caught his breath in a half sob, as he rose in the stirrups, cast one look backward, and then, with a low cry of "On, on!" to Fanuella, dashed forward with the speed of the wind. He had had no time to think, no slightest wish to demur. Yet from Lord Weymouth's first word, one vision had been before his eyes. He had seen the long, straight lists, the gay pavilions, the marshals, the heralds, the horses in their fine array, the gathering of the panoplied combatants. Looking down from the high balconies and improvised galleries, gay with hangings of many-colored tapestries, and astir with floating banners, while the royal ensign waved triumphantly over all, were the Queen and her ladies, all for whose approval he cared in the small world of Longleat, all the strength and beauty of Somerset. He heard the summons, the challenge, the acceptance. He saw Lady Anne, with the soft glow on her cheeks, the tender light in her eyes, bend forward in eager search of her knight, her champion, who but last night had sworn himself to her service, he to whom she had given the dear right to "dream awhile," and to wear her favor on his helm. And now! Lord Weymouth's hurried words had made him aware that his was a secret embassage. His absence could, for the present at least, be neither explained nor forgiven. It must be set down to fickleness, or to rank cowardice. His lady had given him the token from her arm, and to all appearance he had dishonored it. He had not even had the grace to restore it to her, unworn and unsullied. For one instant, as these galling thoughts swept over him, he checked Fanuella's headlong flight, and half turned her towards Longleat, now dim with distance on the sky line. Then, with a cry of dismay, he leaned forward till his brow touched her neck.

"Go on, go on, Fanuella!" he cried. "Go on, in God's name!"

For some time he was on familiar ground, and could lessen the distance a trifle by short-cuts through lanes and by-ways, and the leaping of hedges and ditches. Then he struck into a country that was new to him, and the only safe course was to keep to the highway. Men and women at work in the harvest fields lifted their heads, and stared after him as he shot past them; old crones at cottage doors gazed with dull curiosity; children laughed, and clapped their hands gleefully, thinking he but rode a mad race; dogs barked, and hens and chickens scurried out of the way, like coveys of partridges at the tread of the hunter.

The sun was low in the heavens when he reached Salisbury, and threw himself from his reeking mare, at the door of the King's Arms. He was, perhaps, as tired as she; but he followed her to the stable, to oversee the care given her, before seeking a few moments of rest and refreshment for himself. For if she should fail him, what then? Another horse? But who so fleet as she? And who but she knew his very thoughts, read his moods, and could respond to the exigency of every moment?

It was but a short breathing space. Then on, on again, crossing rivers, fording streams, climbing hills, threading valleys, — out of Wiltshire, and into Hants. There was no thought now of Little Lady, or of tournament, or favor. All feeling, all desire, was merged in one great longing, — to do the deed he had set out to do. His heart beat heavily, keeping time to the measured, monotonous thud of Fanuella's hoofs. He looked anxiously at the darkening heavens. He could not yet catch so much as a far-off glimpse of the roofs and spires of Southampton. Oh, for one breath of the salt sea on his forehead, that he might know the goal was near! For he knew it must be almost the hour of ebb-tide, when the *Falcon* would weigh anchor.

Fanuella was growing exhausted. The sweat poured from her steaming flanks. She turned her head slightly from side to side, as if to say, "Why so cruel, good master? Have pity and give me rest."

But still he goaded her onward, now with light touch of spur, now with entreaties, love-words, and caresses. "A little longer, a little further, for God's sake, and if thou lovest me, Fanuella," he cried, stroking her wet mane, and touching tenderly her quivering ears.

And at last,—oh, joy! Southampton was in sight, and he could see the tall masts of the *Falcon* lying at the quay!

He dashed through the Norman archway of the Bar Gate, and down High Street to the sign of the Dolphin. He threw the reins to a groom.

"Care for her well, I pray you, for she is sore bestead. I will be back ere long," he said, and went on his way down the quay.

The gang-plank had been removed, and with many a "Yo, heave, ho!" the stalwart sailors were casting off the lines.

"Too late, my hearty!" shouted some one from the deck, as Robin ran down the pier. "Too late, now,—we're off!"

Already there was a widening strip of black water between the ship and the wharf. He measured the distance with his eye. It was no further than he had jumped many a time when matching himself with Ralph. He gave one great leap and fell headlong,—but it was on the low deck of the ship.

"The captain!" he shouted. "I bear despatches to Captain Sampson."

"The captain deals with no one while the ship

gets under way. Even a landlubber should know that. Bide your time, lad!" said an elderly man in a rough jerkin, who was leaning over the taffrail.

"Nay, but my business is urgent. I must speak with him at once. Where is he?"

"Yonder," with a nod of his head over his left shoulder. "Go your own gait, if you must, but I warn you to leave him alone."

However, Robin faced the redoubtable captain forthwith.

"This from my Lord of Weymouth," he said, bowing low. "To be given into your hands, and yours alone, Sir Captain," and he repeated Lord Weymouth's injunctions.

The captain, with one eye on the movements of the vessel, and shouting out orders with every third breath, scrutinized the packet with the other eye, closely examining the crest and seal. "It is my lord's," he said; "I will do his bidding, though at some cost to myself. But you? Methinks you look blown. Whence come you, my young sir?"

"From Longleat."

"To-day? Then go you below and rest."

"Not so, not so!" cried Robin, startled. "But now that I have done my task, I pray you to put me ashore."

The captain demurred. It was much trouble. It would cause delay. He could do it for no man.

'Twould be a rare chance to see France, such as all gallants craved, and it should cost the young master nothing. And in less than a month he would be home again.

"Nay, nay, Sir Captain," said Robin. "There need be no delay worth the counting. No need to put the ship about. Do but lower a small boat, and let one good oarsman set me ashore. He can over-take you before you are out to sea."

At last, with many protestations that he would do it for no man on earth but the messenger of Lord Weymouth, to whom he was much beholden, Cap-tain Sampson gave the order, the small boat was lowered, and Robin climbed down the swaying rope into the frail shell that was rocking on the black waters beneath him.

By the time the quay was regained, it was quite dark. The moon had not yet risen, and the whole deserted pier was wrapped in dense shadow. With a word of thanks and a douceur to the solitary oars-man, Robin scrambled up the wet planks. His head was in a whirl, his thoughts in strange commotion, and he dropped on a bench to recover breath and composure. As he sat there in the chill, damp darkness, he fell into a dull stupor, thinking nothing, feeling nothing, hearing only the thud, thud, of Fanuella's feet, and the heavy beating of his own heart. It was the thought of her that at last stung

"HE DREW HIS PISTOL FROM HIS BELT."

him into action, and half stumbling, half groping, he finally made his way back to High Street.

But ere he had gone half-way to the Dolphin, out from the mouth of a narrow black alley a roisterous group of men and boys rushed with great noise and tumult, — wild, turbulent fellows, more than half drunk, and wholly bent on fighting and mischief. One or two of the leaders carried dim lanterns, and all were well armed with heavy staves and cudgels. Seeing in their way a youth well dressed, and apparently well-to-do, they dashed towards him with oaths and curses, bidding him stand and render account of himself.

With the stirring of the quick instinct of self-preservation, Robin's brain cleared instantly. He retreated swiftly to the wall, and drew his pistol from his belt. But the movement was observed, and, even before he could raise and cock it, a powerful blow from the cudgel in the hands of the ringleader knocked him prone and senseless.

"There! take that for drawing your fine pistol on the likes of we!" he shouted; and a second blow would have fallen had not one of the men, somewhat less drunk than the others, caught him by the arm. These were troublous times, and there was not too much law and order in the realm, yet there was at least the semblance of it.

"Hold, hold your hand, you fool, as you would not

be fruit for the gallows-tree!" he cried. "See you
not that you have stoven in his head already, Jan
Migglesworth? A pretty kettle of fish, this! Why
did you not parley with him before you felled un
like an ox?"

"Parley with a drawn pistoller?" muttered the
other. "Marry, I be no such curst fool as that,"
and he reeled away while the rest of the group, half
sobered, brought their lanterns nearer. One of
them bent down, pushing aside the man who had
interfered. "Methinks he be gone to judgment,
that fine chap," he asserted, after due consideration.
"But he be a Jacobite, and I tell ee 'tis no sin to
slay a Jacobite. I knows that, if I knows naught
else. I wants no Jacobites! The devil fly away wi'
'em all, say I!"

"Aye! aye! we wants no Jacobites," echoed one
and another, with solemn shakes of the head, but
an air of general relief. "No matter if Jan Migglesworth did fell un like an ox."

"But how know you he be a Jacobite?" said the
first speaker, bending over the prostrate figure. "I
see no sure marks on't. He be a comely youth."

"Let me tell ee," replied the other, straightening
himself up for a speech. "Firstly, he hath long
hair of his own, — like Lord Russell, who meddled
wi' the Rye House plot; secondly, he hath a gold
chain under his doublet; and thirdly, I've seen

him afore!" and with this culmination he grinned triumphantly.

"Where? where? How? how?" burst from the gang.

"This night, good sirs, this night. I was but coming out of the ale-house yonder when I see him flying down the quay, like a dun deer. The *Falcon* was just standing out, — but lo! he gave a great leap, and fell aboard her. I tell ee, the devil he holpeth his own! Parson says so, says he."

"Aye, — the devil he holpeth his own," echoed the bystanders, with preternatural solemnity.

"But how comes he here then, if the devil helped him to board the *Falcon?* Tell me that," said the doubting Thomas.

"I watched un, I did, thinking it summat queer. And lo! after a bit, a boat put off wi' un, and brought un ashore. See you that now? Be he not a Jacobite sending mischief over to France, — letters or summat? I be no fool, I tell ee!"

Suddenly he stooped down and seized the chain of which a glint showed in the light of the lanterns, drawing forth the miniature of Gloster which Robin always wore under his doublet. The man gave a cry of exultation.

"Look ee, look ee, now! said I not he was a Jacobite? Here be the very model of the young prince over yonder," nodding towards the French coast. "I knows un, — be sure I do. 'Tis his very model, I tell ee! I saw un once when I was in Flanders fighting for the crown. He tossed me a penny, he did."

Just then, down another dark alley, came a still, slow procession, — a priest who, with two or three attendants, had just administered the viaticum to a dying man.

"Hist! hist! put out the lanterns! Here comes Father John," cried one, and in an instant all was darkness.

But Father John had good eyes, and, moreover, the moon was just beginning to kindle a faint glow in the eastern sky. He caught sight of the half dozen huddled in the angle of the wall.

"How now, my men," he said, coming to a standstill. "What do you here? Drunk again, Jack Watt? But what devil's work is this? A dead man?"

Before he had said five words, most of the men had slunk away, one by one. Only the two who had been discussing the case stood their ground.

"A dead man? Simon, go you to the ale-house, and light your lantern, — quick!"

The man obeyed silently. A certain reverence for the priesthood was still ingrained in the very bone and muscle of the lower classes. If their so-called betters had outgrown it, they had not. As for this especial priest, — had he not ministered to their own sick and dying in the midst of the pestilence that walketh at noonday, never once asking whether they were Papists or Protestants? And was he not known to be a loyal Englishman, in spite of his cowl?

Presently the lantern was brought, and, by dint of close and rapid questioning, Father John soon became possessed of the facts in the case.

" Poor lad ! " he said, lifting the blood-stained hair and examining a cruel wound. " 'Twas a fierce blow brought thee to this."

" But, good Father, we think he be a Jacobite," said he who had fought for the crown, by way of apology. " See ! he did wear this about his neck ! I claim it as salvage, good Father, saving your Reverence's presence. 'Tis but a worthless figure of the young prince, — him some folk call James III."

The priest took the miniature and looked at it closely by the light of the lantern, and then slipped it under his habit.

" Ye fools ! " he cried, " would ye add robbery to murder? This is but a likeness of your own little Duke of Gloster, rest his soul ! 'Tis not Prince James, though somewhat like him, I do confess, they being near of an age and favoring each other. He whom some of you have slain in your drunken rout weareth on his breast a likeness of the Queen's son,

— your own good Queen Anne. Hear ye that, ye blind fools? Moreover, the young master weareth on his sleeve the cognizance of the noble Lord of Weymouth, at whose mansion of Longleat her Majesty doth tarry even now. See what a coil you are in, my overwise masters!"

But there were none to listen. At his first word about the miniature they had fled. Be it said here that nothing but their disordered wits and their private disputes had saved their victim from spoliation, as well as cudgelling.

Father John knelt by Robin's side, straightened the cramped limbs, and laid his ear to his heart. "I think he yet lives," he said to his attendants, "though 'twas a cruel blow, and he hath lain a good half-hour without help, as I judge from his hair, whereon the blood hath clotted. Yet haply he may be saved. Go you quietly for a litter, Anthony, my son, and we will bear him to Domus Dei, in Winkle Street. I do abide there myself at times, and haply I can stay and nurse the poor lad. My heart warms to him, God wot, lying here in his blood and stains."

And bowing his head, he told his beads till the litter came.

CHAPTER XXII.

WHEN Robin left the room on that eventful day, Lord Weymouth paced the floor for some minutes, and then, gathering his mental and spiritual forces together by a great effort, he rejoined his guests. If he was paler than his wont, and occasionally a trifle distraught, what wonder ? One does not have the honor — and responsibility — of entertaining a queen every day in the year, and but seldom even once in a lifetime.

All was merriment and lighted-hearted jollity. Light badinage and gay repartee ruled the hour. Lord Weymouth passed from group to group, giving a word and a smile here, a clasp of the hand there ; or stood at her Majesty's right hand in the fair balcony that was set apart for her use, the observed of all observers, the man whom the Queen delighted to honor. Little did she, or any of the gay throng assembled at Longleat that day, dream that her courtly host had learned within the hour that which might rob him not only of honor and estate, but even of life itself. And this mark of the Queen's favor had only hastened the crisis.

What was the trouble? Nothing more than this, which was quite enough. The Jacobites were at odds with him, covertly, because he, who had formerly been one of them, and whose own son had fallen at Sedgemoor, had given up the Stuart cause and taken the oath of allegiance, to a Stuart, indeed,. but to one who was not in the legitimate line of succession. The Whigs were at odds with him, covertly, for the same reason, with a different application. He had been a Jacobite; therefore they distrusted his professions of loyalty to the reigning sovereign, pretending to believe him ready on any auspicious day to return to his former troth-plight. Was not the obstinate old Bishop of Bath and Wells, whom no power on earth could induce to renounce his allegiance to King James and his son, the closest friend, the spiritual adviser, the father-confessor, so to speak, of Lord Weymouth? Had not the bishop a suite of rooms at Longleat, where he dwelt a good part of the year? Moreover, covetous eyes looked longingly at the vast estates of this man. Many an impoverished nobleman had been enriched by the attainder of his fellows, and what had happened once might happen again. The charge of treason was a most powerful weapon, and, sooth to say, it was right easily wielded in these days. Thus Lord Weymouth was between two fires.

With this tangle of intrigue and falsehood, however, this story has happily nothing to do, save in its slight connection with Robin at this particular juncture. Suffice it to say that by means of a far-seeing, faithful friend, knowledge of the trap set for him reached Lord Weymouth just in time; and the papers placed by Robin in the hands of Captain Sampson, being duly delivered by that worthy, vindicated him at once and forever.

But Lord Weymouth, not being omniscient, could not know this on that July day; and he would have given the half of his fair kingdom for leave to close his gates on the world, and be alone with his own thoughts. There were minor perplexing questions, besides the one great one. How was he to account to the Queen for Robin's absence? How was his sudden removal from the scene to be explained? For that he had been sent to Southampton was something that could be told neither to king, queen, nor commoner.

Yet, as so often happens, the crossing of this bridge was less formidable than he had feared. The Queen did indeed say, as the day closed:

"I .hoped our protégé was to have part in the tourney, my lord, that I might see if he tilts as well as he dances."

"Your Majesty," was the answer, "such was my intention and desire, as well as his own, and I regret the failure much. But at the last moment an unfortunate contretemps set all our plans agley. I count myself lucky that the tournament did not fall through altogether."

The Queen laughed. "Was there trouble in the camp? I thought you somewhat distraught, my lord," and then the conversation drifted away from Robin, and was not again renewed.

Another critical moment came when, on the next day, the Queen and her retinue left Longleat. Would she call for Robin? Would she command his attendance? It must be confessed that these apparently trivial questions disturbed my Lord Weymouth in the night watches.

But the Queen was tired, and did not leave her chamber till the very last half-hour. Somerset had assembled in full force to escort her on her way; there were many to receive and many farewells to be spoken. As Lord Weymouth led her to her carriage she cast a quick glance to right and left.

"I do not see Robin," she said. "My lord, tell him when next we go to Windsor he will be summoned thither. Can you spare him?"

"Assuredly, if such be your Majesty's will. Yet I confess I would fain keep him as long as I may. I take great joy in him." Then, hesitating a moment, he added, "It is not the lad's fault that he is not in attendance this morning, madam. I found myself unwillingly compelled to place him on duty elsewhere."

Anne smiled. "No apology, no apology, my dear lord. I do not forget that he is in your service now, not mine. Yet, as I said, we shall summon him to court ere long, and mayhap give him a chance to win his spurs in France, — who knows?" and the ordeal was over.

Surprise, sorrow, dismay, indignation, — it would be hard to say which of these held strongest sway in Little Lady's heart as the hours of the tournament wore away. From her high balcony, where she sat with the Queen's ladies, she had watched the lists, expecting every moment the entrance of her knight, her champion, him whom she had chosen out of all the world. He would wear her favor on his helm, or bind it on his arm. No one else would know; no eye but hers would see. The trifle was too slight, too inconspicuous, to attract attention. But he knew, and she knew, and that was enough. It was their dear secret, sacred to them alone.

But other champions came and went; and Robin did not appear in the lists. The tourney was over at last. What did it mean?

No out-and-out love-words had passed between them. She acknowledged that. He had not said, bowing low at her feet, "Lady, I love you," — but only, "I would serve you." Yet she had understood, or had thought she understood. Was not service the very soul of love? And she had responded with

none of the coy delays and hesitations born of co-
quetry, but freely and honestly, as a true maiden
should.   She had met his frankness with equal
frankness of her own.

Had she misunderstood him?   Had she childishly
mistaken the simple friendliness born of old associations and companionship for the strong love of man
for woman?   And had he seen this with wonder and,
mayhap, repulsion?   Such things had been, she had
heard.   Her cheeks burned at the thought, and then
grew white with indignation.   For what had he
meant when he implored leave to dream awhile?
What could he have meant but that he loved her?
Yet now, though she could not say he had put her
to open shame while what had passed between them
was known only to themselves, he had acted the
unmanly part of craven, or deceiver.   One was as
bad as the other.

If she had been older, her woman's wit might have
found some way out of this dilemma.   But as it was,
her very self-consciousness sealed her lips.   No one
knew of the interview between herself and Robin in
the picture-gallery, and now no one must ever know.

So she asked no questions and made no comments,
but sat through the long hours of the tournament,
half blinded and deafened by the tumult of her own
thoughts ; and she danced and smiled with the gay-
est at the masque and banquet that followed, only

conscious of one great longing, — to be alone. On her way to her chamber, when the last pageant was over, she paused a moment at the open door of the picture-gallery. It was late. The candles had, one by one, burned low and gone out; but the newly risen moon poured a flood of silver radiance through the great mullioned window with its triple lancets, making the room as light as day. The laughing, chattering maidens, her companions, had passed on, and she heard their voices in the distance, the gay good-nights, and the closing of doors as each passed to her own apartment.

Yet still she lingered here where but last night she had heard his voice, wondering vaguely, as she had been wondering for hours, not where Robin was, not why he did not come to her, but what it all meant, this sudden neglect and desertion, after the only half-veiled passion of yesterday.

Suddenly a new sheaf of arrows from the ascending moon shot athwart the drooping banner and the seat under it, and something on the floor beneath it glittered in the moonlight. It was the little silver arrow that had fallen from her hair as she laid her burning forehead on the cold arm of the settle where but last night his hand had lain. The touch of the insensate wood thrilled her like a caress. But she did not see the arrow. Thus does fate play at cross-purposes with poor humanity. For had she seen it she would have caught it to her heart, her lips, in an ecstasy of remorseful tenderness. All the recollections of childhood, all the sacred memories of Gloster, all she had ever known of Robin himself, — his loyalty, his truth, his knightly courtesy, his unswerving devotion, — would have rushed over her with overwhelming force.

But as she knelt in the cold white light, the moon rose higher and higher; it passed behind the broad eastern tower, it mounted to the zenith, and its rays no longer streamed in at the mullioned window. The room had grown dark and chill when, with a wan, white face, Anne rose from her knees, unnerved and trembling, stole into the corridor again, and fled to her chamber.

One other person, and only one, of the Queen's suite, remarked Robin's absence, unless it may have been some demoiselle who had thought of him as a prospective partner in the dance. But young gallants were not rare in Somerset, and one was not greatly missed. That other person was Lady Marlborough. The next morning, on her way to the Queen's chamber, the Mistress of the Robes met Little Lady in the corridor.

"Look you, my Lady Anne," she said, "our fine young Master Sandys must be in disgrace, for all that my Lord Weymouth made such haste in bringing him to kiss the Queen's hand. 'Tis passing strange he was not put forward with the best of them, in the lists, yesterday. Did he make bold to speak to you of the tourney when you danced with him that first night?"

Lady Anne flushed indignantly. "Nay, I asked him no questions. Why should I? But why do you think him in disgrace, Lady Marlborough? Surely that does not follow. No doubt he did not choose to tilt."

Lady Marlborough nodded significantly. "He did choose," she said, curtly. "Young Montague — ah, there's a gallant worthy of the court! — told me he was to tilt with Lord Hargrave's nephew. 'Tis quite as if he were a lord's son himself, I do declare! But I opine we have heard the last of him. I tell you he is in disgrace, and Lord Weymouth is knowing to it. He was speaking to the Queen last night, and I heard him declare he had fears lest the tournament should fall through altogether;" and she swept on her way, leaving Anne in a maze of bewilderment and consternation.

CHAPTER XXIII.

The Queen's visit was over, and Longleat, after the unwonted excitement, had settled back into more than its wonted repose. Jock and Hobbs had made a slight stir in the stable court, by their graphic story of Master Sandys's sudden flight on the day of the tournament. But Master Sandys was often sent hither and yon on my lord's private business, and this was no nine days' wonder.

For some days Lord Weymouth was not much disturbed by his courier's prolonged absence. The ride had been a hard one, beyond question, and both horse and rider had needed rest. But as day after day passed, and Robin did not return, his anxiety and suspense became unendurable. It is difficult for us in these days, when time and space are not, to realize what potent factors in human life they were two hundred years ago. Distance was distance then, and time was eternity. The lightning had no swift messages for Longleat, and the weekly post was but a tantalizing mystery, a delusion, and a snare. Letters were for the most part sent by private messengers direct, or passed from hand to hand, at the pleasure of the holder.

But there was a post, professedly, between Long-leat and Southampton; and when it brought no letter from Robin, Lord Weymouth at once resolved to go in search of him. It was near night of the second day when he alighted at the sign of the Dolphin, somewhat travel-worn, though he had made the journey as deliberately as his impatience would allow.

But, as the reader very well knows, Robin was not there. He described him minutely, but to no avail. Mine host of the Dolphin was positive no such young gentleman had been under his roof for a month, or had sought entertainment at his hands.

One of the hostlers plucked him by the sleeve, with an explosive whisper like the puff of a bellows:

"The mare, master, — the strange mare! Think you of her?"

"Tush! She hath naught to do with it. Yet, stay! Diccon, go you to the stable, and lead her hither. A mare, saving your lordship's presence, that has been fed at my cost for a full week, having been dropped here one night, without so much as 'by your leave,' by a young gallant in a desperate hurry, who promised to be back anon. And he has never given us scent of his shoe leather since. There, my lord! 'Tis idle to ask it. But know you aught of her ? She's had two quarts daily, at my cost, and a fork of hay, and water to her liking, and — "

But Lord Weymouth paid no heed to this bill of fare. Fanuella, looking rough and unkempt, but carrying her head as proudly as ever, and spurning the very stones of Southampton, whinnied wistfully when she heard the sound of her own name, and trembled with delight as she felt the touch of Lord Weymouth's caressing hand. Her evident joy was pathetic. What with the furious course hither, her master's desertion, and some very palpable neglects since, life had gone hardly with her since she left Longleat.

Mine host was quite overwhelmed with consternation and remorse.

" Here, Diccon, thou lazy varlet," he cried, " take you this fine mare of my lord's to the best stall, and see thou dost clean her well, and make her coat to shine like my silver flagon, or 'twill be the worse for thee ! 'Tis a disgrace to an honest house that she should be so ill-conditioned. And see to it she has her fill of the best oats, and sweet-smelling hay, and a warm mash, as she likes it, and give her — "

" I but did thy bidding, master," growled Diccon, as he led her away. " Thou didst tell me to keep her alive, but to waste no time on her ; " whereat the landlord hastened to change the subject by a flood of exclamations and wonderments as to the non-appearance of the beautiful young gentleman who left her at the Dolphin.

Systematic search of all the inns in Southampton, good, bad, and indifferent, failed to give any clue to the mystery. The ground seemed to have opened and swallowed Robin, and then closed, leaving no trace behind.

Lord Weymouth returned to the Dolphin, ordered a room and supper, and sat down to consider the situation. One thing was absolutely certain, and to his perturbed mind it seemed the only one. Robin would never have left Fanuella in the lurch. If he did not return to the Dolphin and to her, it was because he could not. Where, then, was he?

The landlord, obsequious, smiling, and eager to make himself and his house acceptable, came and went, now bringing in a hot, savory dish, and now a bottle of wine; but Lord Weymouth's absorbed silence gave him small excuse for lingering. On one of his flying visits, however, the latter spoke:

"Landlord, did you see the young man yourself?"

"Nay, sir, I did not. I was at my supper. None about the place saw him, save Diccon."

"Send Diccon to me, then. And, mind you, let him come alone."

He came.

"Now, Diccon, tell me of him who left the mare. Did he seem sore spent, or in ill case?"

"Not he, your honor.   He was red as a lobster just out of the pot, and looked as he had had a hard pull; and the mare, she was all of a white lather. But he were not sick, sir.   Sure I be o' that."

"And did you see which way he went?"

"Straight down the quay, your lordship, where the *Falcon* was lying, on a keen run.   An' I never see hair of him since, though he tossed me the reins as fine as you please, an' says he, 'I'll be back anon,' says he, or summat like it.   An' I never see —"

"That'll do, Diccon.   You may go."

"Thank your honor.   I'll drink your health, sir," as he pocketed some silver.   Still he hesitated, standing first on one foot and then on the other, twirling his thumbs.

"Well, — what is it?" asked Lord Weymouth, impatiently.   "Have you aught more to say? If so, out with it, and begone."

"My lord," said Diccon, drawing nearer and lowering his voice, "will I run round to Domus Dei, an' bring Father John to ye?"

Lord Weymouth laughed satirically.   "Nay, I am in no need of religious consolation, — yet.   I want no Father Johns to shrive me."

"But it was not that I meant," cried Diccon,

"Listen, my lord! I tell ye, mayhap there's more to't. I like not to make nor meddle wi' such doings, for sake o' my own skin. But your lordship be a free-handed gentleman an' no curmudgeon, an' 'tis said there be a young gallant lying at Domus Dei that Father John picked up wi' his head stove in. That's what!"

"Why in the name of heaven did you not tell me this before?" and Lord Weymouth rose hurriedly and seized his hat and cane. "Show me the way to Domus Dei at once, Diccon, and you shall not be the loser. Quick, now!"

They passed out into the darkness of High Street, went down nearly to the quay, and turned into Winkle Street. When they came in sight of the hospital, where dim lights were burning, Diccon drew back.

"That's the place, your honor, and there's a bell to the fore. Please your worship, I never make nor meddle wi' — "

"Run away then, — run away," tossing him a crown piece. Good night to you, Diccon."

When Lord Weymouth rang the bell, it was answered by the sliding of a square panel in the heavy oaken door; and after due parleying he was cautiously admitted and shown into a small parlor, where Father John presently joined him. His guest's person was not unknown to him.

"It is my Lord of Weymouth," he said, advancing cordially. "I thank the Holy Virgin who hath sent thee hither."

"Father John has something to tell me then?"

"Be seated, I pray you, for 'tis a long story, and my lord, — "

"But is the lad here, — and doth he live?"

"Aye, he is here, and he lives. Thanks be to God, I believe he is likely to live. But he hath been sorely dealt with, my lord. He will not know you. Sit, I pray you, for there is no need of haste in this matter."

Gently forcing him into a seat, he drew a chair beside him and in a few rapid, graphic words told the story as he understood it. Lord Weymouth listened intently. To his anxiety for Robin another was being added.

"But tell me," he said, at length, "what think you? Had the lad been on board the *Falcon*? I know he had business with the captain."

"I think so. Indeed, I feel sure of it, unless those varlets lied, — which, forsooth, may well be! But one of them declared he saw him put ashore from a small boat when the ship was well out to sea, and I see no reason for his lying about it, unless from pure deviltry. That was one proof that he was a Jacobite, to their thinking."

Lord Weymouth drew a long breath of relief.

IN THE HOSPITAL.

"So far, so good," he said. "But now about the poor lad himself. Can I see him?"

"If you wish. No harm can come of it, and no good either, unless to satisfy yourself as to his condition. He hath not been himself save for a few moments, now and then, since he was brought hither a week ago. But come you, my lord. You shall see for yourself."

They went up a narrow flight of stairs into a long, low room, sparsely furnished, but scrupulously clean. On a low cot drawn out from the wall lay Robin, his head so swathed in bandages that only the lower part of the face was visible. Kneeling by the cot, Lord Weymouth laid his hand on his, called him repeatedly by name, and tried to draw from him some sign of recognition. But there was no response, not so much as the quiver of a muscle or the clasp of a finger.

"Doth he lie like this all the time? Hath he no moments of consciousness? Look, now! He moves his hands. He seems searching for something."

Father John stooped quietly, and turned back the coverlet. "It is but this he wants. It has slipped from his hand," he said, replacing the miniature that was slung around Robin's neck by its slender chain. "The ruffians that felled him had seized it, making excuse — as if they ever needed excuse for thieving! — that it was a likeness of the young prince, or king, over in France. I knew it at once for the miniature of the Queen's son, who died some years ago, — the Duke of Gloster."

"Yes. He was fond of this poor lad, here. The picture was the Queen's gift."

"In a day or two," went on Father John, "whenever he was not quite unconscious, he began feeling restlessly, for I knew not what, — feeling, — feeling, — his hand creeping about his neck continually. At last I bethought me of the picture, and put the chain on him. He hath been quieter since, and keeps it in his hand save when he chances to lose hold of it, as he did but now. But, my lord," he continued, as he crossed the room to a cupboard, and came back with a little packet, "What make you of this?"

Lord Weymouth took it, held it to the light, and examined the superscription critically. It read, "For Little Lady," — just that, and nothing more.

"What is it?" he asked. "I make nothing of it; nothing whatever. Who is Little Lady?"

Father John shook his head. "That is more than I know. I hoped you might help me out. It may be a mere vagary of his wandering brain, and it may not. But let us go below, my lord. The lad seems to hear nothing, to regard nothing. But one never knows, and it is not well to converse by a sick-bed."

He called a brother who was telling his beads in the chapel hard by, and they returned to the parlor.

"Now tell me," said Lord Weymouth. "What is it?"

"Well, my lord, I can soon tell you all I know of the matter. One day, — 'twas the third, — he seemed a trifle clearer in his mind, and as I sat by his cot he looked steadily at me, and moved his lips as in an effort to speak. When I bent my ear, he caught hold of me with more strength of grip than seemed to belong to him, and cried, softly, 'The favor, father, the favor!' Then I, knowing naught about favors, made as if I did not hear, and after a brief while he fell away into delirium again. As I sat watching him, trying to read his poor wandering thoughts, — for I have been much with the sick, my lord, and know they must be humored in their wild fantasies, — I noticed that he was ever making a motion as if to wind something about his wrist. And then I remembered me of a trifle that had fallen from his doublet that first night, when we undressed him. 'Twas a long thread of gold, such as a lady might wear for an armlet; and hanging thereon was a little trinket, like the amulets the Crusaders brought from Eastern lands. The Church has many such in her treasuries."

"But the lad had no such toy," cried Lord Weymouth. "If he had had such a curious trinket, I should have seen it. He has lived with me long."

"I know not how that may be," said Father John; "I only know it fell to the floor as we were getting his doublet off, and I picked it up and put it in my pouch for safe keeping. Seeing he slept at last, I got the toy and put it where he might see it on awakening. I was right, my lord. When he saw it he smiled, and put it to his lips; and then, as if striving to bring back something that was fading out of memory, he looked at me with eyes that were like a prayer. 'Little Lady, Little Lady,' he whispered, and put the trinket in my hand. Then, to help him, I said, 'And what am I to do with it, my son?' and again he whispered, 'Little Lady, Little Lady.' I know not how it was, my lord, for it was like a dream to me afterwards, and sure am I he spoke few words, and those not clearly. But somehow he made me understand I was to put it up in a packet; and then he motioned to the inkhorn on the table where I had been making up my accounts. 'And who is it for?' I asked, seeing he meant me to address it. And as I live, and believe in God, he answered, 'Little Lady,' — and then not another word could I get out of him. So I wrote it down as you see, and there it is."

"And has he thought of it since?"

"He has not spoken of it, nor of any Little Lady.

No doubt he has forgotten the whole story. 'Twas a cruel blow they gave him, and his wits are all astray. But keep you that, Lord Weymouth. I like not to have the care of it, lest it should be lost."

They talked long of the case, of its dangers and its problems; and then, after a parting look at Robin, Lord Weymouth, at once distressed and relieved, returned to the Dolphin, promising to come again in the morning.

Seated in his room, he drew the packet from its hiding-place.

"Little Lady," he said, musingly. "Little Lady. 'Tis but the wandering of the poor boy's wits. I know of none whom he doth ever call Little Lady, and he was but a lad when he came to me,—too young for love-fancies. Yet to some, as I know right well, they come early and stay long. He was ever old for his years."

Turning the packet over, he was about to cut the skein of yellow silk Father John had bound about it, when an impulse of delicacy, sensitiveness, tenderness,—what you will,—restrained his hand. "Nay, I cannot do it," he said, flushing. "Whatever it is, 'tis the boy's secret. Let him keep it!"

The next morning he went early to Domus Dei. Father John met him at the portal with a smiling face. "Good news, my lord," he cried, with outstretched hand. "He hath had a quiet night, and hath rested fairly well without sleeping-draughts. His mind seems somewhat clearer, and the fever, which I feared greatly, hath left him. Come you up; come you right up and see if he will know you!"

But he did not, and was lying again in a state that seemed almost unconsciousness.

Some of the bandages had been removed, and Lord Weymouth was able to see more clearly the nature and extent of the blow to which Robin had succumbed.

"Had the varlet's cudgel struck half an inch lower," said Father John, "it had been the last of him. See!" and he bent cautiously over the dark head, disfigured by sundry plasters and cataplasms. "The fracture runneth from here to here, and there are sundry bad bruises, also. But it is healing well, that wound. He will live, my lord, he will surely live. When he first wakened this morning, he was quite himself for five minutes, and took some porridge."

"Shall I try to rouse him, Father John? What say you?"

"Nay, let him be; let him be. Nature is wiser than we are, and knows what is best for him. Let him be quiet. My lord, you can do no good here. It may be many days before the lad can have any converse with you. Go you home to Longleat and be at peace ; and by every post I will send you word of him.   Go you home."

And thus, after much further deliberation, it was settled.   The next day Lord Weymouth departed, leaving the treasury of Domus Dei in much better condition than he found it.

THE next post brought word that Robin was, on the whole, better, though still unconscious much of the time. The second gave a more encouraging report, and in the third letter Father John grew jubilant.

"The lad tires of Domus Dei," he wrote. "'Tis a good sign. He wearies of confinement. By your leave, my dear lord, I will e'en get me a gentle palfrey, such as will not rack my old bones, and bring him to Longleat myself. By slow stages, if need be; but get there we will in due time. Fret not, if we are long, for if aught goes wrong I will find means to let you know. Peace be with you."

And so Diccon brought Fanuella around to Domus Dei, where the gentle palfrey was waiting for Father John; and a proud and happy creature was she when her young master was again astride her. How much she understood, this chronicler does not undertake to say. But she stood quietly on four feet, instead of three, or less, arching her neck, and looking around with long, sidewise glances, as he who was wont to vault to the saddle at one bound, mounted slowly, by the help of Diccon and the horse-block; and then, instead of prancing off in her usual gay fashion, soberly awaited the word of command, and moved sedately up through the Bar Gate, and off into the fair, still country lanes.

As for Robin, it seemed to him that ages had passed since he and Fanuella had taken that long frantic ride together. Something had gone out of him, — youth, and hope, and buoyant energy that knew neither fatigue nor weakness. A very different journey was this. Father John knew the country as one knows a map, every lane and byway. He avoided the great, dusty highroads and the noisy towns; and after a dozen miles, or less, in the cool, dewy mornings, at the slightest sign of weariness on the part of his charge, he would order a halt at some quiet, shady little inn, where Robin was made to undress and go to bed, will he, nill he. And it may be the long, placid hours when Father John sat quietly by his bedside, his very presence a benediction, and the low, quiet talks when, on the borders of some village green, they sat together under the spreading boughs of ancient oaks, or stately sycamores, — talks that touched on all high themes of earth and heaven, — ministered to his needs in a way that was beyond the reach of drugs, however potent.

Robin was a Protestant, and a loyal one. For years, now, he had been under the direct teaching

and influence of Thomas Ken, who wrote himself
"Late Bishop of Bath and Wells;" an influence
as powerful for good over the young men at Longleat as it had once been over the lads at St. Mary's,
for whom he wrote his morning and evening hymns.
Yet here was Father John, with his tonsured head,
his cowl, and rosary; and his "confessions" were
as saintly as those of St. Augustine, coupled with a
worldly wisdom, and a knowledge of common human
nature as profound as Bishop Ken's. Who shall say
that the wider sympathies, the broader outlooks, that
came to Robin through this experience, were not
worth all the pain through which they were won?
In after-years, he looked back to this loitering journey with Father John as to some blessed pilgrimage.

They were a full week on the way, and when they
at last reached Longleat, the great court rang with
welcomes. Even Gaffer Ambrose hobbled forth to
meet them, not being quite clear in his mind as to
the nature of the trouble that had befallen Robin,
yet feeling morally sure that, in some unaccountable
way, Queen Henrietta Maria was at the bottom of
it all.

No need to tell of Robin's last talk with Father
John that night, nor of a still longer one that followed between Father John and Lord Weymouth.
And the next morning Father John and the palfrey
ambled back to Southampton.

He had told Lord Weymouth that Robin had never again alluded to the packet so strangely directed. Either he had quite forgotten the matter, or he supposed it had reached its destination, and was satisfied. But, as the days went by, Lord Weymouth himself was not content. He watched Robin narrowly, seeing that strength and vigor did not return to him as Father John had prophesied. What was wrong with the lad? Had the packet anything to do with it? Its possession became an incubus, a nightmare. It might be of consequence, or it might not. In either case, what right had he to hold it, now that Robin was able to speak for himself?

So one night when Robin, who had insisted upon taking up his old duties, one by one, brought the sleeping-cup to the fair chamber, with the outlook towards Heaven's Gate, he found his lord sitting, as before, in the great chair under the hanging-lamp. A small packet, tied with a yellow thread, lay on the table beside him.

As yet, nothing had passed between them, bearing directly on his errand to Southampton or its results, all mention of exciting topics having been forbidden by Father John. But to-night, as Robin presented the cup, he said, " My lord, I have not asked you, but I long to know. Is all right? I delivered the papers as you bade me."

"Sit here, my son," — a name which brought the swift color to Robin's cheek. "Sit here beside me, and let us talk awhile. Yes, all is right. The net was skilfully woven, but it broke, and the bird escaped. Some day you shall know from what a tangled coil you set me free, — but at what sore cost to yourself! It cuts me to the heart to think of it."

"Think not of it, then, my dear lord. Had I gone on any other errand, the ruffians might have felled me all the same. No doubt, I shall have harder knocks by and by, when I set out to seek my fortune, and win my spurs;" and he laughed lightly.

Lord Weymouth sat in thoughtful silence for a moment, and then took the packet from the table. "This is something that belongs to you," he said. "When you were at the worst you bade Father John deliver it as directed."

Robin received it carelessly, then turned it over. "Little Lady!" he cried, coloring deeply. "Surely I said naught to Father John of her, — of Little Lady! What does it mean, my lord?"

"That is for you to say. I know not. But open the packet. There is something enclosed."

Robin hesitated for a moment, and cut the string. "It should have been sent at once to the Lady Anne Gascoyne, as I directed. See, my lord! 'Tis but a favor she gave me to wear at the tournament. I dishonored it, in seeming, by my non-appearance. All I could do was to return it, as I bade Father John. I did not think he would have played me such a scurvy trick."

"But, my dear fellow, you do not see, you do not understand. How could Father John post the packet to 'Little Lady?' Tell me that!"

Robin turned the folded paper over and over, still bewildered. "He should have sent it to Lady Anne at once, as I besought him."

"But you said nothing of Lady Anne Gascoyne. How was he to know? You spoke only of some child, — this 'Little Lady.'"

"Was I such an imbecile as that, my lord?" in a tone that had even a shade of awe in it. "It must have been worse with me than I knew. I have been in bad case, surely."

He had not yet wholly lost the air of bewilderment, and drew his hand thoughtfully across his forehead with a sigh.

"But why 'Little Lady'?" asked Lord Weymouth, an irrepressible smile just touching the corners of his mouth. "I should hardly think, myself, of calling that tall, lithe young demoiselle 'little;' though, to be sure, she is somewhat diminutive as compared with her Majesty, or even with that stately personage, my Lady Marlborough," and he laughed outright. "Moreover, it seemeth to me rather familiar, considering all things. What think you on that point, my lad?"

Robin was silent for a moment, flushing deeply.

"The reproof is well put, my lord, but indeed I do not deserve it. I have only reverence for the Lady Anne Gascoyne. I have known her these many years. She was often at Windsor with the princess when we were but children; and the name written here is one I was used to give her then."

"Ho, ho! I see. So you had met before? And she gave you the favor?"

"I begged it of her, and then I did not wear it."

Lord Weymouth looked at him keenly from under his shaggy gray eyebrows. He was long past middle age; but more than most men, perhaps, he remembered the heart of youth. Robin's eyes were downcast, and only the firm compression of his lips kept them from a trembling betrayal. The elder man saw very clearly what his prompt, unquestioning obedience must have cost him.

"I see," he said, again. "It was hard, my boy. I would I could have spared you this. And yet —"

It was his turn to hesitate, and he paused long; but for the boy's own sake, his thought must out. He laid his hand on his knee.

"Laddie, perhaps it was as well. Do you know aught of Lady Anne's history? her lineage?"

"Nothing save what she told me herself many years ago,—that her father was slain on Tower Hill, and of her life since, which hath been somewhat lonely."

Lord Weymouth lifted his eyebrows. Confidences, then, had been exchanged between these two young people.

"Yes; but she belongs to one of the oldest and noblest houses in the realm. Lord Gascoyne's unfortunate death does not alter that fact. Then, too, she is her Majesty's godchild, and I am assured she will have a fine dowry. Lady Anne can send her arrows high. Lord Dalkieth is even now a suitor for her hand, and, if I mistake not, there are others."

Robin started as if he were stung,—then rose and walked to the window. When he turned to Lord Weymouth again his lips had lost somewhat of their firm tension.

"I thank you, my dear lord," he said, "and I understand. I have naught whatever to offer to the Lady Anne Gascoyne,—neither wealth, nor name, nor aught else. I will remember. But, my lord?"

"Well?"

Then, greatly touched by the pride and self-restraint that held him in leash, he laid his hand on Robin's shoulder.

"Believe me, I speak thus only to save you greater pain, hereafter. 'Tis but to put you on your guard against yourself, my boy.   Can I do aught for you?"

"You are versed in all courtly ways, sir.   Tell me what I shall do with this bauble?   Have I the right to keep it?"

His lordship pondered a moment.

"I think it would be wiser to restore it to the lady," he said.   "The Queen is at Kensington, and I shall send a courier thither to-morrow.   Write, if you wish.   Surely there is no harm in that."

This is what he wrote:

He to whom the Lady Anne Gascoyne gave this favor returns it because he must.   Though he may seem so, yet he is neither an ingrate, craven, nor disloyal.   But since, as she knows, he did not wear this jewel in the lists, he has no right to keep it.

Long he brooded over this short note.   What more could he say?   A partial explanation, wrapped in mystery, was worse than none at all.   He was chilled, too, by the fresh sense of the distance between them.   What right had he to assume that she cared?   So he signed his name, saying nothing more.

In a week the courier returned.   Robin was summoned.

"Communications from Kensington," said Lord Weymouth, dryly, "and this for you."

Lady Anne had sent the armlet back, without a word. The act was significant, — but of what? Perhaps Lord Weymouth was a trifle astonished, not to say dismayed. He belonged to his age and his environments. Much as he cared for Robin, when it came to the question of love and marriage it must be confessed his inherited prejudices were somewhat at war with his affection. His eyes followed him as he gravely and silently received his treasure and walked off with it, betraying his delight only by a more elastic step and prouder bearing, of which he was himself quite unconscious.

My lord shrugged his shoulders. "I know not what will come of this. Old Lord Dalkieth must fight his own battles, and he may lose the day. It looks mightily as if my Lady Anne had a mind of her own," he thought, as he settled down to the consideration of his own affairs.

Yet the return of the trinket, with no words of explanation, was surely open to two interpretations; and, after the first flush of joy had passed, Robin grew aware of this. The Lady Anne might have sent the little armlet back to him disdainfully, thus paraphrasing the old song, "What you've touched you may take." Or, it might have been returned as a pledge of amity, a token of forgiveness. Which was it?

That night, Robin, whose chamber had been for a

long time one of a suite connected with his lord's private apartments, crossed the inner court in pursuit of Ralph Montague. It was a moonless, starless night. The chill of early autumn was in the air, and the frogs croaked dismally. Turret and tower, barbican and parapet, stood black and frowning against a leaden sky, — a strange contrast to that night of the Queen's visit when they had soared upward in the moonlight, gleaming like molten silver. Robin shivered as the wind swept around the corner, and drew his collar more closely about his ears. But presently he caught sight of Ralph's window, from which the red rays of a lamp were streaming.

The young men of Lord Weymouth's household were not encouraged in any undue luxury, but Montague was a bit of a sybarite in his way, and gathered to himself warmth and beauty, brightness and color, as instinctively as a bee gathers honey. Robin smiled as he mounted the stairs and stood in the doorway of the small chamber, so great was the contrast it presented to the barrack-like quarters with which the other squires were well content.

"Tapestry fit for the King's anteroom," he cried, laughing, — "and, on my word, a rug from Ispahan, and trinkets enough for my lady's chamber! Your finery puts us all to shame, Ralph. Has your lady mother never a girl, that you are so tricked out?"

Ralph shrugged his shoulders, "Aye, plenty of

them, and never a lad but I,—which counts for much in the long run. But as for the tapestry, which is somewhat rare, as you have had wit enough to divine, 'tis but some lengths that same lady mother of mine sent as a gift to my lord; and he bade me hang them here till he could make some changes and find a fitter place wherein to bestow them. As for the trinkets, as you are pleased to call them, I would have you know I have many friends, my Robbie, to say nothing of my sisters," and he laughed significantly. "But come in, come in, and try the comfort of this divan, which is by no means to be despised. Beshrew me, Robin, but why should a man sit on a hard bench when there are soft cushions to be had?"

"Some of us are born to soft cushions, my lad, and some to hard benches. 'Tis not all a matter of choice, or liking. Perhaps not a matter of chance, either. But what is this new toy?" and he took from the dressing-table a small dagger with a delicately carved handle of ivory.

"Take heed, take heed!" cried Ralph, as Robin lifted it carelessly. "If it be but a toy, as you call it, 'tis of the best steel of Damascus, and has an edge keener than any razor. Take heed!"

Robin examined the fine workmanship for a moment, and then replaced it carefully, letting his eye move idly over the medley on the table. Suddenly his heart gave one wild throb, and then stood still. Side by side with richly wrought pouncet-boxes, rare bits of Bohemian and Venice glass, a hand-mirror in a frame of arabesque design, a couple of miniatures, and an ebony crucifix, lay Lady Anne's little silver arrow.

Leaning against the adjoining casement, he stared at it as if it were a basilisk.

Meanwhile, Ralph had thrown himself on the divan in one of the picturesque attitudes that were as natural to him as its airs and graces are to a cock-sparrow, and silently awaited his pleasure.

"Come, come," he said, at last, "when you have studied my curiosity shop long enough, what if you were to sit down on a soft cushion for once in your life, and tell me what brought you hither at this hour o' the night ? It was not pleasure, merely, — that I know right well. For it is well past nine o' the clock, and I was just about to go to bed when I heard you come stumbling up the stairs."

Robin collected his scattered senses, as best he might, and looked about him as one awakening from some vivid dream.

"What I came for ? Oh, yes ! I remember," he said, blankly, pulling a paper from his pocket. "My lord sent me hither with these instructions as to some duty of the morrow."

"Bother me, but I hope 'tis not to send me off on

some wild goose chase through all this mud. What may the duty be?"

"Indeed I know not. The script explains all. There, take it! Good night."

"Good night to you, Robin. But what ails you?" and he started from the couch. "Are you ill, lad? You look as if you had seen a ghost."

"I have," said Robin, striding down the stairs, and out into the darkness.

Ralph Montague had been the chief victor in the tournament. This much Robin knew already. Had he laid his trophies at the feet of Little Lady, and received from her in exchange the silver arrow?

A few days after this, as Lord Weymouth was walking on the terrace, as was his wont after supper, Robin approached him, with the usual obeisance.

"Can I speak with you, my lord?"

"Certainly. Say on."

But permission having been given, Robin continued silent, his features working.

"Out with it, my lad. Anything wrong?"

"My lord, will you think me ungrateful? I am homesick! Since I was ill I have had a great longing for the gray cottage, and the dim forest. I pine for the humble places and things I knew when I was a child. I have hungered for them for a full month. I pray you let me go for awhile, if I can be spared."

His lordship gave swift consent.

"Moreover," he added, "I have long been thinking it was time you left this quiet Somerset."

Robin smiled faintly.

"For the stir and bustle of Windsor Forest, my lord?"

"As to that, it will not be Windsor Forest long. The Queen will summon you to court. I have her own word for that. Indeed, she more than hinted that you might have a chance to win your spurs in France, — the spurs you spoke of not long ago."

"I did but jest, speaking idle words after the manner of young men."

His eye kindled, nevertheless.

"Think you her Majesty really means that, my lord?"

"She means you shall have a chance to show what mettle you are of. I am sure of that. As for the spurs, — that's neither here nor there. They are not so important to a man's advancement as they once were, even though it be an honor to have the right to wear them. And hark you, my lad! By your leave, I have somewhat more to say to you in the matter of Lady Anne Gascoyne. If there be some slight fancy, some little touch of sentiment, be it more or less, between you two —"

"Nay, nay, my dear lord," cried Robin, lifting his hand deprecatingly, while his face flushed to a deep crimson, and then paled as suddenly. "Nay, nay, my dear lord, I do beseech you speak not thus of the Lady Anne. There is nothing — there has been nothing — between us that would give warrant for your words, or that would make it right for me to listen. If I ever dreamed or hoped the contrary, I thus dream and hope no longer. I have grown wiser. Believe me, I speak the truth, my lord."

The elder man looked at the younger curiously, studying the bowed face, with its averted eyes intently, ere he answered. Then he said, half lightly, half soberly: "Nathless, let me finish my sentence. It can do no harm to you, and it is no irreverence to her. If, as I said, there should be some slight fancy, some little touch of sentiment between you two, see that you raise yourself to her height before you speak, that you may look in her eyes level-fronted. Nay, I want to know nothing now. Do not answer me, but ponder on what I have said. Yet I have one word more for you. If you chance to meet the lady, I give you leave to tell her why you had no part in the tournament. Tell her, if need be, that your lord was in sharp and sudden peril, and that you saved him. But see to it that you say no more than that. Now go and make thyself ready for the journey."

Robin kissed the hand extended to him. "My lord," — and his voice faltered, — "my dear lord, have I pleased thee since I have been of thy household?"

"In all things, my son. I shall miss thee sorely."

"Then give me thy blessing, as thou didst once before. Mayhap I go to worse straits than I found in Southampton, — God knows!"

Three days later Robin leaped from Fanuella's back, with much of his old vigor, and was clasped in Dame Dorothy's arms. He was half cured already; and she and Betty were two happy women, as they made his own old room, with the bay window and the high-carved mantel, sweet and fresh for him, a low fire burning on the hearth, and the scent of thyme and rosemary and lavender floating in from the garden. He looked around him with tender, smiling eyes, almost fancying himself a child again, as Dorothy hovered about him wistfully, and Betty fluttered in and out, tempting him with sweets.

"Thou art much changed, Robin," said the former, when, supper being over, they were at last alone. "But thou art mine own laddie still, though thou art a fine gentleman, fit for the Queen's court."

"'Tis well I was sent away from thee to find my level," he answered, laughing, but with a shrug of his shoulders. "Thou didst ever make too much of me, granny, thinking thine own swan the whitest of all. But, tell me now, for it is long since I had a letter from thee, — "

"Aye, so it is, laddie. Thou wert ever good to write to me, and proud was I of thy letters. But I could not send thee much in return. I can talk fast enow, as thou knowest, but when it comes to pen and paper, — bah! But is it good to be here, Robin? Is home sweet? 'Tis a great fall from Longleat."

"Aye," he answered, laughing. "There are few finer places than Longleat, even among 'kings' houses.' Do you remember, granny, how I used to tease you for stories about kings' houses?"

She nodded, with tears in her eyes.

"But," he went on, soberly, "it is good to be here. Never do you doubt that."

She shook her head, repeating, "'Tis a great fall from Longleat, though."

"So it is; so it is, in one sense. But, granny, have you forgotten what Mat Hansel said when he brought Fanuella here, and I, foolish lad that I was, feared she would miss her fine quarters at Windsor? That reminds me! Mat is not home from the wars even yet?"

"No; Betty gets word from him now and again, through some straggler from the camps. He says war is like that great whirlpool on the coast of Norway. 'Tis easy enow to get in, but hard to get out. Always he says he is coming when the campaign is over. · But when one ends another begins. Please God, he will come sometime."

"And then there will be a wedding?"

"Mayhap. Yet I know not. Time settles all things. But tell me of thyself, laddie. Is all well with thee?"

They talked late that night, and Dame Dorothy listened, delightedly, as Robin told of his life at Longleat, with all its varied experiences, of his affection for Lord Weymouth, and of the latter's increasing trust in him.

"And thou didst see the Queen? Mistress Randee told me of her visit to Lord Weymouth. It was a great honor. 'Tis long since her Majesty hath been in Windsor; but twice, or thrice, since thou wert away. But thou didst see her?"

"Yes."

"And were all her ladies with her? Didst thou see the Lady Anne Gascoyne? She hath grown to be a great beauty, and 'tis said she is to wed with my Lord Dalkieth. Didst thou hear of it?"

"Aye; I heard some such report. But I know not if it be true."

CHAPTER XXV

In due course of time Robin returned to Longleat. The forest, and Dame Dorothy's nursing, had done their predestined work, and all traces of the South-ampton episode had faded away, leaving him as well as ever, if somewhat graver.

He found Ralph Montague's bower, as it was sarcastically styled by his comrades, empty as a last year's bird's-nest. All had flown, — the tapestry, the fine hangings, the luxurious divan, the costly trinkets. His father had died suddenly, and the young heir had been hurriedly summoned to his home in the far north, to assume the new dignities of the head of his house.

Robin had had much time for reflection during his absence, and had returned, fully determined in his own mind to probe to the bottom the matter of the little silver arrow. But it was too late now. He and Ralph had long been friends, it is true; but such searching questions as he meant to put could only be ventured in the close intimacy of daily familiar intercourse. How could he, indeed, ask any questions whatever? What right had he to meddle with the affairs of the Lady Anne Gascoyne, or with those of the House of Montague?

The days came and went, and at last all came about as Lord Weymouth had predicted. In a few months, the Queen came to Windsor and bethought herself of her protégé. In another month, — for events moved rapidly in those days, — Robin was in France, fighting her Majesty's battles in the campaigns of 1706 – 1708. Fanuella smelt powder at Ramillies, minding it no more than the scent of clover, and thought the clash of arms and the thunder of cannon were to be dreaded no more than the patter of raindrops on her stable roof. It was she who flashed like a firefly through the smoke and din of war, bearing her young master proudly when more than once he crossed the bloody field to deliver orders from the great duke to Major-General Webb. It was she, too, who pranced with him into Spain, as gaily as to a festival, when he went thither to join Lord Peterborough at Barcelona.

But there are strange and unlooked-for meetings in camps and on battlefields. Before this flitting into Spain, on one dark, dreary October morning when the English army was entrenched before Lisle, Robin was picking his way through mud and mire from one quarter of the camp to another on a tour of inspection. It was raining, — not a good, sharp, resolute shower, bound to attend to business and be done with it, but a slow, persistent drizzle, irritating as a weak woman's causeless tears, or the fretful wail of a peevish child. The wind howled dismally, and the chill dampness penetrated to the very bones and marrow, making English soldiers think gloomily of warm fires on the glowing English hearthstones they left across the channel. It is one thing to rush cheerily into the forefront of battle when bugles call and trumpets blare and the whole world watches the onset breathlessly; it is quite another thing to lie idly in camp listlessly waiting, waiting.

Suddenly, as he sought temporary shelter in a sentry's box, he heard the voice of one approaching, — the strangely familiar voice of a man, growling at wind and weather.

"By Saint George and the dragon, what a day! More fool I to have come out in such weather. Look at me, James! Hat drenched, feather drooping and all awry, doublet dripping, hose bespattered, and not a dry thread about me. 'Tis worse than a walk in Hades — Heavens and earth, man! Is that you, Robin Sandys, hiding there like a hen in a coop?"

For at that instant the occupant of the sentry-box stepped forward, with extended hand.

"It surely is, Ralph. But no need to ask if it is you, bemoaning the fate of feather, doublet, and hose. How came you here, man? Are you with the army?"

"Not I, indeed. I have no mind to stand up to be shot at, — nor to shoot, either, unless it be in defence of home and hearth. And mine are not in this beggarly land of France, God be praised! I am but a poor bearer of despatches from her Majesty to the duke; and my errand once done, back I fly, straight as a homing pigeon. But do but look at me! I can never present myself to his Grace in this plight. 'Twould mar all."

Meanwhile Robin had drawn him under shelter, laughing at his discomfiture.

"His Grace has little time to consider feathers down here, be they dishevelled, or no," he said. "I have nearly made my rounds. Stay you here while I finish, and then go with me to my quarters, where James will soon put you to rights."

"Nay, let us get out of this mire. Go you with me to my chambers, where we can be quiet and comfortable, and I can lay hands on my own dressing-case. Robin, lad, but 'tis good to see you again," he added, heartily. "What changes hath time not wrought since we were lads at Longleat! I, head of my house, and you, a target for French bullets."

Half an hour later they were in the best quarters the place afforded. Trust Ralph Montague for that! When, after submitting himself to James's ministrations, he emerged from his dressing-room, fresh from the bath, spick and span as ever, and with a certain air that hung about him as of one made of finer clay than other folk, yet, after all is said, with no real trace of weakness or effeminacy, Robin could but admit to his own heart that he was as fine a specimen of young manhood as one need wish to see. But lo! the folds of his laced cravat were held in place, not by jewelled clasp, or golden ring, but by a little silver arrow that was itself half hidden in the airy meshes. An eye less keen than Robin's would scarcely have noticed it. His heart sank.

"Now, for a sip of something hot to cheer us up, a bright fire, and a good talk about old times," said Montague.

"But, — the duke and the despatches?" suggested his companion.

"Bah! there's no hurry. I am twenty-four hours ahead of time, and I don't get hold of an old comrade every day. How goes the world with you, Robin?"

Robin was silent so long that his friend stared. Then he said, quietly, "I can answer that question better, Ralph, after I have asked one of you. Where got you that little silver arrow?"

"This? this?" responded Ralph, his color deepening while his hand sought the head of the tiny bauble. "This? Ho, ho! Is that the way the wind blows? After you turned so white that night in my room at Longleat, and stalked off, saying you had seen a ghost, I turned back to my table and examined it curiously, wondering if, by chance, I might find any clue to your discomfiture. Yet now I do bethink me this was lying there."

"But you do not answer my question. Where got you the arrow?"

"In the picture gallery at Longleat. 'Twas the night after the Queen left. In truth we were all somewhat upset after the fine doings. My lord was glum and silent. You had flown, nobody knew whither. All who did not win prizes in the tournament looked askance at those who did, and Gaffer Ambrose went hobbling up and down the courts shaking his old head and maundering on about Queen Henrietta Maria, till I thought I should go crazy with it all. So I strayed off by myself into the gallery, which was still bedecked as for the festival, and there on the floor, under the settle, I saw something shining in the moonlight. It was this arrow."

"And did you know to whom it belonged?"

"Of course I did. I had seen it hidden away in Lady Anne Gascoyne's hair when I danced with her at the ball. 'Twas for her sake I kept it. But, laddie," he went on, nervously, glancing at Robin's grave face and questioning eyes, "it was but a trifle, a mere hairpin, as one might say, not worth making a pother about, or returning to one of the Queen's ladies. A knight may keep a lady's glove if he is lucky enough to find it, or a knot of ribbon from her breast. This is no more than that, surely, and all is fair in love and war."

"In love? Ralph, let me take the arrow for an instant. See here," — and holding the trinket to the light, he showed him Gloster's initials in very small letters on the shaft. "Look you, Ralph! I won that arrow in an archery contest on the Duke of Gloster's last birthday. I gave it to Lady Anne myself, when we were children."

Montague gave a long, low whistle.

"The deuce you did!" he cried; "and I supposed you had never seen her any more than I, till the night of the ball. So much for your confounded reticence. Robin, tell me the truth now, remembering that we are men, not children, do you love the lady?"

"There is nothing between us," he answered, speaking low and with evident constraint, "nothing whatever."

"That is not what I asked. Do you love her? What there may be between you now is nothing to the point."

Robin hesitated for a moment.   He *was* reticent. Lord Weymouth was the only one on earth who had ever so much as suspected that he cared for Lady Anne beyond the bounds of childish friendship. But he must speak the truth now.

" Yes," he said, under his breath.   " I love her. I have loved her all my life.   I shall love her till I die, — and afterward, if God wills."

There was a moment's silence, and then Ralph, searching his friend's face with a strange, scrutinizing glance, placed the arrow in his hand.

" Take it, Robin, it is yours," he said, very gravely. " That is something that is vouchsafed to few men, — to love one woman all their lives and to cleave unto her only.   Take you the arrow."

" But you said all was fair in love and war, Ralph. As I told you, I have no possible claim on Lady Anne, — not even the claim of an outspoken love. She is not mine, to have or to hold."

" Perhaps not.   Yet this makes many things clear to me.   She would not wed Lord Dalkieth, in spite of the Queen's furtherance of his suit and Lady Marlborough's manœuvering.   Surely you have heard that ? "

" Something to that effect."

Ralph hesitated a moment, and then, with a sudden snap of his fingers, as if tossing something from him, he went on :

"By her Majesty's command I have been much at court, and no obstacles have been thrown in the way of my meeting the Lady Anne. In fact,"—and he laughed a little shamefacedly,—"I have sometimes fancied that our royal mistress would not be unwilling to see her fair goddaughter mistress of Montague Hall. But I have known from the first that it could not be. The lady made it clear enough. She smiled and sang and danced as she was bidden, but no more. And—'if she be not fair to me, what care I how fair she be?' Go you in and win, Robin, and never bother about me or my loves. I am not worth it."

Robin was gravely silent for a moment. Then with an unfeigned humility, while his eye studied the gay, debonair young figure beside him, he said, "What possible chance is there for Robin Sandys where there is none for Ralph Montague? Moreover, if you take the matter so lightly, why have you kept this toy so long?"

"'Twas a mere whim. I hardly know, myself. Possibly because, as things turned out, I dared not let the lady know I had it, and yet was loath to get rid of it in any other fashion. Look you, Robin Sandys, and mark my words. I know nothing of love as measured by your standards. As I said, it is vouchsafed to few men to love one woman with a lifelong love. Truly it is not vouchsafed to me.

I have had a dozen light loves, or fancies. I shall have a dozen more, no doubt, before I make my lady mother a dowager."

The two rose, and with clasped hands looked steadily into each other's eyes. Then, " God bless you, Ralph," said Robin, and they went their separate ways.

CHAPTER XXVI.

In less than three years from the time he set out, Robin was home again. He was older, wiser, graver, yet, perhaps, on the whole, happier than when he went away. He had been tried and tested; and to stand any test well makes for happiness.

Not that he had immortalized himself. He had had occasion for none of those displays of superhuman valor that now and then lift a man suddenly out of the ranks of common humanity, and set him at once and forever among the stars. No one expected it, and he least of all. There had been some slight badinage as to his winning his spurs. But there was little of that business going on. Its day was pretty well over before he was born. The accolade belonged to the days of jousts and tourneyings, for the most part; the days of splendid armor and all the pomp and circumstance of chivalry.

But he had done his full duty. He had proved himself a valiant soldier, ready to fight when fighting was to the fore, and, after it was over, humane and generous to friend and foe. He had received honorable mention more than once, and felt that the path of preferment was open before him. On the whole, all who cared a straw for the young fellow, from her Majesty down to Betty Macthorne, were well pleased with him. Even my Lady Marlborough had only smiles for him now. Had he not been with his Grace the duke? And the duke had said, in his private letters to the Queen and to his wife, that no man of his age in all Flanders deserved more honor than young Robin Sandys. Whatever else my lady did, or did not, believe, she believed in her brave husband, who loved her so devotedly. This much must in justice be said of her: that in spite of the dominating, overmastering ambitions that made her often cruel and unrelenting, in spite of the ingratitude that must be laid to her charge, in spite of all her greed and selfishness, there must have been noble qualities in the woman who commanded her Queen's love for two-thirds of a lifetime, and held that of Lord Marlborough forever. So now she gave her lord's new favorite her white hand to kiss, forgetting he was the boy she had flouted.

As soon as Robin had made his obeisance to the Queen at Kensington, and received, as he did, her congratulations, he begged permission to retire for awhile to the gray cottage. But first he had had a few whispered words with Lady Anne. He had made his peace with her as to the matter of the favor and the tournament, and had shown her the slender thread of gold that he had secretly wound about his sleeve whenever he went into battle, assuring her, no doubt, it had been the talisman that had kept him safe through many perils. He had restored to her the little silver arrow that had known so many vicissitudes, replacing it himself in the thick coils of her golden hair. His fingers trembled at the touch of the soft, odorous folds, and he dared not meet her eyes, that shone with such subdued and tender light.

"My lost arrow!" she cried. "I did not think to see it again. But how came it in your hands, pray tell me, sirrah?"

"Ask me not, dear Lady Anne," he answered. "I can tell you only this. It was delivered to me by one who found it, and I would fain say no more."

So, though there was no out-and-out love-making between them, — for the time was not yet ripe, — it cannot be denied that there was a pretty fair understanding between the two. Love is its own interpreter; and oftentimes it finds the spoken word superfluous.

And who should ride home with Robin, but Mat Hansel, — Mat, browned and bronzed, and looking every inch the soldier in his buff coat and jack-boots? The one gray hair he had shown to Betty had increased by many dozens; but he was still a man in the prime of life, with many long years ahead before he would be old. The two had met by chance one morning in Spain ; and the elder man, overjoyed, had managed, by hook or by crook, to get himself exchanged into the company of the younger, to their mutual satisfaction.

Mat had seen enough of fighting, and was tired of the wars that seemed so endless, and accomplished so little. What did it all amount to, beyond the killing of brave men and the making of widows and orphans? It had seemed grand and glorious at first, but now he had had enough of it ; and when he rode up Castle Hill, and around to the stables where all was unchanged, and just as he had left it when he enlisted five years before, he felt surer than ever that England was the fairest land sun ever shone upon, and Windsor the fairest spot in England.

At any rate, it held Betty, — Betty for whom he had waited so long and so faithfully. Was he to have his reward now that he had come back ?

One cool evening, early in September, a few days after Robin's return, a bright fire was blazing on the hearth in his room, and he sat in a big chair, his head resting on his hand, and his eyes watching the flickering flames and the glowing coals beneath them.

"Where are you, granny?" he called. "Come hither, and sit with me."

"Soon, soon," she answered, from the room opposite. "Let me finish spinning this skein of fine yarn first. I promised Mistress Randee she should have it on the morrow."

By way of response Robin dashed across the entry, caught up the little wheel, and set it down before his own fire.

"There!" he said. "If thou must needs 'sit by the fire and spin,' like the old woman in the song, thou art to do it here by my side, granny. There is no sweeter music on earth than the humming of thy wheel."

She laughed happily. "Thou wert ever a masterful lad, and wouldst make me do thy will. How will it be now that thou art a man? But now tell me of thy adventures. Thou must have a store of them," and, as she spoke, she drew out a long, shining thread of flax, while Robin watched her, feeling as if he were a boy again.

"'Tis thy turn to tell stories now," she insisted, as he remained silent.

"I was thinking where to begin," he said. "Granny, many strange things have befallen me, but one seems strangest of all, as I look back. Wait now, and let me think a bit. It was in Barcelona, late in June, not long before Lord Peterborough threw up his command. One evening I was wandering through the crooked, narrow streets of the old city, as it is called, to distinguish it from the modern part where the fine new buildings are, when suddenly Mat came running towards me with a peasant woman at his heels.

"'Well met, master,' he cried, as he caught sight of me. 'Can you tell me what 'tis this woman wants? I can make nothing of her outlandish gibberish.'

"'Alms, most likely,' I answered. 'They are all beggars.'

"But she still pulled at Mat's coat, and when he pushed her from him, somewhat rudely, she seized mine. Had she been younger I might have thought her one of the women that hang about the camps. But she was old, and withal she had a saintly face as I caught glimpses of it under the shawl drawn around her head. Now I do not know the Spanish tongue, but I can make out to understand a little by hook or by crook, my knowledge of the Latin helping me somewhat; and I knew she was entreating us to follow her, with much rapid talk and many gesticulations.

"'Come on, Mat,' I said. 'Let us see what the old creature wants. She is trying to ask if we speak the English.'

"'Thank God, we do,' said Mat. 'The devil take me if I ever speak anything else. 'Tis not quite safe, master; but anyhow we be two to one, and that one an old woman. So let us on, in God's name!'

" We followed her up one lane, and down another, out towards the open country, till she stopped at last before a low cottage near the walls. It was hardly more than a hut, and stood somewhat with-drawn from the highway. Mat drew back, and put his hand to his belt, as she proceeded to unfasten the door. 'See here, old woman,' he said, quite for-getting she could not understand him, 'if you are playing a trick on us, and getting my young master here into a snare —'

" 'No, — no,' she cried, understanding the voice and action, if not the words ; and again I made out something like 'Anglees, Anglees.' Clearly she was in pursuit of some one who could speak English.

" It was but a little place, only two rooms, the walls hardly to be distinguished in the light of one feeble candle. At first I thought them empty. But as my eyes grew wonted to the dim light, I saw the form of a man stretched on a pallet in the inner room. The woman dragged me to his side, and I saw he was lying with closed eyes, very near to death. She lifted his head, and put some wine to his lips. It is strange, granny, how much one can understand without words. Those Southern folk, — they talk with their eyes and their hands. Somehow she made me know that this man had been wounded in a skirmish, many days before, and left for dead. She had found him lying help-less, and half dragged, half carried him to her hut, where she had done her poor best for him, foe and stranger though he was. All this I made out, partly by my own wits, and partly through her endeavors; and it came to me that the man, who perhaps could make her understand his Spanish, had implored her to bring to him some one to whom he could speak in his own tongue. For I saw at once that he was an Englishman.

"Twice, thrice, she put the cup to his poor lips, and chafed his hands, and cooed over him in her soft, motherly voice, before he opened his eyes. When he saw me, such a glad light came into them as I never saw in mortal eyes before. 'You are my countryman,' he murmured, taking my hand. 'God hath sent you to me in my need.'"

Dame Dorothy had pushed the wheel away, and was leaning forward, listening intently.

"Go on, laddie," she said at length, as Robin remained silent, lost in his own memories. "There must be more to tell."

He started at the sound of her voice. "I will not try to give you his own words, for he could speak but few at a time, and that with long pauses. Often he would lapse into stupor, and then through the woman's ministrations would rally again. Somehow,

I felt he could not die — nay, that he would not —
— till he had finished his story.   So I sat waiting
patiently, holding his poor hand, and bending my ear
to his lips, whenever he had strength to speak.   I
saw from the first moment that there was no possible help for him.   All I could do was to listen.

"Broken and disjointed as the story was, it was
yet coherent.   He made me understand him fully.
He had been one of the many who had followed
the fortunes of King James, and cast in their lot
with his, feeling that, whatever his errors and weak-
nesses might be, he was still England's anointed
king."

"Aye, there were many such," said Dame Dorothy, nodding her head gravely.   "Good Protestants, too.   'Tis a mistake to think that all, or
even most of those who followed the banner of
King James, were Papists.   'Twas not so.   They
were but loyal Englishmen, faithful to their sworn
sovereign.   But go on, laddie, my old tongue runs
away with me, when I think of those dark days."

"This man was a Protestant," said Robin, "and
loyal to England, though not to one whom he
regarded as a usurper.   But for this he was outlawed, and a price set on his head.   He tried to
give me details of wherein he was falsely accused;
but seeing how fast his strength was failing, I
begged him to say only what he must.   Then he

told me this : that when James and William were both dead, and Anne was on the throne, he felt that the cause of the young prince was hopeless ; or if it were not, that the new order of things was established, and its maintenance best for England. So he joined the armies in France and Spain, not as an officer and gentleman of rank, but as a common soldier; trusting that, after he had done good service under the Queen's banner, he might venture to again tread English soil, and to throw himself on her mercy. And now, death was to end all, leaving him attainted, and his son a beggar. For he left a little motherless boy in England, when he was forced to flee for his life ; and 'twas for his sake he longed to retrieve somewhat of his losses in rank, and in estate."

Perhaps it was well that the room was lighted only by the glow from the hearth, for at this juncture Dame Dorothy's fine old face grew white as a snow wreath, and she left the chamber, with a brief word of excuse. When she came back, she drew her chair farther into the shadow.

"And what was the gentleman's name?" she asked, in a steady voice, though, if one had looked closely, he would have seen that she held the arm of her chair as in a vice. Her finger-nails were white with the pressure.

"That is the saddest part of all, granny. I can

hardly forgive myself. I was intent on hearing what he had to say, and he was only intent on saying it. It did not once occur to me until all was over that he had not given me his name. Dawn was just breaking, and he was about to draw something from his bosom, when, suddenly, he gave a sharp cry, and caught my hand. 'Say a prayer!' he gasped, and I fell on my knees, and said one of the little prayers you taught me when a child, and 'Oh, Saviour of the world.' In the whirl of my thoughts I could remember nothing else. As I rose and bent over him, with tears in my eyes, he smiled. 'Kiss me, lad,' he said. And, as I stooped and did his bidding, the spirit departed."

Dorothy rose silently, and laid her hand on Robin's head.

"'Twas a mercy thou wert there in his dark hour," she whispered. "Thy story hath moved me much, laddie. Let me leave thee for some little while, and then we will talk farther of this."

It was half an hour before she returned. "Hast thou nothing more to tell?" she asked, taking his hand.

Robin looked at her, anxiously. "I am sorry I told thee anything," he answered. "Art thou not well to-night? I never saw thee so pale."

But she made an impatient gesture. "Talk not of me. I am well enow. Was there nothing more to't?"

"Not much. I —"

"But surely thou didst find what it was the man had hidden in his bosom?"

"Yes. I will show thee presently. I hesitated just a little, seeing he was quite unknown to me. Yet, after what he had told me, it did not seem like prying into his secrets. So I called Mat, who had remained in the next room, and when we had made the poor body ready for burial as best we could, I took a small pouch of green leather from beneath his shirt. It hung around his neck by a black cord. You know nothing about war, granny. You cannot understand. But we could not give him what you would call Christian burial. The town was in tumult, and the hut, or cabin, was on its extreme northern limit, almost in the open country. We dug a grave under a low, wide-spreading ilex-tree, and there we left him. The woman looked on silently, crossing herself, and telling her beads. I gave her all the silver I had about me, and before the sun was fairly up we were back to our quarters again. It had been a long, strange night."

"But the pouch! What was in the pouch, lad?"

He crossed the room to his chest. "Here it is," he said. "See for thyself."

She unfastened the string with nervous fingers that would hardly do her bidding, and took from the small pouch the miniature of a lovely, dark-eyed woman, a flat brown curl, evidently cut from a child's head, and a ring, — an amethyst with an engraved crest thereon. Dorothy gave a low cry as they fell into her lap; then checked herself, and looked deprecatingly at Robin, while her lips trembled.

"They are so beautiful it quite took away my breath," she said, smiling faintly. "And — and — it is all, as you say, so pitiful."

"It is a sad story, indeed," he answered. "To-morrow I must find a merry one to make up for it."

"Nay; I like the sad ones better. Laughter is but the crackling of thorns under a pot."

"But tell me, granny, you who are so wise," he went on, while she studied the miniature and the crest. "What shall I do about this matter? If I do nothing, that man's white face will haunt me till I die."

"Let me think. Let me think it over," she said. "But the hour grows late, and now I must to bed. I will e'en take the pouch with me, by your leave, and dream on't."

An hour later, Betty, hearing a slight stir in her mistress's room, stole softly down-stairs, to see if aught was wrong with her. The door was ajar a trifle. Dame Dorothy was kneeling by her bed-side, with her arms outstretched upon the coverlet.

"Lord, I thank thee," she said, under her breath; "now lettest thou thy servant depart in peace."

"My dear old mistress," thought Betty, as she crept quietly away with tears in her eyes. "'Tis but because our Master Robin is safe home from the wars. And my Mat, too. Truly, we have much to thank God for, and I will surely go to matins and even-song to say my prayers three times a week till next Michaelmas."

CHAPTER XXVII.

"Did you dream it out, dear heart?" asked Robin the next morning, following Dame Dorothy into the garden, gorgeous with the late splendor of the year, and glowing with heat again. The sun shone warmly after the early chills, and the bees were coming and going as in midsummer. "Sit here in the sunshine, and let us talk it over."

"I have thought it all out, Robin. You are to tell the whole story to Queen Anne, just as you told it to me. She comes to Windsor next week; for so Mistress Randee was telling me but yesterday when she came to speak with me about the yarn. You must tell her of the poor gentleman, and what he said, and show her the miniature and the ring; and mayhap God will incline her heart to help you find the little lad if he be living. For she hath a kindly heart, — our good Queen Anne."

"She has indeed. I have much cause to know that. But she has been taught to believe this man a traitor. He told me as much. Still, I know not what else to do, and it may prove worth the trying. When do you say she comes?"

"Next week."

"And next Monday Lord Weymouth is to be in London. I will see him. If any man can help me with the Queen in this matter, it is he."

A few days later, young Master Sandys went out to the stable just before sundown, to have a little confidential talk with Fanuella.

"Sleep well, my lady," he said. "Thou must be in fine trim on the morrow when we go up to London to see our dear lord and master. Thou must carry thyself proudly, as befitteth one who hath been in the forefront of battle, and never quailed ; and thou must remember thou art a giddy young thing no longer, my Fanuella! Why, thou art middle-aged at the very least, while I am still but in the heyday of my youth. Art thou not sorry? For surely it is good to be young, and life is sweet."

Ah! life and youth were very sweet to Master Robin Sandys about those days!

Fanuella answered him with neighs and whinnies, as was her custom, lowering her head for his caresses, and assenting to all he said, with much pricking of her small ears and most intelligent glances, until with a laugh he gave her a lump of sugar, bade her good night, and returned to the house again, where he and Dame Dorothy talked late and long.

"Wilt thou tell the whole matter at once to my Lord Weymouth?" she asked.

"Nay, I think not. There are always many to see him, and a crowd of folk coming and going when he is at his house in London. I will but pay my obeisance, as in duty bound after my long absence, and bear to him the Queen's mandate that he come to Windsor on Thursday. 'Tis a rare chance that he is up from Longleat just now."

"Thou wilt stay at the castle thyself, Robin?"

"Yes. The Queen bids it. And she was pleased to say I must have had many rare adventures, and must relate them some evening for her amusement, and Lord Weymouth's. I made answer that I was no Scheherezade, like her of the 'Arabian Nights,' but that some strange things had indeed befallen me, one at least of which might possibly be worth her hearing. So the way is open. Her Majesty will not forget, for she dearly loves a story."

"Wilt thou not see to it that Mat Hansel be somewhere within call? 'In the mouth of two witnesses,' the Scripture saith, thou knowest," she said, anxiously.

"He can be called if it seem needful; but I think the Queen will take my word as far as it goes. Would it went further! Yet the miniature and the crest, — surely they will help me out. Granny, it is borne in upon my mind that I shall find the little lad."

"God grant it! But the 'little lad' must be well-nigh as old as thyself, Robin, — a man grown by this time. Tell me, lad. Are there many at the castle whom you knew in the old days?"

"Not many. Lady Marlborough is at Woodstock just now, looking after the building of her fine palace of Blenheim. I had a moment with Mistress Hill in the east corridor. You know she has changed her name and estate, and is Mistress Masham now?"

"So Mistress Randee told me but last week; and she added that Lady Marlborough was wroth because her Majesty went to the wedding, forsooth!"

As usual, there was some fine darning to be done at the castle; and thus it happened that on Thursday morning Dorothy was in the Queen's bedchamber busily plying her needle, while Anne, from the depths of a capacious chair, with her hands folded, and a smile on her lips, watched the movements of her deft fingers.

"Dorothy," she said. "Hearken to me! You are to have such a treat as you never dreamed of. Hear this now. My Lord Weymouth is coming hither to-day, and I have bidden Robin hold himself in readiness to tell us somewhat of his happenings in foreign parts. What think you of that? 'Twill be fine sport, and you shall have a share in it. I have set my heart on't."

Dorothy clasped her hands in delight, for all

things seemed turning as she had almost hope-
lessly prayed. "Thou art only too good to me,
my Queen," she said, "and I would I could hide
behind the arras, and hear the lad's stories. But
thou knowest I have no part nor lot with great
folk. Yet, dear my lady, tell me if it please you,
where will this story-telling be?"

"In the green and silver chamber. And now I
do bethink me, there is a screen there, — the fine
japanned screen Mistress Dalrymple brought down
to me from Scotland, it being her own handiwork.
If you choose, you can sit quietly behind it, and none
will be the wiser, not even Master Robin Sandys
himself. How will you like that?" and she laughed
merrily.

"I shall like it well, madam, and I promise you
I will be stiller than any mouse, hiding behind the
arras."

And so it happened that when a small but somewhat stately company, consisting of her Majesty,
Prince George of Denmark, Lord Weymouth, and
two or three of the Queen's ladies, met in the
beautiful chamber where Robin first saw Little
Lady bending, with wistful eyes, over her embroidery-frame, Dame Dorothy, in her purple gown, and
cap and lappets of sheer, fine muslin, sat behind
Mistress Dalrymple's tall screen. Over her shoulders, that were still unbent by the weight of her

more than seventy years, she wore a soft white shawl with a narrow needle-wrought border that Robin had brought her from the South. A crimson spot burned upon either cheek, and her hand trembled as she drew the shawl closer about her, laying her cheek upon its folds caressingly.

"God help him now," she sighed, inaudibly, as she listened to the light talk going on beyond the screen, the jests and the laughter, the Queen's silvery voice, Prince George's gutturals, and Lord Weymouth's deeper tones. Robin was at the lower end of the long chamber awaiting his summons, and, meanwhile, solacing himself with Lady Anne.

At length her Majesty called him ; and Dorothy's heart gave a great throb as, through a crevice in the screen, she saw him come up the long room, his head erect, his hair thrown back, his dark eyes kindling, and a smile on his lips as he knelt to the Queen. She beckoned to the younger ladies, and they drew nearer.

"Now, prithee, Master Sandys, — for I must not call you Robin now that you have a beard, and his Grace the duke says such fine things of you, — tell us the story you spoke of as being, perhaps, worth our hearing."

He bowed low, and drew a step nearer. "If it please your Majesty, let me tell of some lighter matters first. The adventure I spoke of, though

I hope it may prove to be of interest, is yet a sad one when all is said, — fitter to move tears than laughter."

"As you please, as you please, Master Sandys. Only, I pray you, let the tales be of Spain, of which we know much less than of France."

Robin was not a bad story-teller, and the presence of his old friend and master, to say nothing of Lady Anne's rapt listening, was of itself an inspiration. With a light and airy touch, as of one who scarcely dealt with matter-of-fact realities, he told of two or three merry happenings of camp and court and bivouac, amid much laughter and jesting. Then his face changing, he again bowed.

"Will your Majesty listen to the sadder story, now?"

She nodded.

"Go on. 'Twill be a pleasant change if it make me cry, for I have laughed till my sides ache."

Prince George rose with some difficulty. "If it please you, madam, my wife, I will retire. My breath comes hard to-night; and sad stories are not for sick men."

Anne looked after her husband anxiously, as he made his slow way to the door.

"Bid Masham prepare the bolus for you, dear heart," she said, "and make ready the night draught. I will come soon, and do my poor best to make you comfortable for the night. This high Windsor air seems always bad for him!" she added, with a sigh. "He is better in Kensington. But go on, Master Sandys."

Dorothy, behind the screen, held her breath, and leaned forward, hearing her own heart beat. In almost the words he had used in telling the tale to her, he told of the dark streets of Barcelona, of the appeal of the peasant woman, of following her to the lonely cabin on the outskirts of the town, of the dark inner room, and the wounded man stretched on that forlorn pallet; of the long, weird night-watch, of the death, just as the faint gray dawn was breaking, and of the hurried burial under the ilex-tree. But he did not tell of the prayer, nor of the kiss. They were too sacred. Neither did he tell what the dying man had said to him. That should come later.

When he ceased, the Queen was in tears.

"And this was one of mine own gallant soldiers, wounded in mine own cause," she cried. "This bloodshed, this bloodshed, — oh, my God! when shall we be done with it? But go on. What said the man? It must have been of much import, seeing how he strove to speak in the very death-agony."

Robin hesitated, and his color changed. The crucial moment had come, the moment that should test all. Lord Weymouth watched him curiously, seeing, as the Queen did not, that there was some strong purpose underlying this story-telling. It was more than the pastime of an hour. Something of weight hung thereon. What was it?

"It was indeed, madam. Would I could give the story in his own words! Broken as they were, and with long pauses, as for breath, they were far more eloquent than those of any other tongue can be. Madam, your brave soldier dying there was one who had loved King James, and followed his fortunes. For this he was outlawed under William, and forbidden to return to England, under penalty of death. He was stigmatized as a traitor to king and country. I cry pardon, your Majesty,"— for the Queen's face flushed, and she made an impatient gesture. "I do but repeat the words of a dying man. Shall I end here?"

"No, no! Go on, sir. Let us hear the whole, seeing we are in for it. We are all friends in this presence, or I would give a different answer. Say on!"

"The man said, 'I was no traitor. William was no king of mine. Yet I bred no treason, even against him; and I had part in no plots. I did but follow mine own anointed king in his flight, because I loved him.'"

"Aye," said Lord Weymouth, rising and taking

his stand by Robin's side. "Aye, madam, 'tis one thing to love, or even to hold enmity, and quite another to breed treason."

Anne made a quick motion of the head, but said nothing in response to this. Presently, however, she bade Robin proceed.

"How came this martyr to be fighting my battles, then?" she said. "Faith, they be all martyrs! Beshrew me, if I can understand. What more said he? Speak out!"

He explained in a few quiet, yet graphic words, most studiously chosen, as Lord Weymouth perceived, with a view to avoiding offence, telling of the man's determination, after both James and William were in their graves, to earn the Queen's favor by good service under his country's banner, and then to return, and throw himself at her feet, with a prayer for mercy.

Her face softened, and she listened silently, and without manifest impatience, as Robin told of the little son, thus bringing his story to an end.

Then came the momentous question.

"Who was this man?"

"Your Majesty, strange as it may seem, I do not know. I can hardly forgive myself for not knowing, for not having asked the question directly. I had often seen men fall on the field, in the fury and tumult of battle, and had not minded it much. But

I had never stood by a death-bed until then, nor spoken with a dying man, face to face. I was a good deal unnerved, and was only intent on hearing what he had to say. And he, — he thought only of telling his story while he had breath to do it, and death took him unawares. It did not occur to me, till it was too late, that he had never once spoken his own name."

"But," said Lord Weymouth, "there must have been papers, letters, something to identify him?"

"My lord, he had been stripped of his outer garments when left for dead. If he had papers, doubtless they were in his coat. But here is the pouch I spoke of, which, being worn beneath his shirt, was overlooked. The poor woman who befriended him had thought it an amulet, and left it untouched, as something sacred."

Dropping on one knee, he untied the little leathern pouch, or tiny bag, and poured the contents into the Queen's lap.

"Faith, but this grows interesting," she said, as she took up the miniature. "'Tis a lovely face, and does not seem unfamiliar. Methinks I must have seen the lady. Look, my Lord Weymouth. Do you know the face?"

He took the little case from her hand, and examined it long and closely, carrying it into the full blaze of the sconces on the wall.

"No, madam," as he returned it. "It reminds me strongly of some one I have known well. Yet I cannot place it, strange as it seems."

She held the little lock of hair tenderly for a moment. "'Twas cut from some baby's head," she sighed, dropping it as if it hurt her. "'Tis a tiny curl. But here is this ring. Can you make anything of that, my lord?"

Dorothy behind the screen rose softly and clasped her hands with one imploring glance upward. Then she stood listening, with one hand on her heart as if to still its loud, pulsating throbs. The moment for which she had been waiting eighteen years had come at last.

"Nothing whatever, your Majesty. If you look closely, you will see the device is a crest merely, not the entire coat of arms. 'Tis a pity. Yet no doubt it gives a clue. It may be traced in due time."

As he ceased speaking, Dorothy, to the astonishment of every one in the room, her Majesty included, glided out from behind the screen and knelt at the Queen's feet.

"Wilt thou look at this, my Queen?" she said, her voice scarcely rising above a whisper. "This" was a ring, the exact counterpart of the one in the pouch, except that it was a trifle larger, one being evidently a man's ring, the other a woman's.

"Dorothy, Dorothy, what means this?" cried the

Queen, while Robin took a step forward as if to draw her away. What could be the significance of this? What could she possibly know of this matter? How could she have any connection with it? Then he remembered her strange emotion when he first told her this very story, and he drew back again, breathless and in dismay.

"What is it?" repeated the Queen. "Speak, Dorothy."

But the woman hesitated, growing so white that Lord Weymouth, unbidden, brought a glass of wine from a tray in the corner and bade her drink it. When her color returned, forgetful of all but the one thing she had to do, she leaned forward with clasped hands.

"Look, my dear Lady Anne Stuart," she said, addressing the Queen by the old familiar title of long years ago. "Look! dost thou not see the ring I gave thee is like the other in all things save that it is larger?"

"Yes. But what does it mean? I like not mysteries. Speak, I command you. Speak out at once if you know aught of this matter. Whence came this ring, and how happens it to be in your possession?"

"Both rings belonged to Sir Henry Valdegrave, please your Majesty," Dorothy answered, her self-possession returning under the stimulus of the

Queen's sharp questioning. "The miniature is that of his wife, Lady Valdegrave, who died twenty-two years ago last April. And this — and this — and this," she cried, rising to her feet and turning to Robin with all the majesty of a sibyl, while her voice grew stronger and steadier with each reiteration, "this, my Queen, is their son, Sir Robert Valde-grave."

Even her Majesty rose to her feet at this climax. A low sound that was like a smothered sob came from the little group of ladies at the left. Lord Weymouth sprang forward and grasped Robin's shoulder, while Dorothy, erect, her head lifted, her eyes shining, stood motionless, looking from one to another.

Then Robin, gently freeing himself from Lord Weymouth's clasp, dropped on one knee.

"Forgive her, I pray your Majesty to forgive her and let me take her home," he entreated. "She is distraught, madam. She has been strangely wrought up for some days, — ever, in fact, since I told her this story and showed her the pouch. It hath upset her wits. Let me take her home, I pray you, and end this scene."

Dame Dorothy burst into tears. "Oh, laddie, laddie!" she cried. "Beware, lest you mar all!"

She tottered, and would have fallen had not Lady Anne, at a glance from the Queen, pushed forward a chair and beguiled her into it; while Lord Weymouth strode forward and again laid hands on Robin.

"Not so fast, young man, not so fast," he said. "Here is matter that must be sifted. Your Majesty, have I permission to cross-question this witness?" and his smile did something, if but little, towards lessening the tension of feeling by which all present were held.

The Queen nodded assent as she reseated herself, and he turned to Dorothy with great gentleness.

"Do not be alarmed," he said. "Speak out and tell whatever you know, without fear or favor, Dame Dorothy. As her Majesty was pleased to say, but a few moments agone, we are all friends here, and would know the plain truth. What have you to say of Sir Henry Valdegrave?"

She looked imploringly at Robin; and with a rush of irrepressible tenderness, as well as of sorrow for the stress into which he believed her love for him had led her, he crossed the room to her side, and bending, took her hand.

Lord Weymouth repeated his question. "Tell the story in your own way, and take your time," he added.

"It was Sir Henry," she said, after a moment's delay, speaking now in a low, calm voice, — for Robin's remark as to the upsetting of her wits had steadied her as nothing else could. "It was Sir Henry, who at the time of the Great Plague, or shortly thereafter, got me place as nurse to the Lady Anne Stuart. He was then in the household of his Grace, the Duke of York. Ever after that, as indeed he had been before, he proved a true friend to me and mine, and made us greatly his debtors in many ways. Sir Henry married late in life, and his wife lived but three years, having borne him one son."

Her voice trembled for a moment, but steadying herself by the close clasp of Robin's hand, she went on :

"Troubles came at last, as all the world knows; and he who had served the Stuarts all his days was on the Stuart side then. That is the long and the short of it.

"One night, — it was when I was living alone in Deptford, my husband having long been dead, — there was a knock at my door, and when I opened it, lo! there stood Sir Henry Valdegrave, all dishevelled and distraught, with a little child in his arms. He stepped in quickly and shut and locked the door behind him. The child was sleepy and tired, and dazed with the light, but it stretched out its little hands to me at once, and I took it to my heart forever, — took *him*, for that child is standing by my side in your presence now."

Questions sprang to many lips, but Lord Weymouth raised his hand, with an authoritative gesture, that silenced even Majesty itself. "Hush!" he said. "Let her speak as she will. Go on, Dame Dorothy."

"Then Sir Henry told me he was outlawed, and must flee for his life; and he begged me to take his child and care for it, keeping his secret until he gave me leave to speak.

"Now all Deptford knew I was daily expecting my little grandson, Robin, from the colonies in America, where his father and mother had lately died. But the post had just brought me a letter from one who had the child in charge, telling me that he died on the voyage over, and was buried in the deep sea. This no one yet knew, no, not a soul,—and I saw my way clear. 'Sir Henry,' I said, 'your child shall take the place and name of my son's son, who has just died on the way to me. I will care for him as if he were my very own, and keep your secret and his till you give me leave to tell it, so help me God.'

"We talked for an hour. Much can be said in that time when the heart is full, my lord. He told me that, foreseeing the evil days, he had tried to make what provision he could for his child by the sale of one of his estates at the north; and he drew from some hidden place where he had bestowed it a small bag of gold pieces. 'My boy shall not be a beggar, nor a pensioner, while I live,' he said. 'Father Hunt knows all, and will be faithful unto

death.   When this is spent, he will know where and
how to get more.   I will send word to you through
him as I am able, and he will advise you about the
rearing of the lad as he grows older.   Yet ere that
time comes, all may be well and I at home again,
please God.'

"Then he tore himself away, covering the child's
face with kisses, and wringing my hand, and was off
in disguise for Southampton.   That is all, my lord.
I never saw him again."

"But you heard from him?"

"Yes.   Several times through Father Hunt.
And as the years went on, — so many more than
he had counted on, — he sent money, now and
again, through some unknown hand.   It came, but
I knew not whence or how.   The child's purse was
like the widow's cruse of oil, my lord, — never quite
empty.   But since Father Hunt died, now three
years gone, I had heard nothing of Sir Henry, and
I thought him dead.   As you know, he was not.
The end came as — Sir Robert has told you."

During all this time Robin had stood behind
Dorothy's chair, one hand clasping hers, immovable
as a statue.   Dazed, bewildered, he was as one in a
dream, who is yet conscious that he dreams.   Yet
slowly, inch by inch, moment by moment, he felt
that the web of a new life was being woven about
him.   He knew that Dorothy spoke but the truth.

Something within him, some hidden pulse of his own being, made quick response to this strange revelation, and he knew it was his father he had kissed in that extreme hour. Yet when Dorothy called him "Sir Robert," with something in her voice, half triumph, half pain, — a note that he had never heard before, — forgetful of the Queen, forgetful of Lord Weymouth, forgetful even of Lady Anne, who stood a little withdrawn in the shadow of the screen, scarcely daring to look up lest her eyes should betray her, forgetful of everything but the long years of brooding, watchful love this woman had given him, he fell on his knees by her side, and buried his face in her lap.

"Nay, nay," he cried, "Call me not 'Sir Robert.' I am thy Robin till the day I die!"

She passed her hand tenderly over his dark hair, and her lips quivered, but she spoke no word.

Lord Weymouth stepped forward and raised him, whispering, "Courage, lad, courage;" then turned to Dorothy again.

"But the two rings. What of them?"

"I had nearly forgotten them, sir. That night in Deptford, when he brought the child to me, Sir Henry took from his finger the one I gave the Queen, bidding me keep it for — Robert. And he showed me the smaller one, making me see how that the device was exactly the same, and telling me it had been worn by his wife. Which, indeed, I knew without being told, as I had often seen it on her hand. I have nothing more to say, sir, save that I knew the picture as soon as ever I set eyes on it. I was with my Lady Valdegrave when her son was born, — and she had that ring on her finger."

There was a moment's silence.

"Your Majesty, I resign the witness," said Lord Weymouth. "The chain of evidence seems to me complete."

Taking Robin's hand, he led him to the Queen's feet, where he knelt silently, his eyes cast down, his lips compressed but tremulous.

Thus far Anne had given no intimation of her purpose, or even of her feeling. The stillness grew appalling, as moment after moment passed, for there was not an audible breath or motion. Dorothy had risen and was leaning forward, her face white as marble, with yearning eyes fastened on the two. Lord Weymouth had withdrawn a little, and stood motionless, but the hand that rested on the high mantel trembled. The ladies were in tears, — all but Little Lady. She was past tears.

One person only — Lord Weymouth — saw that the Queen's silence grew out of her emotion. Seconds counted for hours as she toyed with her fan, compressing her lips, and not even glancing at the kneeling figure before her. Then suddenly, as with an effort, she threw the fan aside, and laid her hands on Robin's shoulders as he knelt before her.

"Child," she said, "it was not I who made your father an outlaw. It does not become me to decide as to who was right, or who was wrong, in the first place. But he was slain in my service; and so for his sake, and for my son's sake, who loved you, and for your own sake, because I know you to be noble in word and thought and deed, I restore to you your father's dignities, and the estates he forfeited to the crown. Rise, Sir Robert Valdegrave, and would to God my Gloster were alive to see this day!"

Leaning forward she kissed his forehead. "Rise, child," she repeated, softly. Then as he obeyed her mutely, and stood before her, white, dazed and trembling, she rose, also, and, beckoning to her ladies, left the room.

Dame Dorothy had disappeared, without a word or sign. Only Lord Weymouth and the new Sir Robert were left in the green and silver chamber.

CHAPTER XXVIII.

IT was the morning of August 2, 1714. Raneleigh, the fair estate of Sir Robert Valdegrave, was
never fairer than it was that day, when over the
whole wide landscape, hill, and valley, winding
river, fertile meadows, and deep green forest, hung
the soft haze of lingering summer. Afar to the
right the horizon line was broken by cathedral
towers, grand, sombre, majestic. To the left there
was a glimpse of the blue sea, shimmering in the
sun ; while at the foot of the long, sloping descent
of Raneleigh Hill nestled the village buried in
masses of verdure, above which soared the spire
of its old gray church.

On the lawn in front of the stately Elizabethan
mansion, a white-haired woman, in a purple gown
opening over a gray petticoat, was caressing a little
child.

"Wait thee, now, and be patient, laddie," she said.
"Hark ! Dost thou not hear old Fanuella coming
around from the stables ? Listen ! Her hoofs go

craunch, craunch, on the gravel. Thy daddy will give thee a ride presently."

In a moment, Sir Robert, followed by Fanuella, came around the corner, and Dame Dorothy led the little boy to his father.

"Come on, youngster," he said. "Up, now, like a bird! There! Cling to her well, lest you tumble. If nothing will do but you must mount Fanuella, see that you hang on."

"Careful, careful! Keep fast hold of the bridle, Robin!" called Lady Anne from the terrace, where she was arranging a tall vase of lilies. "You're not to be trusted with that child," and she turned a half laughing, half anxious, face towards him.

"Never you fret, Little Lady. I'll not let him break his neck, — which, by your leave, is as precious to me as to you. Neither will Fanuella. She is trustworthy, if I am not."

Turning to her flowers again, she laughed by way of answer. "See the lilies, Robin! Are they not lovely this morning?"

"They are like the great sheaf you gathered in the garden at Windsor that other August day so long ago," he answered. "How much has changed since then!"

"Hast thou any news yet?" asked Dorothy, in a low voice, stepping from the velvet greensward to the gravelled path, and smoothing Fanuella's mane, while the boy spurred her impatiently with his small heels.

"Not yet. I sent Mat over to Brently early, when the sun was scarce four hands high, but he has not got back. Ah! There he comes this minute," as Mat Hansel galloped up from the lodge with a package of letters and papers. "Down with you, little man. Daddy has something else to attend to, now."

But the little man whimpered.

"Let me have the young master and he shall not lose his ride," said Mat, lifting him to the saddle again. "And then I will take him around to Betty. Go you in, Dame Dorothy, for I fear me I brought bad news."

Sir Robert had torn open his letters, and was rapidly glancing through them, while Lady Anne leaned on his shoulder. Her face had lost the slight veil of sadness that had shadowed it in her early girlhood. As she stood by her husband's side, in her superb womanhood, she was almost as tall as he. Literally, as well as figuratively, they — to use Lord Weymouth's words — looked in each other's eyes level-fronted.

"Well, what say the despatches? How is it with her this day?" asked Dorothy, as she came up the steps, and joined them on the balustraded terrace.

"Sit here, dear heart," and Sir Robert drew a

chair forward. "It is as we feared. All is over. Our dear Queen died yesterday morning."

"God rest her soul," said the older woman, while the younger was silently weeping. "Ill, childless, and a widow, life hath gone hardly with her, for all her high estate. Children, give thanks for her that she is at rest."

"Aye," said the young master of Raneleigh, "hear what our good Doctor Arbuthnot says in this letter, — 'I believe sleep was never more sweet to a weary traveller, than death was to her.' Yet it seems hard that she could not have lived, now that the long wars are over. Through all these years, it hath been she who hath stood steadily for peace, — peace. She hath cried out against blood-shed, and wept over the slain of, her people, as Rachel wept for her children. And now that the land is at rest she is not permitted to behold it."

"Neither her children's children, nor peace upon Israel," said Dorothy, with a slow shake of the head. "I wonder was it a judgment, as she sometimes thought? Yet I know she grieved for her young brother. She sorrowed, — she sorrowed. Robin, what dost thou think? Hath he any chance at the throne now?"

"Not the slightest. 'Tis said"—and here the voice was lowered ; there were many things in those days of which men spoke only in whispers. "'Tis said his Royal Highness hath been in London lately, even if he be not there at this minute, and that her Majesty's heart yearned over him. There were those in high places who thought his succession might be brought about, — for we Englishmen like not that foreigners should reign over us. I have been approached myself more than once. But as for the young prince, even though he be lovable as men say, yet is he not to be trusted in great affairs. The reins were in his hands even now, and he failed to grasp them. George I. is already proclaimed, and no Stuart will ever again sit on the throne of England."

"Unstable as water," cried Dorothy, throwing up her hands with a long sigh. "'Tis a fated race, yet oh, how well beloved!"

"Let us talk no more of it," said Robin. "'Tis all over now. Weep no longer, Anne. Why, sweetheart, I did not think thou wouldst so take this death to heart. Didst thou then love the Queen so much?"

"Nay, 'tis not that, 'tis not that alone, though I learned to know her better, and to love her as I never did before, after that night when she laid her two hands on your shoulders, and said, 'Child, it was not I who made your father an outlaw.' Those words laid my father's shade, too. But I was thinking of them all, — of those two, and of the mighty hosts that have marched to their deaths as proudly and gaily as to a revel, if the Stuart did but call. And 'twas all for naught, all for naught!"

"Not so, not so!" cried her husband, drawing her yet closer. "As long as valor is, and loyalty and devotion endure, so long shall the noble men who followed the Stuarts to defeat and death live in the hearts of mankind. 'For naught?' Nay, cease your crying, Anne. They are all at peace now, — your father and mine; the slayers and the slain. God rest them!"

For many minutes they sat in silence, the three whose lives had been so strangely linked with that of the dead Queen.

"Dear heart," he said at last, turning to Dorothy, and addressing her by the tender name he had given her since "granny" had been handed down to Robert the second. "Dear heart, when thou dost tell my boy thy stories of 'kings' houses,' even as thou didst tell them to his father, teach him to hold Queen Anne's name in reverence, not only for what this house owes her, but for the good she did her people, and the greater good she willed to do. Tell him she left behind her a united people at peace with all the nations. Tell him of Gloster, and of the love we bore each other. Tell him of our tender compact made in thine own old garden. Tell him — "

His voice broke.

" Let us go in," he said, rising abruptly.

The three entered the wide, lofty, oak-raftered hall, and the door swung to behind them.

THE END.